CW00853773

Philip Bentall is a novelist and poet. He is the author of the novels *Stray Dog* and *Wild Flower*. He lives in the south-east of England.

ALSO BY PHILIP BENTALL

Wild Flower

STRAY DOG

Philip Bentall

1

La Seine, Paris. A phone was ringing in Martin Decker's bag that wasn't his. He knew his own ring tone well enough and this wasn't it.

Walking along the riverside, he stopped just before Pont du Carrousel and, resting his canvas backpack on the wall, retrieved the phone. A green light pulsed around its edges. It was just after five in the afternoon on the 29th of September and Decker was on his way home from work. A fine drizzle was falling. Sliding the rack of the phone, Decker said, 'Hello.'

There was a delay, like you might get on international calls, then a click.

A man's voice said, 'It's been a while.'

Decker recognised the voice in an instant. Squinting into the wet breeze, he wondered who had planted the phone in his bag. He recalled sharing the lift with the new girl from sales that day, her joking about being too lazy to use the stairs; then seeing a bike courier at the front desk, and a woman taking pictures by the kiosks on Quai des Grands Augustins; and later a guy jogging round the corner of Rue de Savoie. Not that it mattered now.

'Almost a year,' Decker said.

'Doesn't time fly?' the man said in that gentle manner of his.

'Depends,' Decker replied.

'I believe you've been keeping well,' the man said.

'I've been getting by. What do you want?'

'Something has come up. We have a job for you.'

Decker looked across the grey waters of the Seine; a river barge was passing under the bridge carrying freight to the southwest of Paris.

The man said, 'A straightforward pick-up and drop-off. What do you say?'

'That nothing is straightforward.'

'You will be away for a while. There is a target.'

'What else?'

'You will need to pick up and deliver a package – the usual arrangements.'

The breeze gusted. Decker turned and faced the traffic coming down Port des Saints-Pères. His eyes narrowed. He didn't expect the call. He never did. He let himself forget there was someone out there who knew him for who he really was, imagining a time when they wouldn't need him again, and he'd be free of all this. Then the call came. And whatever cover-life he had at the time – such as now, with his job at the travel agency, his apartment with his girlfriend, Annie – was revealed for what it really was.

The man said, 'We really need your help on this, Martin.'

'Funny that,' Decker said, scanning the rooftops and pavements, the cars braking at the lights, but knowing, deep down, there wasn't ever going to be an end to this. 'That's not what I need.'

The man said, '18:30, Cardinal Lemoine station. Line ten, fourth carriage.'

Then the click; the dead line.

Decker checked his watch, a Seiko chronograph, given to him by his employers at Corpus all those years ago. It was 18:14. He set the timer for 18:30, which gave him less than an hour.

Decker walked down Quai Voltaire and crossed the road at the lights. Traffic barrelled in both directions; the zip of tyres on wet tarmac.

Already, Decker could feel his old life slipping away from him, like the rain running off the pavements – a life growing further and further away, until it no longer seemed to belong to him.

At Metro Rue du Bac, Decker slipped through the ticket barriers and headed down a wide tunnel where a busker was singing *California Dreamin'*, his guitar covered in stickers and scratches, with a kid accompanying him on a recorder:

'Stopped into a church
I passed along the way
Well, I got down on my knees
And I pretend to pray.'

The song followed Decker down the tunnel along with the sound of money being tossed into the guitar case at the busker's feet.

Decker boarded a train in a huddle of people and turned to the window as they sped into the darkness. Electric sparks lit up graffitied walls. He recalled being told it was a straightforward pick-up and drop-off but knew nothing was straightforward.

As the bevelled white tiles of Sèvres Babylone appeared in the window, Decker moved towards the doors. Here, lines 10 and 12 intersected on the border of the 6th and 7th arrondissements and he needed to change trains.

Decker switched platforms, timing his next train to the minute, where he boarded the fourth carriage and rode the train straight through to Cardinal Lemoine.

At 18:24, the doors slid open. And a man wearing jeans and white trainers boarded the train just as Decker was getting off. The man was carrying a small North Face rucksack. He brushed shoulders with Decker as he went past. Neither of them looked at each other as they switched bags.

Once off the train, Decker moved swiftly through the crowd of people on the platform, then turned right down an exit tunnel, and stood on a moving walkway. Slipping his arms through the straps of the rucksack, Decker kept looking straight ahead.

Decker knew what was about to happen was likely the result of months of planning by his employers at Corpus, but he thought only about the rucksack, its contents, and receiving his next set of instructions when he left the station. Understanding the chain of events that had led to this moment was not Decker's concern. He couldn't do this job and survive by allowing himself to ponder why it was someone's turn to die and not another's. He had a target. That was all he needed, or wanted, to know.

Decker passed through the ticket barriers just as two armed police officers walked through the station. Probably come in from the rain, Decker thought.

He exited Cardinal Lemoine station, taking out the phone he'd found in his bag as he was climbing the steps onto Rue Monge.

As soon as he had a signal, the phone started to ring.

'Everything all right, I trust?' the man said.

'Yeah, everything's fine.'

'Good. Your appointment is at 19:30. Be ready.'

Decker returned the phone to his pocket and reset his watch for 19:30.

It was getting dark, the drizzle still falling.

There was a café on the corner of Rue Malus. The awning flapped in the breeze.

Decker turned left and then right onto Rue de la Clef, where cars were parked bumper to bumper. Crossing the road, he took a set of keys from his pocket and scanned the windows above him. He stopped in front of a large wooden door and looked in both directions. A couple rushed past under an umbrella; two North Africans were unloading crates from the back of a van. Satisfied the area was clear, Decker opened the door and went in.

A light came on in the hallway. There were metallic lockers along one wall, a wooden staircase, and discarded newspapers on the floor. Decker headed straight up the stairs. On the second floor, he selected another key and opened the door with the number 3 on it.

Decker entered the apartment. The room had a wooden floor and high ceiling. There was a bed in one corner and a table and chairs in the other. Decker dropped the keys on the table and, digging in his coat pockets, removed two mobiles. One of the phones was the one he had just received and the other was his own. He noticed the message light blinking on his own phone. Ignoring it, he crossed the room and drew the blinds over the windows. He then turned on the bedside light, tilting its metal shade, and opened the rucksack on the bed.

Inside was a 24cmx16cm snap-lock carrying case and a waistband holster. Decker opened the carrying case and inside was a SIG Sauer P229 Compact 9mm and TiRant silencer. He screwed the silencer on the threaded barrel, checked the magazine, then laid it on the bed. Next, he pushed the bed to one side and lifted a loose floorboard. He reached underneath and took out an envelope with a rubber band round it. He removed the rubber band and tipped out the contents on the bed. There were several passports, a wad of cash, a newspaper cutting and a photograph. He sorted through the passports and, selecting one, stuck it in his coat pocket. The wad of cash went in another pocket. The photograph, which was of a young couple skiing, Decker wiped with his thumb then stuck in his pocket along with the newspaper cutting. The rest of the contents of the envelope went into a plastic shopping bag. He replaced the floorboard and pushed back the bed.

Decker checked his watch again: 19:02. He had 28 minutes.

He walked across to the kitchen, remembering how he used to smoke. It was a year ago on his last job. Parked up in a hire car, he remembered, along the coast of Costa Smeralda in Sardinia, looking at a large pleasure boat through a pair of binoculars, and bagging up his cigarette butts each day just so there wasn't a trace of him left behind. He realised he hadn't thought about cigarettes in a long time. He couldn't even remember giving up now.

Decker opened the fridge and took out a carton of orange juice. He poured some into a glass, drank the contents, and then rinsed the glass under the tap and left it upside down on the draining board.

Walking back into the main room, he removed his Gore-Tex jacket and put on the waistband holster, fastening the Velcro flaps at the front. Then, picking up the SIG, he removed the magazine, pulled the slide and looked inside the chamber. Clear. He fired the dry round, returned the magazine, and tucked the gun into the holster. Then he put his jacket on again, pulled up the zip and looked at his watch: 19:12.

Walking round the flat, Decker threw other things into the plastic bag, then grabbed the keys and phones off the table. As he crossed the room, one of the phones started to ring. This time he recognised the ring tone: it was his own phone. He hesitated, knowing it was best to get it over with now.

'I've been trying to ring you,' Annie said. 'Where have you been?'

'Work.' Decker glanced round the room for the last time before flicking off the lights.

He'd been with Annie for nearly eight months now. Even Decker had to admit they'd grown close in that short time. But he'd been trained to keep up the illusion until the last – a business trip; a sick aunt. He'd be back in a few weeks. He'd miss her. Keep it short. Keep it sweet. He knew the drill.

'When are you coming home?' Annie said.

'Listen, Annie,' he said. 'I've got to go away for a couple of weeks … for work. It's just come up. I'm sorry.' His voice was soft. Only Annie heard this voice.

'What! We're meant to be meeting Paul and Sylvie tonight. I've booked a restaurant. Have you forgotten?'

He hadn't forgotten. 'You know what my boss is like,' he said. 'It's the new offices in London. He needs my help. I'll make it up to you.'

'I don't believe you,' Annie said. 'You're always doing this. Look. I'll come and meet you. What time's your flight?'

'Annie,' he said, raising his voice. Stopping himself, Decker drew a breath, and steadied himself. 'I haven't got time,' he said. 'Not tonight. I'll explain later.' Decker looked at his watch: 19:16. Fourteen minutes. 'Look, Annie,' he said. 'I've got to go.'

'I don't understand you sometimes, Martin.'

Decker remembered his trainer at Corpus telling him: 'There'll be few people who can understand what you do, and even fewer who could do it. You are a rare breed, Martin, make no mistake. You'll be dealing with the rubbish in society that no one else wants to touch. But what you have to remember is this: "It is the greatest happiness of the greatest number that is the measure of right and wrong." And you, Martin, will bring about the greatest happiness in what *you* do.'

Still holding the phone to his ear, Decker said, 'Listen, Annie. I'll ring you later, okay?'

'I don't believe this.'

'Please, Annie, not now,' letting himself out of the flat, reminding himself it was better like this – for everyone's sake. There was Annie's safety to think about; his security. Maybe he'd come back, he told himself, when it was done, and find her. There were no rules against that. Maybe she'd wait for him and they could start again. Maybe one day they could live like a normal couple. It was worth believing for now, he thought.

'You can be so selfish, you know that,' Annie said. 'What is more important – me or your job?'

'Annie, I haven't got time for this now.'

'Where have I heard that before?'

'I'm sorry.' The other phone bleeped with a message.

'You're sorry! What good is that?'

'I'll be back as soon as I can. I promise.' Decker walked down the stairs, scrolling on the other mobile.

Annie said, 'And then what – you'll go away again?'

A picture came through. It was a surveillance shot of a suited man passing through glass doors. The man was about 40, 6ft 1ins, with greying temples. Not a person, with friends and family, but a target. There was no more time to think about it than that. Decker had to move, to react; it was happening now – *The greater good*.

He said to Annie, 'Look, I've got to go,' and hung up, dropping the phone into the plastic bag.

2

Decker dropped the plastic bag into a bin down the road. He studied the other mobile, drizzle spotting the screen, as he stepped onto a bus. The GPS tracker was set in motion. A pulsing icon marked his target to be just off Rue Monge about a mile away.

Decker looked from the bus window, studying street signs. The bus progressed along Rue Monge, with its ground floor shops, cream-coloured building facades and wrought iron balconies. Decker checked the target's position on the phone. About a street away, he stood up and walked down the aisle of the bus.

The bus doors swished open, the sound of tyres in the wet.

Decker pulled up his hood and crossed the road. His eyes tracked in every direction as he walked.

Concealing himself in a shop front, Decker studied the GPS on the phone and saw his target about 80 metres away. He scanned the pavements and tall buildings, trying to get a feel for the area.

Traffic fizzed along the road; it was just after rush hour; a glass-fronted office block; restaurant awnings; a T-junction and traffic lights – symmetrical Parisian street lines.

He looked at the phone again. His target was on the move.

Decker walked forward to the T-junction and stood at the lights. On the other side of the road, a suited man was walking along the pavement. He was carrying a slim black briefcase in one hand, no bigger than a small laptop. The man turned left at the lights and continued along Rue Monge. The cursor on Decker's phone moved in the same direction as the man.

Decker crossed the road through moving traffic and fell in behind the man. He closed in to about 50 metres and followed him down Rue

Monge.

The man turned left into Rue Navarre, tall residential buildings one side, a green overhang of trees the other.

Decker stopped on the corner, sighting the man about 30 metres ahead of him. The man was speaking on his phone now, heading uphill past the Roman amphitheatre, Les Arènes de Lutèce.

Decker checked the windows above him, the balconies, the rooftops, then started along the pavement, hands in pockets, head bowed.

The man was still on his phone. Decker closed in to about 20 metres. Streetlights thinned out. Rain ran off buildings and tree branches.

The man stopped ahead of him, pocketing his phone and removing a key fob. Decker kept walking towards him, closing in … 15 metres … 10 metres.

The man bleeped the central locking on his keyring. A BMW flashed in the line of parked cars. Decker put a hand behind his back, lifted his jacket, and removed the SIG. He slid the slide, keeping his hands low.

The man was opening the driver's door of the BMW. He reached in and put the briefcase on the passenger seat.

Decker drew level. The suited man turned round. Decker computed his face, crosschecking it with the one he had memorised off his phone: an exact match. The surveillance pictures must have been done a couple of days ago, he thought: same suit.

Rainwater had settled on the gun's silencer. Decker fired twice: chest and head. The man slid down the side of the car, an arm getting caught between the door.

Decker pocketed the SIG, looked along the street again and up at the windows.

The rain was already diluting the blood on the car window. Decker took the man's arm out from between the door and lifted him into the car. He sat him upright in the driver's seat, closed the door, and walked round to the passenger seat. He removed the case, slipped it inside his jacket, and shut the passenger door.

Decker checked along the street again, the windows, then crossed the road and walked in the opposite direction.

When he got to the end of the road, his phone rang.

The man's voice said, 'Position?'

Decker said, 'Rue des Arènes. BMW 5 series, registration WW1 2BX.'

The man's voice said, 'Status?'

'Clear. Heading south on Rue Linné.' Decker turned down hill, scanning in either direction as he crossed the road. He held the phone to his ear, the line hissing like the mouth of a tunnel. In the distance he heard the gear changes of a diesel van. He pictured the clean-up van pulling up beside the BMW, the quick wash down, the blanketed body, the BMW being driven away, heading south for the ring road.

The man on the phone said, 'Okay, we have you. Keep going ... on the corner of Rue Cuvier, next to the park. He'll be wearing jeans, white baseball cap.'

Decker saw the park ahead of him. He checked the GPS on his phone, crossing the road to the east side to join up with Rue Cuvier. He focused on the junction ahead of him, the rain coming down in lengths.

A man in jeans, parka coat, grubby white baseball cap, turned the corner of Rue Cuvier. He was swinging an orange carrier bag in his right hand. He dropped the bag into a bin without stopping, the rain pummelling car bonnets.

Decker crossed the road, scanning his surroundings, and lifted the bag from the bin as he walked past.

His phone rang as he was turning into Rue Lacépède.

The man said, 'Keys, tickets are inside. We'll move in the morning.'

*

A dog was barking. The rain had stopped. Drains gurgled in the darkness. Decker turned down a narrow residential street, with a park opposite. A kid's playground occupied one half and flower beds the other. There was graffiti on the benches.

Decker walked up a flight of steps to a single door. The slide in the playground glinted in the streetlight. He opened the door and went inside.

Another room, another bed – the organisation had dozens of such safe houses scattered throughout the city. It was just past midnight.

Decker ate half a baguette with some Brie de Meaux that he found in the fridge, then drank a glass of tap water and lay on the bed, fully clothed. He needed to rest, to recharge. The importance of sleep could never be underestimated – something drummed into him in training. 'Sleep whenever you get the chance,' he was told, 'as your chances could be few and far between.' Decker knew without sleep, your judgment suffered as did your reaction times. Like this, you could end up dead, or worse still, open to capture and possible interrogation – not a position you wanted to put yourself in if you could help it.

Decker turned off the bedside light and lay there with his eyes open. On the bedside table was the dead man's briefcase; under the pillow was the SIG. As he lay there, he focused on his breathing. He breathed in through his nose over a slow count of four, held it for another count of four, then exhaled through his lips over the same time, and then held empty for another count of four before beginning again. As he did this, he felt his heart rate come down, his peripheral vision improve and hearing sharpen. He kept his mind clear, focused. Everything in real time, no thoughts yet of the life he had left behind, or the life ahead of him. Just the moment he was in now.

Lying there like this, Decker could hear the sound of cars passing in the distance, the swish of tyres on wet tarmac, the gear changes through corners; a couple of times an ambulance siren receded into the darkness, while closer by, gentle gusts of wind sounded in treetops and rainwater dripped on pavements.

Decker lay like this for about an hour before sleep came.

3

Decker was a boy again, standing in the garden of his parent's house. He was holding a green hose. There was a big coil of it at his feet. He was watering a flowerbed with it when blood started colouring the water. The hose was soon pumping out blood. The flowers were dripping with it. Now his father was there, calling for him to come inside.

Decker looked over at this father. His father was smiling, but there was a hole in his chest, and blood was streaming from the hole. A puddle had formed round his feet. Decker tried walking towards him but the blood came up to his waist and was as thick as treacle.

Now his father had disappeared. The house looked increasingly small in the distance. Then there wasn't a house. Decker was somewhere else now. He was sitting on a floor looking at a photo album. And there was his parent's house in one of the photos – like he had been looking at the photo all along.

*

Suddenly Decker was awake.

Whether it was a change in temperature or a different type of darkness that had woken him, he didn't know. But he felt someone was there in the room with him. The dream faded into the shape of the room, a presence beside him, a sense of fear.

Decker rolled out of bed, pulling the SIG from under the pillow.

The intruder fired twice, shots that fluffed into the mattress like nothing more harmful than blasts of compressed air. The intruder appeared North African, late 20s, his clumsy gun-handling telling Decker that he lacked training.

From under the bed, Decker shot the African through the leg. The African yelped and wriggled against the wall, clutching his thigh. He dropped the dead man's briefcase, blood soaking through his jeans, and looked at his hands in astonishment as blood dripped off his curled fingers. Then he slumped to the floor.

Decker heard a car door slam and footsteps on the stairs. He stood up.

A shot came through the door, taking out a chuck of masonry from the wall.

Picking up the case, Decker went through the window, shoulder first. He landed on the bonnet of a car and rolled across the tarmac, glass showering the pavement.

Two muffled shots fizzed above his head. The dog started barking again.

Decker picked himself up and crept below the line of cars.

A third shot ricocheted off a car rooftop, the bullet whining across the park.

Decker spotted a man at the window. The man was pointing a silenced firearm through the broken glass. He was wearing a long overcoat and had a pale face.

Decker saw a house light go on and then heard the sound of voices.

Decker moved between the cars, the overcoat in the window letting off another shot. The bullet went through the side window of a car, ripping into the seat foam.

Reaching the end of the line of cars, Decker saw a bike coming down the road towards him, headlight juddering across the tarmac, the driver pulling a gun and shooting.

Decker dived onto the ground, a car wing mirror shattering above his head. Rolling across the pavement, Decker drew the SIG and fired twice. The bullets caught the driver in the shoulder, throwing him off the bike. The bike skidded across the road, indicator lights splintering across the tarmac and headlight pointing at a crooked angle.

Decker looked up at the window but couldn't see the overcoat guy anymore. He heard a shot come from inside and suspected it was the overcoat finishing off the African, for whatever reason. Decker then looked at the driver laid out on the tarmac taking his last breaths. Whoever he was, he couldn't help him with anything now, he thought.

Sometimes the only thing to do was to put as much distance between you and the source of trouble. Decker knew it was such a moment. And within seconds, was up on his feet, jacket hood up, and moving in a low crouch below the line of cars. He was bleeding and could feel a pain in his ribs – possibly one of them was broken – but adrenaline was about the best anaesthetic there was when drugs were low on supply.

When he got to the end of the street, Decker straightened up and ran as fast as he could in a northerly direction and didn't stop for quite some time.

*

The call came an hour later. Decker was crossing the river, the sunrise beginning to catch the grey Paris rooftops and distant tower blocks.

The voice said, 'Can you confirm your position?'

Decker looked across the river, a cold breeze pressing against his face, 'Pont Neuf, heading north. There was trouble.'

'We know. Keep walking. You still have the case?'

'Yeah.'

'Good. We're putting you in position.'

Decker scanned along the riverbank. He saw a car pulling into a bus stop about 200 metres away, a man jogging alongside the river.

The voice on the phone said, 'Okay, we have you now. Your train leaves in an hour. Someone will make contact when you arrive in London. Remember: "April is the cruellest month."'

The line went dead. Traffic barrelled along the highway below him.

4

'April is the cruellest month,' the woman next to him said. She had short blonde hair and had just sat down on the stool beside him, a cup of coffee in one hand and a newspaper in the other, the announcement outside warning passengers not to leave their bags unattended.

St Pancras, London. The time: 9:54. The Eurostar had been quiet. Decker had managed to catch half an hour's sleep in the tunnel. Waking up, the train zipping through the Kent countryside, he'd eaten a bar of chocolate and sipped from a bottle of water.

'How was your journey?' the woman asked, laying the newspaper on the narrow window ledge in front of them. There was an address written on the front page, a set of keys showing underneath.

'Fine,' Decker said, glancing at the paper and memorising the address.

Sipping her coffee, the woman stared ahead out the window. In her late 20s, thought Decker, not long out of college, but playing it cool, wearing a black suit jacket and fitted white shirt.

'London has been experiencing something of a heatwave,' she said. 'Apparently, it was the driest September on record.'

'Is that right?' Decker said, looking at the woman's shirt, the top buttons left undone, giving a glimpse of bra lace.

'That's what they say,' she said.

A station employee drove an electric buggy through the station concourse, people stepping aside to let it pass.

The woman went on, 'Anyway, now they're saying it's going to rain for the next two weeks. Can you believe it?'

Decker said, 'That's British weather for you.'

Without looking in his direction, the woman said. 'We need you to keep an eye on someone.'

A muscle flexed in Decker's jaw. 'They never said.'

'It's not a problem, is it?' the woman sounded to have taken offence.

'No. No problem.'

'Good. You're Extension 8003.'

Decker closed his hands over the keys on the table. 'The drop-off?' he said.

'We're putting you in position.' The woman's eyes fixed on the distance. 'You have some luggage to pick up.'

Decker looked across the concourse.

The woman said, 'South exit, 10:05.'

Decker's eyes flicked up to the large departure board. The digital clock was changing to 10:04.

The woman drained her coffee and stood up. 'Enjoy your stay.' She picked up the newspaper and walked out of the café. Wearing tapered black suit trousers to go with the jacket, there was a sway to her movements.

Decker watched her for a moment as she crossed the concourse, feeling as he did a longing to be somewhere else, but the feeling didn't last. Within a second or two, he'd snapped back into the moment again; and standing up, he slipped the keys into his pocket and dropped his cup into the bin on his way out.

The time: 10:04:23.

He walked across the station concourse, keeping his eye on the large departure board as he headed for the south exit. 10:04:36

… 37 … 38 … 39 …

Decker stopped at the south exit, paused, and scanned the concourse. 10:04:56.

Four seconds.

The man approaching him was wearing jeans and Barbour jacket. He was carrying a grey rucksack through its loop.

At exactly 10:05:02, just out of shot of the CCTV, Decker brushed past the man, taking the rucksack from him.

The sun was shining. Decker turned right out of the station, slipping his arms through the straps of the rucksack. After about 200 metres, he turned down a narrow street. Half way down, he descended some steps. He reappeared wearing a baseball cap and quilted jacket.

He scanned the street in both directions and crossed the road. He continued for another 300 metres and flagged down a taxi.

The cabbie glanced at him in his rear-view mirror but not for long enough to remember him in an hour. There was a folded copy of *The Sun* newspaper on the passenger seat. Decker could just make out the headline: "Paris shootings". They headed south on Tavistock Square.

Decker abandoned the taxi on Charing Cross Road, walked through Chinatown, and headed south on Garrick Street. He was breathing hard. Putting his hand under his jacket, he felt his ribs. It felt like one of them was indeed cracked from the fall the night before.

Checking over his shoulder, he turned down Bedford Street and entered a barber's, where a man gestured to a chair, wrapped a gown round his neck, and took a shaver to his head. It was all over in 15 minutes. At the till, Decker paid in cash and, putting on a pair of yellow tinted glasses, left the shop.

A little while later, Decker stopped at the bottom of some house steps, fronted by black iron railings and porch columns. He stood there and scanned his surroundings. He noted a suited man crossing the bridge, a woman walking her dog in the park opposite, a man on a bicycle. All appeared normal.

Fishing out the keys from his pocket, Decker felt like he had been here many times before, and in many ways he had, or in houses like it.

Entering the flat on the first floor, Decker placed the keys on the table and the grey rucksack on the floor. He then stood by the window, observed the small park opposite, with its line of plane trees and black iron railings, and further along the road, the terrace of three-storey houses. He also noted the main road along the riverside, the suspension bridge, and the position of bus stops. He spent no more than 20 seconds at the window before drawing the blinds. He then walked next door into the bedroom and did the same there. While he was there, he also checked the cupboard and found clothes and fresh linen. He then returned to the sitting room and unpacked the bag.

Inside was a laptop, a camera/USB lead and his SIG 9mm. He laid these things out on the table. He then stood up, took off his jacket and removed the dead man's case, which he had stored inside. He was familiar with the type of case – foam lined, about the size of an A5 notebook, probably containing a hard drive or documents. He looked for somewhere to put it. Next door in the bedroom, he opened a cupboard where there was a water tank. He removed two screws with a fork and peeled back a wall panel. He forced the case inside and then replaced the screws, taking care not to damage the screw heads.

Returning to the sitting room, Decker set the laptop up on the table.

He typed in a website address and logged into a bulletin board with the code extension 8003. A surveillance shot of a man jogging came online.

"Name: Daniel Howell. Age: 33. Height: 184cm. Weight: 74 kg."

Decker clicked through the pictures in the file: Howell crossing a footbridge; entering a tube station; leaving a Starbucks. There were also some attachment files of known associates and contacts of Howell. All very routine.

Decker logged out of the bulletin board and googled "Paris shootings".

He turned up several articles. The coverage was perfunctory. Two men had been shot. A third gunman had escaped on foot. There were fears of another motorbike serial killing following a recent shooting in France involving the killer fleeing on a motorbike. Terrorism had not been ruled out as a motive. A police investigation was ongoing. There was no mention of the guy in the BMW, which meant his employer, Corpus, had likely cleared all the evidence. And there were no mugshots or names.

Decker read each article twice, then tried other searches and read other articles of similar style and content. Clearly government agencies were in control, he thought, working overtime to shut the story down. The overcoat at the window, the moped driver and the North African – likely none of them could be traced anyway. Dead doubles, contracts. Like himself.

Agencies never employed their own men for this sort of work, just as nothing was going to explain why the overcoat had shot the moped guy – different instructions; different jobs.

Decker wondered how long before the story disappeared altogether. A week, maybe less, he thought. Government agencies would be moving in, pulling files, visiting witnesses. Evidence would be mislaid. The police would be left to stonewall the media. Then a tip-off, rumours of a celebrity affair, fresh scent for the media, and things would get back to normal.

In the meantime, Corpus would track down Annie. Feed her a story: your boyfriend was shipping drugs; a phoney looking for cover. They'd replace him at work. Annie would turn to friends. And over glasses of wine, the memories would come flooding back, of the times he'd gone away at short notice, of his demands for his own space, and reluctance to socialise. He'd never been right for her anyway, they'd tell her. Then along the line, someone else would step in, and she'd consider him a narrow escape. One more relationship put down to experience. In such ways, people moved on with their lives. Decker knew how it went. That's not to say this didn't hurt – because it did.

*

Decker stood under a shower with his eyes closed. He stood like this for at least a minute before starting to wash himself. He knew how important it was to stay in the moment. Showers, press-ups – anything physical – all helped. In time, he knew the loss of his old life would be numbed by the routine of the new one. It was all just a matter of time and focus.

Getting out of the shower, Decker dried himself in front of the mirror, running his hand over his new haircut and inspecting his bruised ribs. Then he put on some jeans and a sweatshirt and sat in the chair by the window.

Streetlights were coming on, illuminating the tops of plane trees. Someone had picked up a black woollen hat and left it over the spike of a railing. A bus stopped at the top of the road and picked up a mother with two kids. Cars moved in both directions along the riverside.

The time was 19:43.

Decker sat with the lights off, and began to feel sleepy. After a while, his head lolled forward on his chest. He tried sitting up, looking out the window, but it lolled forward again. Rain hammered on the window. The wind picked up. Decker dozed in the chair in the dark.

When he woke up, a taxi was pulling up outside the row of houses opposite.

5

A light came on inside the taxi. A man got out under an umbrella and paid the driver. Rain bounced off the pavements. The taxi made a U-turn in the middle of the road and drove off. The man walked up the steps to one of the houses.

Grabbing the camera, Decker photographed the man opening the door and letting himself in, then closing the door, and finally in an upstairs window as he was drawing a blind.

The rain beat against the window. Decker looked back at the photographs on the camera's display screen. The man's face was partially obscured under the umbrella. Decker then opened the laptop and clicked through the surveillance shots he'd received of Howell. When he got to the photo of Howell leaving the Starbucks, he stopped and zoomed in on his face. He noted Howell's hollow cheeks, sharp nose, and sensitive-looking eyes. On the surface, an unassuming, mild-mannered looking guy, but you never knew.

Decker compared the surveillance shots on the laptop with the ones he'd just taken. From the photographs alone, it was impossible to say with one hundred percent accuracy that it was his target Howell, but instinctively Decker knew they were a match. He'd have to wait a little while longer though to be sure though, he thought.

Decker shut the lid of the laptop and waited by the window, watching lights go on and blinds being drawn in the building opposite. Then he went to the kitchen and filled the kettle and took down a cup from a cupboard and added coffee and sugar to it. He held the handle of the kettle as it boiled, then added the water to the cup and stirred with a spoon. The clinking sound of the spoon made Decker think about why he was here but he didn't think about it for long.

He sat down by the window again, sipped his coffee, and watched the rain stream down the sides of the road and pool round debris-covered drains. Across the park, treetops gusted and clumps of leaves fell to the ground.

All the while the lights remained on in Howell's apartment – if it was Howell's that was. Decker had the camera on the table at the ready. And as he sat there, he imagined Howell inside the flat, playing back phone messages, getting out of his wet clothes, maybe making a drink, or watching TV from a sofa.

After an hour, the lights went out and Decker concluded Howell must have gone to bed. The time, according to Decker's watch, was 24:54. Decker made a note of it on a pad of a paper. He would sit up for a little longer though, he thought, just to be sure.

To pass the time, Decker stripped and reassembled the SIG, screwing the sound moderator in place and inserting a loaded magazine. Then he fetched a small package from his rucksack and tipped out the contents on the table. It contained bankcards, cash, and the photograph and newspaper cutting he had taken from the flat in Paris. He put the bankcard and cash to one side and opened the newspaper cutting. It was dated January14th, 1989.

"Young couple die in avalanche:

Avalanche hits Swiss ski resort"

Decker read the first paragraph of the article and then looked at the photograph of the young couple skiing. The couple in the picture had been dead over 20 years. The photograph was beginning to show its age.

The young couple were his parents.

6

Decker's parents used to go skiing every winter together.

In the photograph, Decker's father was wearing a bandanna and mirror shades, kicking up powder snow as he made a deep turn between pine trees. Decker's mother was beside him, her trailing hair and skis neatly aligned as she prepared for a jump. It was taken days before they were found dead, buried in an avalanche near the ski resort of Saas Fee, Switzerland.

Decker was seven years old when they died.

Decker put the photo away and sat by the window in the dark. The last time he'd looked at the photo was the last time he'd been called away on a job, about a year ago. The photo went with him whenever he went. Always after leaving a life behind, Decker would look at the photo. It had become part of the routine. For Decker, the photo was a reminder of something in his life that didn't change. Somewhere he could always go.

As he sat there, Decker listened to the rain. His gaze drifted round the ceiling and walls. The swish of the trees played in the background. Another empty room, he thought, another city.

The hours passed. Traffic thinned out along the river.

Around two in the morning, Decker allowed his eyes to close. The sound of the rain, the memories of his parents, the empty room … soon his head fell forward and rested on his chest.

*

Annie was sitting next to him on the bed. Their hands were tied and they were blindfolded. The guy in the overcoat from Paris was pointing a gun at Annie, saying, 'You've no idea who your boyfriend is, do you?'

Decker heard the lid of a bottle being unscrewed, then a cellophane packet being opened. No one was speaking. Footsteps came towards them. The footsteps of a woman, he thought. Decker realised now he was seeing all this through his blindfold. It was the woman he'd met at St Pancras today.

A shot was fired – a muffled thump through a pillow met by a crack of bone. Annie slumped over on the bed next to him.

Decker stood up, trying to wrestle free. The woman pushed a needle into his arm. A heavy liquid filled his system. He fell on the floor. His heart was beating hard. Trying to stand up, he fell over again. No sense of arms or legs. He squirmed on the floor like an amputee. He heard voices in the distance and the beating of his heart.

*

With a jolt, and instantly alert, Decker rolled out of the chair and pulled the SIG onto an empty room.

It was still raining.

A lorry passed in the distance, beating the lights.

Decker got up and walked through to the sitting room. Peeling back the curtain, he saw it was still dark. He thought he had probably been asleep for about three hours, which was better than some nights. He boiled the kettle and made another coffee. He sat at the desk in darkness with the curtains open.

Soon, the sky streaked grey and red. Building silhouettes glimmered on the South Bank.

The coffee tasted good. Decker began to feel hungry and realised he hadn't eaten in a while. Later, he would fry some eggs, he thought, and make some toast.

Just then, a downstairs light went on in a building up the road

Decker took out the camera.

The front door opened and a man stepped out wearing Lycra shorts and a hooded top. He pulled the door closed behind him and walked down the steps, programming his iPod and stretching his legs on the wall.

Decker clicked away on the camera. It was the man from the taxi the night before.

The man secured his iPod on an armband and set off running, his shoes throwing up rainwater and hood flapping on his back.

About 30 metres down the road, the man glanced over his shoulder to cross the road. There was no traffic and he didn't have to stop, but in that split second, looking up from the camera Decker got a good look at him – the slim, athletic build, the short-cropped hair and sensitive-looking eyes – confirming the man's identity beyond any doubt.

It was his target, Howell.

Decker watched him run to the end of the road, where a seagull took off from the back of a bench. He was running quickly, Decker thought, like someone who ran every day.

7

Decker ate a bowl of kimchi noodles in a Korean restaurant off Endell Street, Covent Garden. He'd never eaten Asian food until he'd met Mr Charles. It was one o'clock, the sun was shining, and the call had been made. He was off to meet his handler, Mr Charles.

Decker left the restaurant putting on a pair of fake Ray-Bans and entered the underground station at Tottenham Court Road where he got on a Central Line train, heading west. He read a free newspaper on the train and exited the underground at Lancaster Gate, still wearing the Ray-Bans, and crossing the road towards Hyde Park. He walked west along the Bayswater Road until he came to a hotel, situated on the opposite side of the road, with a front portico, double doors and bay trees in planters at the entrance.

Decker checked the time on his watch – 13:32 – and scanned the front of the hotel, then checked the adjacent road for people sitting in parked cars, or standing about for no obvious reason. The area looked clear. Decker dropped the newspaper he was carrying in a bin as a signal, and a moment later a man left through the double doors at the front of the hotel.

The man was in his 60s, wearing thick brown corduroys, suede desert boots and a blue Musto jacket. His hair was grey and side-parted. Decker knew the man by the name of Mr Charles, and he was his handler.

Decker watched Mr Charles walk along the pavement, giving it a last chance to flush someone out. Still everywhere looked clear.

Mr Charles stopped and waited at the traffic lights to cross the road. He was carrying a golfing umbrella and was tapping the pavement with it. The wind blew his hair out of its parting.

Once across the road, Decker followed him into Hyde Park, keeping at a distance of about 40 metres, head slightly lowered, hands in pockets. As he followed him, he monitored his periphery for any unexpected movement. Ahead of him, Mr Charles swung his umbrella at his side. About 100 metres into the park, Decker closed in on him.

Coming up behind him, Decker said, 'Why did they send you?'

Mr Charles kept looking straight ahead. 'A familiar face.'

Decker, glancing from left to right, half a step behind him, said, 'Not that familiar,' for he hadn't seen Mr Charles for a while now.

'How have you been keeping, Martin? It's been a long time.'

Decker saw himself lying between trees, a .300 magnum in hand, a steep slope, a car parked in a lay-by below, a hole through the windscreen.

'Two years,' he said.

'That's right.' Mr Charles kept looking straight ahead as he spoke. 'I heard you had a girlfriend.'

'Yeah,' Decker said, 'until you called.'

'I'm sorry. We should have given you more time. But you know how it is. You understand everything will be taken care of.'

'I understand,' Decker said.

With his right hand, Mr Charles smoothed back his hair where it had blown out of its parting. Decker thought he looked older: the wrinkles on his hand, the hollowing of his cheeks. He would be about his father's age, Decker thought, had his father still been alive.

Mr Charles said, 'I trust the noodles were up to their normal standard.'

Decker nodded. 'Kim sends his regards.'

Mr Charles turned his attention to a group of kids playing football on the grass. One of the kids scored a goal and, celebrating, pulled his T-shirt up over his head and ran in circles. Mr Charles smiled as he watched them, then said, 'His name is Daniel Howell. You received the photos, I trust.'

'Yeah.'

'We need him watched – who's coming, who's going. You have the case?'

'It's at the flat.'

'We'll confirm a drop-off when the time comes.'

A bar of sunlight swept across the park, as if scanning for a code.

Mr Charles said, 'There are other interested parties … people on the inside. You'll be on your own for a while.'

A woman approached, pushing a double-seated buggy with two kids onboard. Mr Charles glanced up to the sky, and said, 'What a lovely day it is,' and stepped to one side to let her pass.

The woman mumbled a 'thank you' as she went past.

They continued walking.

Decker said, 'How long have I got?'

'Six days. You're looking tired. Are you sleeping?'

'On and off.'

'It's not going to be a problem, is it?'

'No. No problem.'

'Good.'

They approached the Speke monument where another path intersected the one they were on.

Without turning round, Mr Charles said, 'Be a tourist for a few days. Take some pictures. Get some rest. The organisation will be in touch,' and he turned left at the junction, heading towards the Italian Gardens, east of the park.

Decker kept walking straight ahead.

8

Decker had known Mr Charles longer than he had known anyone else alive.

It all began when his parents died in the avalanche and he went to live with his grandmother. He was seven at the time. Despite having just lost his parents, Decker always reckoned this to be about the happiest time in his life. His grandmother lived in the countryside, kept chickens and had a Cocker Spaniel that followed you everywhere. He went fishing for tench and carp in a nearby lake and learnt how to shoot with a rusty BSA air rifle he'd found in his grandmother's garage. His grandmother was a sweet lady who cooked for him, read him stories and let him do just about anything he wanted.

But it didn't last. His grandmother died just before his 11th birthday. After that, he moved between foster homes, which weren't such happy times. Then at 13, he went to boarding school, thanks to money and instructions left by his father.

In many ways, boarding school kept him out of trouble and proved a good escape. That's not to say it was easy at the start. Up to that point, Decker hadn't really noticed the impact that not having parents had on other people. As far as he was concerned, it was no big deal, he was used to it. But for others it was a shock, especially for his cloistered, well-to-do private school contemporaries who'd mostly only known other rather perfect lives similar to their own. What Decker noticed most was how cautious it made people around him, like he was carrying a contagious disease they were worried they might catch. Not having parents set him apart. People were a little wary of him. He was 'the boy without any parents'.

Decker was already a fairly independent and self-sufficient kid and this experience only made him more inclined to seek out his own company. Not that this worried him – he was more than used to being on his own. Besides, he told himself, what did he care what these rich kids thought of him, anyway. In a school environment, though, this had the strange effect of bringing people to him. And within a short space of time, he went from the disease-carrying kid to someone who was seen as being able to take care of himself. It won him many admirers and followers. This, coupled with the fact he showed an aptitude for sport, allowed him to forge out an identity aside from 'the boy without any parents'. All in all, this meant school wasn't an unpleasant experience, although he remained remote and untouchable to some, which he probably was.

As well as being good at sport, Decker also out-performed his contemporaries in the school cadets. In his first year, he won the .22 rifle shooting competition at Bisley, a fact he repeated every year. He also led the assault course team. With the school's strong military tradition, it seemed perfectly normal to think about joining the army. Boarding school to army barracks wasn't such a big leap after all – a fact pointed out to him by the school's career officer at the time. It turned out he wasn't wrong. While his friends went off to India or Thailand or some other remote location on gap years, Decker signed up to the army, where he excelled. He was a natural soldier, he got told. He was physically strong and mentally resilient. But most importantly, he was a good listener who took orders well.

But once again it didn't last. After serving three years in the army, Decker woke up one night and knew the time had come to move on. He wasn't long back from his second tour of Afghanistan and was on post-operational leave. He got up and looked out of his window at home, trees swirling in the breeze, and remembered how he'd often woken in the middle of the night at school – the dormitory full of snoring bodies, the moonlit quads outside, the vast stillness of the old stately home. It was the same then as now, this feeling of emptiness, of his life passing him by, that he felt like he didn't have any choice but to act. And with only a year left to serve, he went missing.

He had nowhere to go of course. He ended up in Israel, working on a kibbutz near Tiberius where he picked fruit, drove a tractor and worked in the packing plant. It was the summer. In the evenings, he and the other workers sat round a fire drinking bottled beer. On his days off, he would lie in a hammock and read books, mainly thrillers that were left in the hostel by other travellers. He slept in a dormitory to begin with then got his own room. A simple set up: a metal bed, blanket and sheet and light bulb on a dusty flex.

Then one day, a young man drove up in a beaten Toyota 4x4 pickup. His name was Raffi and he was commissioned to work on the packing plant.

Although Raffi slept in the dormitory like everyone else, Decker sensed from the start there was something different about him. He had a way of making eye contact that told you he was recording events. He also had an ability to get people talking about themselves within minutes of meeting them without giving much away about himself. With Raffi around, the atmosphere on the kibbutz soon changed.

Decker kept himself to himself to begin with, disappearing to his room to read while Raffi and the others talked. Several nights passed before Raffi knocked on Decker's door and invited himself in. Sitting down on the floor, Raffi swigged from a bottle of wine. 'You were a soldier, weren't you?' he said, wiping his mouth with the back of his hand and handing the bottle to Decker.

Decker hesitated, holding the bottle to his lips, but without drinking.

'It's all right. I won't say,' Raffi said. 'As it happens, so was I.'

And that's how it started. From then on, they drank together on a regular basis. Decker found Raffi to be good company: funny, intelligent, with a gift for seeing the absurdity of life. And Decker enjoyed listening to his stories just as Raffi seemed to enjoy telling them.

The day Raffi finished his contract at the kibbutz he came to Decker's room, only this time he wasn't making jokes in his normal way. He stood by the window and, glancing outside, lit a cigarette. 'All you have to do is pass on a package,' he said. Decker realised then Raffi's whole stay had been working up to this moment. 'Your contact will arrange a time and a place.'

Decker suspected the reason he agreed to do the job had something to do with the fact he was missing from the army and wasn't ready to turn himself in yet and face another year. Besides, he didn't want to work on a kibbutz for forever. So what did he have to lose?

Leaving an envelope of US dollars on his bed, Raffi climbed into the 4x4, flicking the cigarette out the window, and drove away. It was the last time Decker would see him.

The time and place turned out to be a nightclub in Jerusalem, just outside the old city walls. Decker was surprised there was even a nightclub in Jerusalem.

He was there in good time. The nightclub in question was called "The Underground", and borrowed the London underground's logo. It was hidden down a side-street just outside the Old City walls, in walking distance from St David's Gate, where Decker was staying at the Jaffa hostel. He wasn't in the nightclub long when two Americans, recognising him from the kibbutz, came over and said hello. Both of them were a little drunk. 'Come and meet the others,' they said. Making up some excuse, Decker left them talking to two Danish girls and went outside for a cigarette. But just as he was about to spark up he heard a voice behind him say, 'Raffi says hello.' Decker went to turn round when the voice said, 'Keep still. You will pass a man with a red bag. You will tell him you're looking for the pyramids.'

Decker saw the Americans dancing with the Danish girls when he returned back inside. Pushing through the crowd, he spotted the man with the red bag at the bar. He was more of a boy in fact, thought Decker, with bum fluff moustache, darting eyes and a hollow chest. Decker went over and stood beside him and repeated the line about the pyramids; without anything more being said, the exchange was made.

A couple were kissing in the doorway when, leaving the club, Decker heard a loud scream, followed by a burst of semi-automatic fire. Blood splattered the kissing couple and a young Israeli guy went down on his back, blood welling up from holes in his chest.

People panicked and started running. There was another burst of fire and Decker dived behind a line of bollards outside as bullets fizzed over his head.

There were four Israeli soldiers in the club that night – young army recruits armed with guns could often been seen out enjoying themselves at night – and they ran out of the club and returned fire. Two of them quickly took bullets and rolled about on the ground, squealing in pain.

There was a break in the shooting for a moment as masked gunmen walked through the crowd, pushing people to the ground as they searched for a face. Decker watched as one of the gunman went up to a wounded Israeli soldier and, pointing a pistol at his head, fired twice, the sound of the empty cases ringing out in the street as they hit the pavement.

The acrid smell of gunpowder hung in the air. Decker looked round the side of a bollard and spotted the two Americans standing outside the club with the Danish girls, blood covering their faces. Not far away, Decker saw the remaining Israeli soldier struggling with the magazine of his M16, his hands shaking as he tried to clip the magazine into the place. But one of the gunmen saw what the Israeli soldier was trying to do and let out a burst of fire. The soldier's body jigged about on the pavement like it had received an electric shock.

The masked gunman then came together, speaking on walkie-talkies, while people lay on the road, hands over their heads, whimpering.

Decker remembered feeling remarkably calm at that moment. He looked at the dead Israeli soldier nearby, his M16 lying across his chest, his finger still in the trigger guard. He was about 20 years old Decker remembered thinking, too young to die. Noting the position of the gunmen – three in total – then a van parked across the road, its driver smoking a cigarette, Decker rolled across the tarmac until he was alongside the body of the dead soldier, and taking his M16 off him set it in his shoulder. One of the gunmen turned his head at this point, but Decker had already pulled back the charging handle and let out a burst of fire.

The three gunmen crumpled one after the other. The driver was drawing his weapon through the window of the van when Decker turned the M16 on him. Another single burst of fire and the driver cracked his head against the windscreen.

Decker wondered later whether this was what he had been called there for. Even he was surprised how prepared he had been. The next day, he fled the country. For several weeks, he kept moving. Eventually Raffi's money ran out and he ended up in the south of France, sleeping rough.

The months passed. He learnt to speak French and then found work on a farm in the South-West. It was there living with a French girl called Sylvie who worked on the farm with him that his life would change again. One morning, a silver BMW pulled up outside his farm cottage. Getting out the car, the driver of the car looked up to the window where Decker was getting dressed. It was six o'clock in the morning. He was a grey-haired man of about 55 wearing a tweed jacket and brogues. This was the first time Decker set eyes on Mr Charles.

9

The morning after meeting Mr Charles, Decker made himself breakfast at the flat. Two slices of bacon, an egg and toast. It was 6:30, and just getting light.

As he ate, he looked out the window and sipped coffee. When he finished eating, he continued to look out of the window.

At 7:30 he saw Howell leave for his run, in Lycra shorts, hooded top and with earphones in. Decker wondered what he was listening to, figuring it was going to be an extreme – either Beethoven or some gangsta rap.

Howell followed the same route as yesterday, turning left at the end of the road, and heading east along the river towards Blackfriars. Decker made a note of the time, then watched passing traffic and pedestrians until Howell returned about half an hour later, when Decker made another note of the time.

Decker remained by the window like this for the rest of the morning without seeing Howell again. For lunch, he made a sandwich and more coffee. In the afternoon, to break up the monotony, he did a series of exercises on the floor, ranging from crunches to press-ups. A couple of times, nature called. But all day he was never away from the window for more than five minutes.

At 19:06, Decker observed Howell leave his building again. He was wearing beige chinos, a blue shirt and hooded black windbreaker, and carrying a leather satchel over his shoulder. He headed north.

Decker left the flat, putting on a beanie, and followed him all the way to Sloane Square where Howell waved down a cab and set off up Sloane Street. Decker jumped into the next available taxi just as the driver was resetting his meter. 'Sloane Street, please,' he said.

On Piccadilly, Decker saw Howell get out his taxi and enter a hotel with a line of flags hanging out the front. Decker abandoned his taxi a little further down the road, doubled back and entered the same hotel a minute or two later.

In the foyer, Decker saw Howell shaking hands with three men – an Arab in jeans and blazer and two Caucasians in suits.

They moved through into the bar, sat at a table and ordered drinks. Decker hung back in the adjacent corridor, pretending to take a call on his mobile. Howell placed various documents and brochures on the table. The three men looked at the documents. From the hallway, Decker managed to take a picture of them.

A little later, Howell left the hotel alone and walked in a westerly direction. The time was 20:22 according to Decker's watch.

Near the Charing Cross Road, Decker photographed Howell entering an Italian restaurant, where a young couple were waiting for him. They seemed to know each other well – old friends, perhaps – hugging each other as they said hello. A waiter showed them to a table and Decker positioned himself across the road.

At 21:51, Howell was on the move again, walking through Soho, having said goodbye to his two friends at the restaurant. The streets were full of people. Decker had to work hard to keep him in range.

At 22:09, Decker observed Howell entering a pub just off Frith Street. Decker walked past the bar and went into a Chinese restaurant. He asked for a table by the window. He ordered dim sum and oolong tea. He was hungry and now was as good a time as any to eat, he thought. He ate with the chopsticks provided and took his time. As he ate, he watched people come and go from the bar. Finishing the tea he ordered a refill. When he finished that, the waiter brought him a plate of sliced oranges.

At 23:20, Howell left the bar with a young guy, joking and laughing about something. The young guy, in skinny black jeans, white Converse trainers and hooded grey top, stopped on the pavement and lit a cigarette in cupped hands. It was then Decker recognised him from notes attached to Howell's file. His name was Will Fenton and was thought to be Howell's boyfriend.

Decker watched them from the opposite side of the road as he removed orange pith from his teeth with a toothpick he'd taken from the restaurant. When the two men set off in the opposite direction, Decker dropped the toothpick and followed them.

They walked back towards Soho Square, turning right onto Bateman Street, then left down Greek Street. At one point, they held hands. Then, just off the Charing Cross Road, they got into a cab and headed south.

Decker took a picture of the departing taxi, noticing as he did so a man standing on the opposite side of the street to him. The man was wearing a black denim jacket and looking at his phone, or at least pretending to. Decker saw him avert his eyes when he looked across the road in his direction. Something about him, Decker thought, didn't feel right.

Pretending not to notice him, Decker crossed the street and headed down the Charing Cross Road. He walked quickly, turning left just before Leicester Square station, where a group of drunken girls stood outside a bar on the corner of Long Acre. There was lots of screaming and laughter as a bottle smashed on the pavement

Decker turned left down a narrow alley onto Floral Street and flattened himself behind a pillar and waited. Several minutes passed. Then he heard footsteps and the man in the black denim jacket appeared at the top of the alley. Decker could see his reflection in the shop glass, hesitating, looking back. Decker could tell the man was nervous – probably hadn't expected anything like this when he was offered £50 to keep an eye on him.

The man edged forward, keeping close to the wall. Then appearing at the other end of the alley, he stopped and looked in both directions. He was breathing heavily.

Decker stepped out from behind the pillar and drove his fist into his face. Blood spurted from the man's nose as he rocked backwards. Decker then kicked him in the ribs and the man folded over, groaning, at which point Decker grabbed him by his neck and dragged him behind a wheelie bin.

'Who sent you?' Decker said.

'I don't know.'

Decker slammed his face into the wheelie bin. 'Who sent you?'

'I don't know. Honest.' Blood bubbled from the man's nostrils. 'I am just meant to follow you.'

'Who's your contact?'

'I don't know. I've never met anyone.'

'A number?'

'He calls me.'

Decker drew the SIG from the waistband and stuck the silencer into the man's neck.

The man said, 'No, please. Don't kill me.'

Decker looked up and down the street, then struck the man with the butt of the SIG, and rammed his head into the wall. He was unconscious when Decker emptied his pockets, taking his phone, wallet and a packet of cigarettes. Later, Decker got on a bus at Embankment.

10

The unconscious guy's phone rang as Decker was getting off the bus. It rang three times before Decker answered it. There was a hiss on the other end, a click, but no voice. A second or two passed then the line went dead. Decker dropped the phone in a bin along with the man's wallet. He kept the packet of cigarettes because someone had written a number on the lid and he thought it worth checking out.

It was past midnight when Decker got back and another hour before he saw Howell and his boyfriend return. They must have stopped somewhere on their way, he thought. An hour later, Decker fell asleep in the chair.

*

Three hours later, Decker was gasping for breath, fingers digging into the chair's armrests. For a moment, he was somewhere else: an explosion, building masonry, dust, limbless bodies, blood. Another dream.

He sat up and took deep breaths and looked out the window: the lights still off in Howell's flat … halos round streetlights … treetops barely moving. He saw a fox trot down the pavement, stop and urinate, then slip through the railings into the park…

It seemed like hours before he saw anyone.

Howell opened his front door at 7:32, ten minutes later than yesterday. Decker sighted him through the camera as he was programming his iPod and stretching his legs on the wall. Zooming in … click, click … click, click.

Decker moved back from the window continuing to snap him as he ran past.

Howell turned left at the river and disappeared out of view.

Cars stopped at the lights, cyclists snaking forward in the queue. Across the park, the wind gusted in treetops, causing rainwater to shower the pavements. Decker sat and waited, his eyes moving from the window to the table-top where he'd left the packet of cigarettes he'd taken from the unconscious guy.

Decker picked up the packet and read the number written on the lid. He read it several times, his lips moving as he read, thinking it looked like part of a vehicle registration number.

Decker then opened the packet and found a small lighter tucked inside. He took it out and sparked it up. On the side of the lighter was the word "Corus". It was the name of the hotel where he had met Mr Charles, which meant the unconscious guy had probably tracked him from there, so was likely to be someone on the inside – another 'interested party', as Mr Charles referred to them.

Decker looked at the word "Corus" again and realised it was only missing the "p" of Corpus, the name of the organisation he worked for. Was Mr Charles trying to tell him something by this?

Decker removed one of the cigarettes, sniffed its barrel, and put it in his mouth. He could remember smoking on his last job in Sardinia, but not much after that. He couldn't remember exactly when he'd given up, for example, or where, just as he couldn't remember *why* he'd given up. Was it because of Annie, who'd often complained of the smell?

Decker thought about Annie for a moment. He wondered what she had been doing these past few days. He imagined her back at the flat, with all those cushions and candles, speaking to friends on the phone, telling them: 'He's not answering his phone, he's just disappeared.' Her friends would be saying: 'Just forget him, Annie. Just forget him.'

Decker sucked on the cigarette and pretended to exhale. He remembered he'd first smoked at school – in the churchyard – then out of windows at his foster home, and later with his girlfriend, Julie, at her parent's house in Surrey, overlooking Black Down where they'd sat up late with the windows open, the moon rising behind a belt of fir trees. Decker felt a sense of loss for this part of his life – life before the compound and Mr Charles and Corpus. It was a familiar feeling to him.

He returned the cigarette to the packet.

It was getting light outside.

He watched Howell returned from his run, running all the way up the steps to his front door and stopping the timer on his watch. Decker snapped several pictures through a gap in the curtains and then made a note of the time.

Twenty minutes later, the door opened again and Will Fenton appeared, wearing the same skinny black jeans and grey hooded top from last night. He stood on the doorstep, fluffing his hair with one hand. Howell stood back in the doorway, wearing a white dressing gown. He must have just had a shower as his hair was still wet. The two of them kissed. Decker was ready with the camera to capture the moment. Then Howell retreated inside, closing the door, while Fenton trotted down the steps and turned left at the end of the road.

A minute later, Decker left his building and walked down an adjacent street. He came to the main road where cars zipped past in both directions and Fenton was waiting at a bus stop, checking his mobile, the breeze blowing his hair in his eyes.

Decker walked towards him just as a bus was approaching. Fenton stuck out his hand and flagged it down, letting an old woman get on first, then taking a seat near the front. Decker got on after him and sat several seats back.

The bus followed the course of the river and crossed at Chelsea Bridge. Decker observed Fenton looking out the window, with one knee pulled up between his hands and the seat in front of him. According to his file he was 26, which made him seven years younger than Howell.

Fenton got off the bus just south of Chelsea Bridge and Decker followed him. Fenton, squeezing his hands into his jean pockets, rounded his shoulders as he walked along. Decker kept a distance of about 50 metres between them.

At a junction, Fenton went into a Starbucks and Decker waited on the opposite side of the road where a rubbish truck was stopped on the corner, its crew chucking bin bags into the back. A few minutes later, Fenton left the Starbucks clutching a lidded cup and Decker started following him again.

They turned off the main road, Fenton stopping momentarily to light a cigarette, then passed railway arches, a line of industrial units and a greasy spoon café where a train passed along an overground line above them and Fenton turned right down a cobbled alley. About 50 metres down this alley, Fenton stopped outside a metallic door and took a call on his mobile, while Decker stood on the corner and photographed him.

Continuing his call, Fenton unlocked the door and went inside.

It was 9:09.

Another train was passing along the track when Decker turned for home, having seen enough.

*

Drawing the blinds across the flat windows, Decker opened the laptop and uploaded the photographs to a secure bulletin board. He also searched the internet for news about the "Paris shootings". There was mention of the French police putting all their resources into the affair. They were calling for witnesses and following up various leads. There was speculation of a professional hit. The African found shot in the flat was named as Omar "B", a postgraduate student from Algeria with known links to a terrorist organisation. There was no more mention of the moped driver, which meant Corpus wanted it that way, hiding the real story and leaving the police, the media and the public with an erroneous terrorist story because that was the easiest fit. Decker knew how it went.

Shutting down the laptop, Decker did 30 press-ups, followed by 30 sit-ups; then he took a shower. In the shower, he thought about Annie again. He hoped she was okay. She hadn't deserved any of this. Maybe one day he could make it up to her. Then he thought about the woman he'd met in St Pancras yesterday and wondered what her story was. Then he thought how he never used to think like this, about people and their lives, how in the past, he'd been better at putting things behind him.

After his shower, Decker sat on the edge of the bed with a towel round his waist and looked at his reflection. He hadn't shaved for a week. He hadn't slept properly for years. He ran his hand over his bristly hair and inspected his ribs again. The bruising was still there.

*

Howell was working from home today, periodically appearing at a top window on the phone. He went out for milk and biscuits at 12:23, wearing a tracksuit and baseball cap.

Decker made coffee, studied the packet of cigarettes again, and wrote down what he had so far: Howell jogged every morning for approximately 30 minutes; had people he met with in the evenings, some socially, some for business; had a boyfriend, with a flat across the river, who stayed over some times; but otherwise was alone.

Thinking ahead, Decker thought, the morning jog would probably provide the best opportunity – for Decker knew he wasn't there for his photography skills. He could gain access to the house and wait for him to return. Alternatively, there was somewhere along the jogging route, but that brought its own complications and risks.

Decker recorded times alongside every activity. Time made sense to Decker in a way that nothing else did. He knew from past experience the value of time. People fell into natural rhythms, often without knowing it. He was yet to observe a life that wasn't just a series of repetitions. Time and recording it soon revealed these repetitions and, in turn, what you needed to know.

*

It was 15:24 when it started to rain.

Decker observed Howell sign for a package at his front door. He was in the middle of a call, trapping the phone against his shoulder as he signed.

At 15:54, the rain letting off, Decker saw a couple enter the ground-floor flat with suitcases. Decker photographed them opening and closing the door, then again, half an hour later when they went out shopping.

At 17:25, Decker photographed the woman putting out a bag of rubbish.

At 18:40, the man walking up the road and posting a letter.

On Google maps, Decker checked the front of Howell's building. He estimated there to be another six flats. Already he had identified five other tenants. That left one on holiday.

At 19:04, Decker drank a bottle of beer and gazed at the cigarette packet on the table that he'd taken off the unconscious guy. Picking up the packet, Decker read the number on the lid again and wondered who was paying the unconscious guy, and if they'd found his replacement yet, and if this replacement was somewhere out there watching him, just as he was watching Howell.

At some point, he lay on the floor and stared at the ceiling, then did as many press-ups as he could before taking another shower.

He cooked pasta for supper and sat by the window.

One by one, Decker observed house lights going off.

He saw no one leave or enter Howell's building.

He went to bed around one o'clock, lying in the dark with his eyes open for about an hour before sleep came.

11

The next day, Howell walked south on St George's Square and turned left onto Grosvenor Road. It was 16:12 after an uneventful morning of coffee refills and window gazing. The sun was shining on wet pavements.

Decker followed Howell along the river, past Lambeth Bridge, and round Parliament Square, then onto Victoria Embankment. The traffic was heavy in both directions. Howell took a call on his mobile that last no longer than 30 seconds.

They passed under the bridge at Embankment.

Howell turned left into Victoria Embankment Gardens. Decker continued along the pavement towards Savoy Street. Through the railings, he observed Howell walking under the plane trees where a woman in black Lycra was jogging along the track, and a tramp was laid out on a bench with his belongings stuffed into two Sainsbury's bags. Then on the corner with Savoy Street, he lost sight of Howell through the trees.

Breaking into a run, Decker turned left into Savoy Place, the narrow road that ran round the back of the park, and there he was, exiting the park at the back. He was carrying a white carrier bag now. There had been a pick-up in the park.

Howell headed up Savoy Hill and Decker followed him. They came out onto Savoy Street, where the traffic was stopped at the lights, and Howell went into the Café Nero just up from Waterloo Bridge. The time, 17:45.

Decker passed the front of Café Nero and saw Howell taking a seat at a booth with a cup of coffee and removing an A4-sized document from the carrier bag he'd received and slipping the document inside his jacket.

The traffic stopped and started at the lights. There was a never-ending stream of pedestrians along the pavements.

Then at 17:48 Howell left Café Nero and headed up Kingsway towards Holborn where he deposited the white carrier bag in a bin and checked his phone for messages, then headed towards the underground.

Decker stood on the escalator behind him.

They boarded the same carriage but sat at opposite ends. A busker, with a brylcreemed black quiff, walked through the carriages playing *Ring of Fire* by Johnny Cash. Several people gave him money. They changed at Victoria and rode one stop to Sloane Square.

Howell walked down the King's Road, passed the Saatchi Galley, and turned left into Duke of York Square where a grey-headed man was waiting for him on a bench. Decker estimated the man to be in his early 70s and he was wearing a tweed coat and holding a wooden-handled umbrella and had a jacket in a polythene bag folded over his arm.

Howell sat next to him. They spoke. Howell passed him the envelope. From across the road, Decker caught them on camera.

Pocketing the envelope, the old man stood up and set off down Cheltenham Terrace. Howell crossed the road, turned left and cruised down the King's Road.

Decker followed him.

Along the way, Decker watched Howell stop and browse in several men's shops. He wafted through hangers of clothing, checking labels, but declining help when approached by shop assistants.

Next, Decker recorded Howell entering a kitchen utensils shop near the library. After ten minutes of browsing, he had two small gadgets wrapped in brown paper at the till. He paid in cash.

Lastly, Decker saw Howell enter a Waitrose and leave with two bags of food. Then saw him waiting at a bus stop checking his phone again. Decker noticed Howell smile at one of his messages and wondered if it was from Fenton. It was that sort of smile, Decker thought. In the next few minutes, Howell boarded a bus and headed home.

The time: 20:14.

*

It was just starting to rain when Decker entered his flat, dropped his keys on the table and plugged the camera into the laptop. While he waited for the photos to upload, he poured a glass of milk. He drank the milk and looked through the blinds. Howell's lights were on but the blinds were drawn. Spots of rain ran down the windows.

Decker looked through 12x mag binoculars up and down the street: a boat passing along the river; a cyclist freewheeling up to the lights; a girl texting on her phone at a bus stop.

Decker felt hungry. For some reason he thought of Annie again and wondered what her plans were for tonight. He pictured her eating out with friends or maybe having someone over. For some reason he found it hard to picture her face. He recalled some of their conversations, remembering when they had first fallen for each other, standing waiting to be seated in a restaurant. He was with work colleagues; she was meeting friends. They were seated at opposite tables and then bumped into each other at the bar. A week later, they were having sex on her sofa. 'I don't normally do this so soon,' she'd said. He told her he'd just moved to Paris, and nor did he. Smiling, she didn't look like she believed him.

Soon Decker stopped thinking about Annie and noticed the rain hitting the window and falling through the streetlights and then another tenant entering Howell's building – time 21:43 – who Decker had seen before. But tonight, he was back from work a little later than normal and carrying a shopping bag, which may explain it, Decker thought, as he snapped his picture.

Then Decker thought about Howell upstairs alone in his own flat. Pictured him making some fancy dinner, pouring himself a glass of wine. He imagined classical music playing in the background. No boyfriend tonight though. Then he thought about him in the park today: the envelope; the old man in Duke of York Square; then shopping for clothes and food. Then he thought about having to kill him in a few days and him no longer doing these things.

It was still raining when Decker fell asleep.

12

'Are you still there?' a voice said, in his dream.

*

Decker sat up in the chair, knocking a cup off the table. He pulled the slide of the SIG, spinning round as if there had been someone in the room with him.

He was sweating. Coffee dripped off the table. He looked at his watch. It was 4:50. He calculated he'd been asleep for three hours.

He picked up the cup and stood it on the table then, parting the blinds, checked along the street. A van passed along the riverside, a spray of wet under tyres. Then he looked across at Howell's building, the blinds still drawn, and imagined him asleep in bed: a router light blinking in the corner of his room; a pile of books; a laptop; memory sticks. He imagined a sparsely furnished room: a towel folded over a rail in the bathroom; a toothbrush; razor; shaving cream; his running kit laid out on a chair for the morning.

Rain dripped down the fronts of buildings and ran along the sides of the road. Treetops swayed in gusts of wind and rain.

Scanning the street again, Decker then noticed a red moped parked several doors up from Howell's building. After five days of watching the same street, you tended to notice when something looked out of place.

Decker picked up the camera and set it between the curtains, zoomed in and snapped a couple of pictures. Then lowering the camera, he looked at the bike again, its wheel turned at an angle, an armoured cable pulled through the spokes and a plastic cover protecting the seat.

It was then he made the connection: the cigarette packet he'd taken from the unconscious guy; the registration number.

Decker picked the packet off the table and opened the lid and compared the number with that of the moped. They were the same.

Decker stood back from the window, feeling as if someone was watching him now. Another figure in another room somewhere, waiting like him for the call. He reached for the SIG and turned towards the flat door, listening for sounds of movement in the corridor outside; then side-stepped across the room, keeping close to the wall, with two hands on the gun. Reaching the door, he flattened himself against the wall and listened … but couldn't hear anything. He waited like this for about a minute, then went back into the room and took the laptop out from under the sofa, turned it on and started looking for the moped in other photos he'd taken.

With the rain drumming against the window, Decker zipped through photo after photo, stopping on certain photos and zooming in on different points of the street, studying the parked cars, making a note of their registration plates, and the cars that were in some photos but not in others, trying to calculate which vehicles belonged to which address. Before long, he could account for nearly every single vehicle – except the moped. Maybe if he stayed here another few months, he thought, it would appear again. Perhaps it was a new pattern emerging. Or another assignment was taking shape.

He looked at photos of Howell running along the river, and sitting in the hotel with the Arab and two suited Caucasians, then inspecting the contents of the envelope in Nero, and sitting on the bench with the old man on the Kings Road.

Then he looked at the cigarette packet again, the writing on the lid …

*

The rain stopped around 6:30 that morning.

It was still dark. Two seagulls were walking along the pavement. A sheet of newspaper skidded towards them.

Decker was dozing in the chair with a blanket pulled over him when a man left Howell's building and the seagulls took off. The man trotted down the steps, glancing in both directions. But it was enough to wake Decker. And before the man had reached the bottom step, Decker had the camera poking through the curtains.

The man had the appearance Decker knew from experience the police would later describe as 'Mediterranean'. He was carrying a black bike helmet under his arm. As he walked along the pavement, he zipped up the olive green parka jacket he was wearing. He reached the moped and removed the security cable and seat cover, taking a look around him, then climbed on the back and put on the helmet and some gloves and started the bike. Decker took several pictures of him as he performed these actions and then as he drove off down the street. He turned left at the end of the road. It was 6:44.

*

Decker remained at the window and waited for Howell to appear, expecting to see him coming down his steps in his running gear at any minute.

An hour passed. Decker saw the other tenants leave for work, the postman deliver mail, the sky brighten.

But Howell's blinds remained drawn.

Decker reviewed the latest photos he'd taken of the moped and the Mediterranean-looking man, studying the number plate again and double-checking it with the number written on the cigarette packet. They were still the same.

He saw an elderly woman in a chequered wool coat walk a Scottie dog through the park. He watched a cruise boat pass under Chelsea Bridge and seagulls soar over the suspension cables. Later, he observed an electrician park a Vauxhall van down the road and carry rolls of insulated cable into a house.

Mid-morning, the sun broke from clouds. Wet pavements gleamed, wood pigeons flapped about in the plane trees and the first leaves started to fall – but still no sign of Howell.

Decker left the window for a moment and went to the kitchen to fetch some bread and cheese for his lunch. Carrying the food back to the window, he sat down and buttered two slices of bread and cut up the cheese and made a sandwich. As he ate, he watched a street cleaner push a yellow cart towards Embankment, picking up rubbish with tongs along the way.

Then at 13:34, he saw a bus pull in along the riverside and Fenton, Howell's boyfriend, get off.

Decker sat forward in the chair, putting down his half-eaten sandwich, and picked up the camera. Zooming in, he followed Fenton down the street, checking his phone. He was wearing the same skinny black jeans and grey hooded top as yesterday. He crossed the road, looking up from his phone, and approached Howell's building. Decker photographed him ringing on Howell's buzzer.

Getting no answer, Fenton walked back down the steps and looked up at the windows, hands in back pockets, jeans hanging off his hips.

Howell's blinds were still drawn.

Fenton stood there for a moment then walked back up the steps and tried the buzzer again. Then lifted the flap of the letterbox and looked inside. Then walked back down the steps and stood on the pavement for a bit, looking around. The breeze was blowing his hair about.

Decker put down the camera at this point and got ready to follow him.

Fenton was turning the corner at the top of the street when Decker left his building and followed him east on Lupus Street towards Pimlico, Fenton walking quickly now and checking his mobile.

Outside the Tube station, Fenton stopped and took a call on his mobile, and Decker hung back, picking up a free newspaper. Lighting a cigarette, Fenton ran his hand through his hair and gesticulated as he spoke on the phone. Then, looking like he lost the signal, stared at his mobile for a second before heading into the station.

Decker stood on the escalator behind him. Arriving on the platform, a train was just pulling in and Decker followed Fenton aboard. Sitting at the opposite end of the carriage, Decker watched Fenton judder his legs and scratch his arms. He hadn't shaved since he'd last seen him and there were dark bags under his eyes.

They changed at Embankment, took the Northern Line, and exited at Euston.

Decker followed Fenton across Euston Square then saw him stop at a set of lights on the Marylebone Road and check his phone. Then the lights changed and Fenton crossed the road and headed west.

Decker tracked him from the other side of the street, noticing him looking over his shoulder with greater frequency. Watching him, Decker remembered reading about an old age pensioner being run over on the Marylebone Road last year. About how she was crossing the road at a zebra crossing, pulling her shopping trolley, when an articulated lorry hit her. The driver never saw her. She was killed outright. You live to your 80s, survive a world war, the threat of heart disease and cancer – and a lorry mows you down. Decker remembered thinking it told you all you needed to know about the randomness of fate.

Now Decker saw Fenton stop outside the Wellcome Trust Museum, look in both directions, then go inside. Decker continued along the road for a bit, then crossed at a set of traffic lights, and doubled back.

He kept his eye on the museum entrance but got stuck behind a family of Chinese tourists wheeling suitcases along the pavement, taking their time, looking up at the buildings, and snapping crooked photos on their mobiles. One of them gave off a strong smell of perfume.

Just as he was about to pass them, Decker observed Fenton leave the museum in a hurry. Decker watched him run for the lights and head back across Euston Square. A second later, he saw a man appear from the museum entrance. The man was wearing a navy-coloured overcoat and had a pale face.

Decker's focus fissured for a second, like a buffering live stream. Memories of the African's blood-soaked leg, the smashing glass, the fizz of bullets overhead, the man at the window, the extended arm, the large sound moderator, the pale face … Soundless freeze frames flicked on and off in Decker's mind.

The man in front of him was the man at the window in Paris.

The man stood on the pavement outside the museum, turned in the other direction from Decker, his overcoat flapping about his legs in the breeze, the ripped lining hanging loose like a homeless guy's hand-me-down. Decker was close enough to see a crust of dandruff round the collar.

The Chinese tourists were consulting maps, jabbering away in Chinese as if their lives depended on whether they took the next left or right. Standing behind them, Decker didn't move. There was still that strong smell of perfume in the air.

The man in the overcoat walked to the kerb, putting his hands in his pockets now, causing the back of his coat to tighten. He had black hair and a complexion as white as chalk. To a passer-by, he had the appearance of an overworked Italian waiter. Decker knew him though for what he really was – a killer, a dead double, someone you wouldn't want to accept a plate of food from.

Decker watched as the killer flagged down a taxi. Gripping the lapels of his overcoat, he got into the back. The taxi pulled a U-turn, crossing the Marylebone Road, and headed back towards King's Cross. Decker watched it go, feeling this wasn't the last time he was going to see the passenger in the back. But he didn't want to think about that now.

At the next junction Decker veered south.

13

'Can you confirm your name and number?'

'Corpus: B four, zero, two, seven, one.'

The line whirred for a second like overhead cables swaying in the wind, then the bleep of the scanner, and a new ring tone started.

Mr Charles answered on the fourth ring, 'Go ahead.'

'I need to come in.'

There was a pause. 'Your assignment is still live.'

'The situation has changed.' Decker turned in the phone box, scanning the pavements.

'Meetings are difficult.'

'I understand.'

The line bleeped again.

'What is your status?'

'Howell is missing.'

'Remain at the flat. We'll get someone to you.'

The line hissed. 'When?'

'Early tomorrow. Use extension nine, two, zero, one.'

Decker entered the Underground at Warren Street and boarded a packed southbound Victoria Line train. He stood by the doors, watching people pushing each other to get on and off, and thought how senseless human life seemed at that moment with everyone rushing around trying to get somewhere important when really there was nowhere to go.

*

It was getting dark when Decker exited at Pimlico. Streetlights shone in the gloom. He walked down Lupus Street and turned right towards the river.

Approaching the flat, Decker saw a guy sat in a dated-looking silver Mercedes playing with his phone, the screen lighting up his face. Late 20s, with his hair shaved round back and sides but left long on top. Maybe he was waiting for his girlfriend or had come to pick up his grandmother. Either way, Decker wasn't taking any chances.

Pulling up his hood, Decker walked past his building and turned the corner at the end of the road and came round the back where there was a side alley.

Think of the world as a vast database. And the people in it, a set of types.

Decker saw Mr Charles turned to The Compound window.

This is what linguists call a corpus. But instead of words we are collecting people and behaviours. What we have is a lexical-like calculator of humanity.

Decker checked round himself, looking along the line of parked cars and up at the windows above him before pulling himself over a brick wall. He dropped down the other side onto a pile of rubble and peered round the side of an outbuilding covered in ivy. He saw a narrow strip of lawn leading to the back of his building.

Martin, people are the same as words. They are mostly predictable, conform to certain rules, and exhibit specific patterns of behaviour.

Decker entered his building through a downstairs window and stood at the bottom of the stairs. He could hear voices on a TV somewhere, then the clatter of plates of someone washing-up. He looked around himself. A free paper was sticking out of the letter box. Someone had parked their bicycle in the hallway.

Decker walked up the two flights of stairs and crept along the corridor to his flat. With his back against the wall, he drew the SIG from the waistband of his jeans and listened at his flat door, then checked the lock for scratches or signs of a forced entry. Satisfied no one had paid him a visit Decker unlocked the door and went in.

At the table, Decker uploaded the remaining photos to the bulletin board then packed a rucksack with a change of clothes, along with the photo of his parents, a passport and some cash. He stuffed the rucksack under the bed to pick up later, then sat in the chair and waited in darkness.

The rain tapped against the windows. He dismantled and reassembled the SIG. A car went past, headlights raking across the ceiling. He remembered the shootings in Paris, the man at the window, and then seeing him again today at the museum, and wondered what he was doing here, and what he wanted with Fenton. Knowing something wasn't right. But that it wasn't his job to work out what. The rain kept up throughout the night.

Intermittently, he slept.

*

It was still dark when Decker left the flat. The Mercedes had disappeared.

A payphone was ringing. Decker answered it. 'Extension nine, two, zero, one,' he said.

It had stopped raining but the roads were still wet, cars zipping past on damp tarmac, a cold breeze coming off the river.

The line hissed. 'Extension nine, two, zero, one confirmed.'

Decker said, 'I'm in position.'

'Please proceed. Username: Clements.'

'Confirmed.'

'Position: East of Eden.' And the line went dead.

Walking along Victoria Embankment, Decker looked across the river: another grey dawn, sunlight leaking across the city, fog swirling round bridge cables.

He covered the ground with little effort, his breathing steady, controlled. His eyes narrowed in the damp breeze.

In a glass-fronted hotel near Blackfriars Bridge, a woman at the front desk said, 'Can I have your name, please?'

Decker said, 'Clements.'

'Here you go, sir.' She handed him a small bag, smiling.

'Thank you.'

A bus pulled in with fogged-up windows. Decker boarded and took a seat near the front. On his lap, he opened the bag and removed a mobile. The bus splashed through potholes. They headed south of the river.

Opposite a warehouse with "For Let" signs up, Decker stepped off the bus and crossed the road. He had his hood up. Half way down a side-street, he entered a café.

Decker bought a coffee and sat at a wooden table, leaving his jacket on. Drinking the coffee, he kept his eye on a park entrance across the road where streetlights glowed in the foggy half-light. Before long, Decker saw a man in a Barbour jacket appear at the entrance, hands thrust in pockets, woollen beanie hat covering his ears. The man looked left and right then removed one of his hands from his jacket pocket holding a mobile.

Decker sipped his coffee and waited. He saw the man in the Barbour jacket press a saved number on his phone, his breath clouding above his head in the cold air. There was a split second's wait before Decker's phone started ringing on the table in front of him.

Decker said, 'Clements.'

'Position?'

'East of Eden.'

Pocketing his phone, Barbour jacket crossed the road and headed towards the river.

Decker left the café, scanning in both directions, and followed him.

At the end of the road Decker saw Barbour jacket turning right along the towpath and followed him.

Mist drifted off the water, the sound of seagulls and tug boats.

After about 200 metres they came to a small car park where a black Lexus was pulling in.

Barbour jacket crossed the car park. The Lexus circled and a back door swung open.

Decker looked over his shoulder. There was no one behind him. Barbour jacket was now standing alongside the Lexus, scanning the surroundings.

Decker started to cross the car park when he spotted a moped pulled in further down the road. He froze, his eyes narrowing, as he recognised the registration plate.

A hand beckoned to Decker from inside the Lexus, but it wasn't Mr Charles. Decker looked back towards the moped, the driver lifting his helmet visor, speaking into a radio mike. Decker didn't like it and started backing up.

He re-joined the towpath. He heard the Lexus pulling out of the car park, types screeching.

He broke into a jog.

Seagulls took off from hand railings, squawking.

He spotted an underpass ahead of him. Glancing back, he saw Barbour jacket breaking into a run, about 50 metres back.

Decker ran down some steps, stopped, and looked for a way out.

Seagulls squawked as they flew across the water.

To his right, there was a restaurant with aluminium tables and chairs. And two teenagers, loose baggy jeans, were skateboarding down the concrete walkway. The restaurant wasn't open. Looking up, Decker saw the moped pulling up on the road above, the driver – parka jacket,

Mediterranean complexion – removing his helmet and descending the steps the other side.

Decker looked back again and saw Barbour jacket was coming to a standstill behind him.

Decker wasn't left with many options. He started slowly towards the tunnel, slipping his hand inside his jacket, clasping the SIG. Glancing back, he saw Barbour jacket following him into the tunnel. The moped guy appeared at the other end. The two men closed in on him.

Decker was drawing the SIG when the skateboarders came through the tunnel, pushing off one leg and gliding in unison. The sound of skateboard wheels filled the enclosed space. Decker waited until they drew level, then dropped to the ground, turned and shot Barbour jacket behind him.

Barbour jacket lent up against the wall clutching his gut, blood filling his hands. Shot in the stomach.

The skateboarders left the tunnel the other end, none the wiser. The moped guy didn't fancy it and started running.

Decker raised the gun and purposefully shot him in the leg, knowing he was going to need him in a minute. The moped guy staggered against the side of the tunnel, slipping over like a shunted deer.

Decker then turned and saw Barbour jacket, sitting in a pool of his own blood, trying to pull a gun from his jacket pocket but it getting caught on the lining.

Decker shot him in the head, twice, the expended shells clinking on the concrete. Then, tucking the SIG into his waistband, he bent down and picked up the shells. Checking round himself, he came out of the tunnel, saw the moped driver limping off down the path, and broke into a jog.

Catching him up, Decker grabbed the back of his coat and rammed him against a wall.

'Call your friend in. And get him cleaned up.'

'You're going to shoot me,' holding up his hands, dripping blood.

'No, I'm not.'

'You're lying! You're going to shoot me. You're crazy!'

Decker looked round, checking windows, CCTV cameras. 'Do it now,' he said, and shoved the man in the direction of the underpass. He didn't want the police on to him as well, Decker thought. He needed this cleaned up, and quickly. Although the police were the least of his worries at this point, they would certainly complicate things. And if he was being set up, if Corpus were pulling the plug on him, which it looked like they were, one thing Decker didn't need was added complications.

The man headed back towards the tunnel, dragging his leg, glancing back, blood trailing along the towpath.

Decker watched him for a second before setting off in the opposite direction.

14

It was almost ten years ago when Mr Charles had come for him and he climbed into the passenger seat of the silver BMW and drove away from another life. He was missing from the army and now under investigation for his involvement in the murder of three Palestinians; the authorities were closing in on him.

'For someone with only basic training you've done remarkably well,' Mr Charles said as he drove away. 'But all things, good and bad, have an end.'

The BMW left a long trail of dust as they barrelled down the track away from the farm. Decker remembered observing a covey of partridges scuttling down the fence line and lifting off in the wind and Mr Charles saying, 'I've come to offer you a job,' checking his rear-view mirror and handing him a business card, then adding, 'You will work for Corpus Industries.'

Decker took an evening flight from Nice back to the UK where he stayed at the Ibis hotel near Gatwick airport. The next day he was taken in the back of a truck to what was referred to as "The Compound". The journey took several hours. There were no windows in the back of the truck and he was never told where he was going. But judging by the landscape when he got there, he guessed The Compound to be located somewhere in North Wales.

His training lasted two years, though such a measurement of time soon became meaningless on The Compound. Some nights it felt like whole lifetimes had passed, that his life in France with Sylvie was something he had dreamt or seen in a film. Yet some mornings he'd wake up and feel like he'd only just arrived, that it was only yesterday he was with Sylvie on the farm.

The mind played tricks. Any normal sense of time was no longer sustainable, a fact made worse by his lack of contact with others. Except for Mr Charles, Decker spoke to very few other people while he was at The Compound. Plus, there was no internet, TV or newspapers, so he'd no idea what was going on in the outside world, or even if there was an outside world anymore. Sometimes it felt like he was the remaining soldier in a once vast army. Empty barracks, firing ranges, assaults courses, and canteens greeted him each day. Anonymous uniforms issued him boxes of ammunition and served him dinner. He trained in the woods and fields surrounding The Compound, seeing only sheep and crows. Sometimes he was left to camp out for weeks on end without any provisions. At such times, he was forced to kill and eat rabbits and drink from streams. He sat through videos in empty classrooms and was given tasks on topics ranging from survival techniques to counter-surveillance. Sometimes, he was locked in an empty room for days at a time until it felt like he'd been abandoned there. Then there would be a knock on his door. And things would continue as before. No explanation.

'A long time ago I knew your father,' Mr Charles said to him one day. They were sitting in a long rectangular office overlooking the courtyard at The Compound where self-seeded trees sprouted through cracks in the concrete. Mr Charles was standing looking out the window with his back to him. The sun was setting though a line of ash trees. 'We worked together on an engineering project in Abu Dhabi,' he said. 'He was a most likeable man. It was a terrible accident.'

Decker remembered rising in his chair, but Mr Charles motioning to him to sit down again, then passing him a photograph of him with Decker's father, adding, 'So you can see our meeting wasn't a complete coincidence.'

Decker remembered feeling immobilised by a sense of familiarity, like somehow he'd always known this moment was going to happen. Looking up, he saw Mr Charles turning the gold signet ring on his little finger and looking back at him.

'Lesson one,' he said. 'Remember: acknowledging something as a coincidence is a sure sign you don't know what's really going on.'

And that was it.

Mr Charles never mentioned his father again. Looking back, Decker couldn't understand why he'd not asked for more details. For some reason, he just accepted it. Like everything else on The Compound, it felt to belong to its own reality. Anything that had happened in his life before seemed increasingly remote and unreal. And the longer he was there the greater this sense of unreality became. With it, Decker felt a growing acceptance of life on The Compound. From the early morning runs, the absence of contact, to camping in the woods, and living like an animal. These things became his reality, his life. The old memories began to recede, like dreams.

Lesson two: given time, you can get used to and accept anything.

The only other person Decker had any significant contact with was a woman called Eunice. She was his language teacher while he was there and taught him French and the rudiments of Arabic and several Slavic languages. 'Learning a second language is one of the few ways to conquer yourself and your ego,' Mr Charles told him once.

Lesson three: Learn to conquer yourself; to disappear; to think past yourself as if you no longer existed.

It was his contact with Eunice that was about the closest Decker got to his old life. Eunice talked about the world outside The Compound; how she had known three languages fluently by the age of five; having a French father and a Moroccan mother, with Spanish and German following at school, making her a polyglot by the time she went to university. Decker looked forward to his lessons with Eunice, though on reflection perhaps even Eunice's stories weren't real either.

Lesson four: Draw a circle. Put yourself inside this circle. And remember: this is your reality.

Decker was never told exactly what he was going to do in his new job, just as he was never told much about the organization he worked for. 'If there are others,' Mr Charles said to him once, 'which you can probably assume there are, you will not have contact with them or their handlers. Each of us, including myself, has contact with only one other operative. From now on, you are as good as alone.'

The funny thing was Decker felt for the first time like he wasn't alone anymore. But that he'd found a home, albeit an unusual one. He realised he'd been living a double-life for as long as he could remember – from one foster home to the next, to years of boarding school and the army. It was like there was now finally someone out there who knew him for who he really was.

When he left The Compound, he was 26 years old. He got a job with a travel agent. He lived in his own flat. He played football at the weekends. He went out drinking with colleagues. He dated a girl called

Lisa. They ate at restaurants, rented DVDs and had sex. It was all very normal. He received a promotion at work. Lisa moved in with him. For all intents and purposes, he was living a regular life again.

Nine months went by and events of the last three or so years began to feel like some kind of dream – the shootings, his disappearance, Mr Charles and The Compound. On his departure from The Compound he'd received no instructions as to what was going to happen next. Sometimes, he wondered whether The Compound was some kind of military prison. Maybe in cases such as his the authorities sent people there to rehabilitate them. And now he was rehabilitated they'd let him back into society. Another thought was that maybe it wasn't the authorities who'd caught up with him in France but the organization behind the shootings in Israel, and he'd been trained by them. Or maybe his training wasn't over yet and everything that was happening to him now was part of an exercise. Or maybe his first assignment had already begun and he just didn't realise it.

Nine months and two days had passed when his doorbell rang and his girlfriend, Lisa shouted, 'The pizza's here.' Running downstairs to answer the door, it never crossed Decker's mind that this would be it – the beginning.

15

A breeze was getting up. Pages of a *Metro* skated along the pavement. Riding the wounded guy's moped, Decker turned left off Nine Elms Lane, past the railway arches, the line of industrial units and the greasy spoon café.

A train went past on the overground. Decker turned right down the cobble alley and parked up against the kerb.

Removing his helmet, he climbed off the bike and checked round himself. Then he approached the metallic door and rang the buzzer.

A voice crackled on the intercom. 'Hi. Who is it?'

'Gas. I need to take a reading.' Decker wiped blood off his hand onto his trouser leg.

The door clicked open.

Decker walked in and Fenton opened the door at the top of the stairs and put his head out and, pointing, said, 'The meters are down there.'

Decker saw the box, but started up the stairs. 'I'll need to have a look inside as well,' he said. 'Is that okay?' He wasn't very good at the small talk.

Fenton frowned. 'Really? You don't normally.'

'Only be a few minutes.'

Fenton looked at Decker's clothes and said, 'Can I see your ID, please?'

Decker put a hand on the door. 'In the van.'

Fenton tried closing the door.

Decker put his foot in the way and pushed.

Fenton, his feet starting to slip on the wooden flooring, said, 'What are you doing?'

'I need to ask you some questions,' Decker said.

'What about?'

Decker punched him in the face through the gap in the door and Fenton fell backwards, a squirt of blood looping over his head.

Stepping into the flat, Decker closed the door behind him and locked it.

Fenton picked himself up, clutching his nose, then looked at the blood on his hands and said, 'Jesus! You just broke my fucking nose!'

Decker glanced round the room, noting a desk, a laptop, and TV, then walked to the window and dropped the blinds, saying, 'Start talking. Tell me everything you know about Daniel Howell.'

Fenton attempted to stand up but Decker pushed him back into the couch, then walked over to the desk and started opening drawers.

Fenton said, 'What is this? What are you doing?'

'Tell me what you know about Daniel Howell.'

'Who?'

'The guy you sleep with.'

Fenton hesitated. 'I sleep with lots of guys.'

'The guy you visited yesterday.'

'What?'

Decker said, 'He wasn't in, was he?'

'Who the fuck are you?'

'Then you met someone at a museum.'

'What?'

Decker walked to the couch and grabbed Fenton round his neck and threw him against the wall. A framed photograph of a suspension bridge in Los Angeles fell on his head. Fenton slumped to the floor, blood smearing the wall.

Decker said, 'I don't have much time. Start talking.'

Fenton spluttered, 'You're crazy,' tears filing his eyes.

Decker said, 'Who did you meet at the museum?'

'No one—'

Decker kicked Fenton in the stomach. 'Who did you meet?'

Fenton groaned. 'I don't remember.'

Decker lifted his foot again.

Fenton said, 'Okay,' holding up his hands. 'Please. His name's Schiller.'

'Go on. What else?'

'That's all I know. I swear. He gets me work sometimes. That's all.'

'What kind of work?'

'Nothing much. Errands; cash-in-hand stuff.'

Decker kicked Fenton in the stomach again. 'What kind of work?'

Fenton coughed. Blood and saliva ran down his chin and he wiped his mouth with his hand. 'Jesus, man,' he said.

Decker said, 'Hurry up.'

Fenton said, 'I tell him what people are up to – where they are, who they're meeting, that sort of thing.'

Decker walked across the room and pulled some books off a shelf. 'Keep going,' he said.

'That's it. I swear.'

'How long have you known Howell?'

'Who's Howell?'

'The guy you visited yesterday.

'Simon, you mean?'

'His name's Howell.'

Fenton said, 'A few months. What's this about?'

'What has he told you?'

'What do you mean? Told me what?'

Police sirens sounded in the distance and Decker went to the window and looked through a gap in the blinds but saw they weren't coming this way. He turned round and looked at Fenton again and said, 'What does Simon do?'

'I don't know … something to do with property development.'

'What else?'

'I don't know. We don't talk much about work. I suck his cock.' Fenton smiled sarcastically.

Decker ignored him, picked up a box of papers and files, and emptied it onto the floor. He didn't know what he was looking for anymore than he knew what this was about. But at that moment, this skinny little runt of a boyfriend was about all he had to work on. 'Tell me about Schiller?' he said.

'What do you mean?'

'What's the arrangement with him?'

'There isn't really one.'

Decker stopped what he was doing and eyeballed Fenton.

'All right …' he held up his hands again. 'Please. Just don't hit me again. I sleep with Simon, or Howell, or whatever his name is, and tell Schiller what he's up to from time to time, you know.'

'No, I don't.'

'That's it. I swear. This shit happens.'

Decker turned out a wallet, dropping cards and money on the floor. 'Do you have access to his computer?'

'No.'

'Have you passed on any information?'

Fenton shook his head. 'Is Simon in trouble?'

Decker chucked the wallet aside. 'Most likely he's dead.' Decker didn't know this for sure but reckoned it wouldn't hurt Fenton thinking it was the case. Besides, if Decker was right about his organisation pulling the plug on him, anyone who was involved in this job, if they weren't already dead soon would be.

Fenton sat up on the sofa. 'What?'

Decker said, 'You've been set up.' He noticed a business card on the floor that must have fallen out of the wallet and he bent down and picked it up. On the front was the name Simon Reeves. On the back was a number written in biro.

He waved it at Fenton. 'What's this?'

'It's Simon's business card.'

'When did you get it?'

'I don't remember.'

Decker reached over the sofa and grabbed him by the face. 'The number on the back … whose is it?'

'I told you, I don't remember.'

Decker started crushing Fenton's face with his hand.

'They wrote it … said if I was ever in trouble to ring.'

'Who, Howell?'

'No. They did. Schiller.'

Decker let go of his face. 'What else?'

'That's it, I promise.'

Decker went over to the window and looked across the street again. 'How did you first meet Howell?' he said.

'At a party.'

'When?'

'A few months ago.'

'When exactly,' scanning the approach roads in either direction.

'September, I think. Yeah, beginning of September.'

'Whose party?'

'I don't remember … something to do with work.'

'What work?'

'I got invited.'

'And Howell?'

'He was at the party too.'

'And?'

'And what? We started talking. I went back to his flat. We fucked. What is this?'

Decker turned from the window. 'The party … where was it?'

'A private club … near Piccadilly.'

'Name?'

'The Solo.'

'What happened?'

'It was a party. What do you mean?'

'What do you remember about it?'

'I don't know. There was a band, food, drinks. Some guy made a speech. Yeah, that was it – it was some Arab guy's party. He was buying houses.'

'What Arab guy?'

'Really, I don't remember.'

'Age?'

'I don't know – early 30s.'

Decker remembered Howell entering the hotel off Piccadilly, shaking hands with the Arab in jeans/blazer, and the two Caucasians in suits.

Decker crossed the room towards Fenton. 'Give me your phone,' he said.

'What?'

Decker grabbed Fenton round his neck.

'All right!' Fenton put up his hands again, then reached into his pocket and held out his phone.

Decker said, 'Open it.'

Fenton entered his password and then handed the phone back to Decker and Decker started scrolling through photos.

Fenton said, 'What's going on? Where's Simon?'

Decker made no response. He stopped at a picture of The Champs-Élysées. 'You were in Paris …' he said, '… when?'

'A week ago.'

'Howell?'

'Yeah, Simon asked me.'

'What for?'

'He said he had some work there. He paid for me.'

There was a photo of a café, outside seating, in the foreground Howell walking towards the camera, mouth open, looking like Fenton had surprised him. In the background, sitting at a café table, was the old gent – tweed coat, wooden-handled umbrella – that Howell had met off the King's Road.

'Who's that?' Decker threw the phone at Fenton.

'I've never seen him before, I swear. We were in Paris. I was meeting Simon. What's this about? Who are you?'

There was a screech of tyres outside. Decker went over to the window and looked through a gap in the blinds again. At the end of the road, he saw two guys getting out of a Vauxhall Astra. They looked over the roof of the car, scanned rooftops, and set off in opposite directions.

Decker walked into the kitchen, opened a door at the back of the flat. A small balcony, fire escape steps … He looked round and said, 'You're in trouble. Do you understand? Get out of here.'

Fenton nodded, wiping his bloody nose with the back of his hand.

Decker shut the balcony door behind him.

16

There was a note left inside the pizza box. It simply said: "Answer the phone". Lisa was drying her hair in the next-door room. What phone, Decker thought, when a mobile started ringing that wasn't his? He tracked the sound down to his bag. He had never seen the phone before. This was his first call.

A voice said, 'Status?'

It took him a moment. Then reeled off, 'Corpus B four, zero, two, seven, one,' without thinking about it. Then it all started coming back – his parents, the army, Israel, The Compound, Mr Charles – like not a day had passed.

'You'll travel up to London tonight. Someone will meet you at the Thistle Hotel, Victoria Station.'

He didn't eat any pizza. He said his sister was ill. That he had to leave right away. Lisa said she didn't know he had a sister. He said she was only a half-sister and that he didn't see her much. He got better with the excuses as time went on.

Crossing the main concourse at Victoria Station, Decker headed for the Thistle Hotel when a man passed in front of him, saying, 'Follow me.' He followed the man out of the station and left onto Buckingham Palace Road. Coming round the corner, Decker stopped to see where the man had gone when a voice behind him said, 'You have a room booked at The Lodge Hotel, Vauxhall. You're on a business trip. Your name is Paul James.'

Decker walked the mile and a half to Vauxhall and checked in at The Lodge Hotel under the name Paul James. He rode the lift to the third floor. His phone was ringing as he was opening his door. He closed the door behind him and, drawing the curtains with one hand, answered the phone with the other.

A woman's voice said, 'You will find a package under the bed. You have 20 minutes. He will be expecting you.'

The phone went dead. Decker pulled out a cardboard shoebox from under the bed. Inside the box was a Ruger LC9 and Silencerco sound moderator. He screwed the silencer in place, checked the magazine, and fired a dry round. He stuffed the gun inside his jacket and shoved the box under the bed again. He was looking round the room, checking he hadn't forgotten anything, when his phone bleeped with a message. He clicked on an icon and watched a photo download of a man leaving a white stucco-fronted building. The man was in his late 30s, unshaven, receding hairline, and wearing a white and green Adidas tracksuit and carrying a leather sport's bag over his shoulder. An address followed. A message confirmed it was to be done tonight, and that a laptop was to be taken from the target's apartment.

Decker took the underground and exited at High Street Kensington. The address was down a narrow side-street, with iron railings at street level. Scanning the upper windows and balconies, Decker approached the stucco-fronted building.

There were two topiary trees at the entrance and a brass plaque of flat numbers. Decker said his name into the intercom. 'Paul James.' And the door clicked open. He rode the lift to the third floor where he rang another intercom. 'Come in,' a voice said.

His target stood up behind a desk when he came in. He was wearing a white Lacoste polo shirt and beige chinos. Decker shot him twice in the chest and once through the head. The man slipped down the leather-backed chair, upsetting a stack of papers. Decker unhooked his laptop and left the house. He checked out of the hotel the next morning.

*

A week later, he went on holiday with Lisa. A cheap ticket had come up at work for a long weekend in Paris. Decker hoped it would make up for his strange disappearance the following week.

They had just checked into their hotel off Rue de Rivoli and Lisa wanted to get some shopping done before dinner. Leaving her to it, Decker found a small square and took a walk, then sat on a bench and watched people go about their business. He was lighting a cigarette when someone sat down next to him. It was Mr Charles.

'Well done the other day,' Mr Charles said. He looked across the square as he spoke. 'You understand meeting like this is difficult. As time moves on, there will be fewer chances. I hope you understand.'

Decker said, 'I understand.'

'How are you finding life on the outside?'

'Fine,' Decker said.

'That's good. You seem to be doing well. But you always did – a true survivor.'

Half a dozen pigeons landed on the track in front of them. Mr Charles placed his hand on the bench between them and Decker observed the gold signet ring on Mr Charles's little finger and then under his hand a set of car keys.

Without looking round, Mr Charles said. 'There is a red Peugeot 205 parked round the corner on St Michel. In the boot is a case. Your target is leaving Paris tonight for his home in the country. It must look like an accident. You will find details in the case.'

Across the other side of the square Decker saw Lisa walking towards them. She was wearing sunglasses and carrying two bags of shopping. He glanced at Mr Charles, who continued to look off into the distance.

'You will tell her you have to meet someone about work …' he said, '… that your company is setting up a branch in Paris, and they need your help. You will see her for dinner later tonight. I have booked a restaurant. There is no need for her to worry. Everything will be fine. Work is work. You leave in ten minutes.'

Mr Charles stood up and walked off. Along with the car keys, he left a business card on the bench with the name of the restaurant.

Decker picked up the card and said the name over to himself, his lips moving as he read, then put the card in his pocket as Lisa walked over.

'Who was that?' she said.

17

Decker went into a pay phone near Pimlico Station. He dialled the number written on the back of the business card he had taken from Fenton's flat. The number rang three times then stopped ringing as the call was diverted. Then anew ring started up, slightly higher pitched. A man picked up on the fourth ring and said, 'Who is this?'

Decker didn't recognise the voice this time. He turned round in the phone booth, checking to see if he had company.

'Hello?' the voice said. 'Who is this?'

Decker switched receiver hands, wiping blood off his face.

The voice said, 'It's you, isn't it?'

Decker said nothing.

There was silence the other end, then. 'Tell us where you are, Martin.'

A vein pulsed across Decker's right temple.

The voice said, 'We can help you, Martin. Just tell us where you are.'

A white van stopped at the top of the alley and Decker turned in the opposite direction.

The voice said, 'Speak to us. You have to trust us.'

Decker said, 'I want to see a familiar face.'

'We understand. When?'

'Tonight, seven o'clock, Covert Garden.'

There was a pause.

The voice said, 'Do you have the case?'

Decker hesitated.

The voice said again, 'Do you have the case?'

Decker said, 'Yeah. I have the case.'

*

Soon, Decker was walking through St James Park.

He crossed over the Mall, up the steps towards Waterloo Place. Pigeons scattered through the trees.

The fact they had asked for the case was significant, Decker thought. It told him two important things. First, it told him what they wanted, which could prove important if he hoped to get out of this alive. Second, asking him if he had it, was as good as saying they didn't, which meant they hadn't recovered it from the flat yet. He would pick the case up later, he thought.

But first he had a couple of house calls to make.

It didn't take him long to find the club. A small brass plaque, with the words "The Solo club, members only", was mounted to the front of a three-storey building tucked away down a secluded side-street. There was a black front door and a large brass claw knocker, but Decker didn't bother with the door. Walking round the side of the property there was a cobbled alleyway leading to the back of the building where a set of iron gates were pegged open. Decker checked in both directions and walked straight in.

A white van was parked up in the courtyard, but there was no one about. Using a large wheelie bin, Decker pulled himself up onto a flat roof, then climbed over a large air-conditioning unit and walked over to a parapet wall. Below was a back entrance to the club. The door was open.

Decker dropped down into the courtyard and walked through the door into what was some kind of storeroom. A trapdoor was open in the floor, steps leading down to a cellar, and Decker could hear voices below. He walked past the trapdoor and turned down an aisle-way between racks of detergents and toilet paper and came to a fire door with a large aluminium handle. He pushed down on the handle and opened the door.

On the other side was a carpeted corridor, with abstract paintings hanging on the walls. There was a vacuum cleaner and trolley of cleaning products left out at one end. The vacuum cleaner was still plugged into the wall but there was no sign of its operator. Decker checked for CCTV cameras in ceiling corners then slipped through the door and set off down the corridor.

Passing the vacuum cleaner, he turned the corner and came to a reception area. On a polished wooden desk was a black flat-screen PC. Decker saw the computer was open on an Excel programme and that the desk chair was pushed back at an angle telling him that someone had just got up, maybe to take a break.

Decker sat down and started looking for names, bookings. He clicked through several files. It wasn't long before he found what he was looking for.

"Hatton Alharbi. 2 September. The function room." On the guest list Decker saw: "Simon Hart, aka Daniel Howell."

Decker grabbed a pen and started writing down Alharbi's contact details on a slip of paper when a voice said behind him, 'Excuse me. Who are you?'

Decker looked round. A man with an orange suntan was standing there with a cup of tea in one hand and a mobile in the other. On his T-shirt was written the word "Zen".

Decker said, 'No one you know.'

'I can see that. What the hell are you doing?'

Decker punched him in the face. The man fell backwards over the printer, slopping tea across the wall.

Decker stepped past him, pocketing the piece of paper he'd written on, and walked out the front door.

*

Time 10:34. Decker exited Sloane Square underground station, checking the address on the piece of paper for Hatton Alharbi.

He crossed the road and headed up Sloane Street. The sun had gone in; a breeze gusted.

He turned left at Cadogan Gardens, walked up some steps and rang on an intercom. A woman answered.

'Sorry, Mr Alharbi is not in now. Can I give him a message?'

'Do you know when he will be back?'

'No, I'm sorry, I don't. He's at work. Who are you?'

'I'm from the Solo club. Mr Alharbi recently had a function with us. I need to speak to him about one of our mutual clients. It needs to be in person.' Decker looked up at the windows.

'I will let him know you called. What was your name again?'

'Simon Hart. I will leave my card.' Decker took out the business card he'd taken from Fenton's flat, crossed out the number on the back and pushed the card through the letterbox. As he did so, he noticed a packet of Dunhill cigarettes on a hall table along with a set of car keys. Maybe Alharbi was in after all, he thought.

Decker reached the end of the road, checking the time on his watch: 10:55. He pictured the woman walking up the stairs to Alharbi's room, one or two floors, perhaps. She would knock on the door and have to wait, Alharbi probably on the phone, drinking coffee in a dainty cup, suede loafers on the table. He'd signal the woman over, hold the call, and listen. He'd look at the card, thank the woman and send her away. Then he'd be on the phone again – to Howell or some other contact? This would all take ten minutes. He would have to change. He would light a Dunhill leaving the house, adding another ten minutes.

Decker flagged down a taxi on Sloane Street and told the driver to take him round the back of Cadogan Square. It only took a couple of minutes. They stopped at the end of the road, Alharbi's house just in view, 80 metres further down the street. It was 11:09.

Decker wondered if his gamble was going to pay off. Then again, maybe Alharbi had nothing to do with this. Maybe he was just another rich Arab buying houses in London and Howell really was an estate agent.

But he doubted it.

At 11:17, Alharbi left the house in a mustard-coloured overcoat, lighting a Dunhill with a gold lighter. He was in his early 30s, dark curly hair, thick lips, and wearing aviator sunglasses. He'd time to take two puffs on his cigarette before a black Range Rover pulled up to the kerb.

Alharbi climbed into the passenger seat with the cigarette hanging between his lips.

Decker waited until the Range Rover reached the end of the road before instructing the cabbie to follow him.

At the top of Sloane Street, the Range Rover turned right and headed along Kensington Road. Then, after about half a mile, the Range Rover pulled into a lay-by and Decker saw Alharbi get out and go into an Arabic restaurant.

Decker abandoned the taxi a little further down the road, doubled back and positioned himself on the opposite side of the street to the restaurant. He needed to put names to faces – to know who he was up against. In his experience, people fell into two categories: they either wanted what they didn't have; or they had what they wanted but were worried other people might take it from them. Either way, it usually ended the same way.

Fifteen minutes passed before a black cab pulled up opposite and the overcoat, Schiller, got out, checking his ground before entering the restaurant.

Decker wondered which category Schiller and Alharbi fell into. Were they the ones after something they didn't have or the ones afraid of losing what they had?

Decker saw Schiller leave the restaurant ten minutes later, hail down a taxi, and head east. Shortly afterwards, Alharbi walked out of the restaurant, lighting another cigarette and making a call on his Blackberry. He stood on the kerb waiting for his lift.

Standing on the opposite side of the road, Decker watched him closely for a moment. He needed to learn as much as he could about him in this short time – how he moved, how he reacted. Decker knew no amount of expensive clothes or gold wrist watches could hide the skin and flesh of the animal underneath.

Whatever was going to happen between them, Decker knew he must be ready.

Alharbi came off his phone and stared vacantly across the street. With his cigarette pinched between his thick lips, he looked to be lost in his own world for a moment. Something was getting to him, Decker thought.

Alharbi looked round as the Range Rover pulled up to the kerb. He took one last puffed on his cigarette and then flicked it away and climbed into the passenger seat.

Decker watched the Range Rover go past, unable to see much through its tinted windows as it headed west towards Piccadilly.

It was getting cold standing in the shade and Decker checked his watch to see how much time he had left before his meeting tonight.

18

He had six hours and 14 minutes left. And knew he had to go back to the flat and pick up the case next. It'd be a risk going back, he knew, but figured he didn't have much choice. Without the case, he was as good as dead.

Turning the corner, a tall black man in a pin-stripe blue suit was feeding coins into a parking meter. Behind him his car door was left open. Inside, Decker saw a Yankees baseball cap resting on the steering wheel.

Passing the car, Decker swiped the cap off the steering wheel and crossed the road and headed back down to Sloane Square where he entered the Underground and got on a train.

*

Decker appeared at the top of his street wearing the black man's baseball cap. He glanced across at Howell's window and saw the blinds were still drawn. Then looked at his flat and saw the blinds were also drawn, as he'd left them.

The street seemed unusually quiet, like a Sunday. Scoping the area, Decker looked up at rooftops and across the park.

It could just be that they hadn't expected him to come back so soon. Why would they? He had the case, or so they thought. Why take the risk?

Decker continued slowly down the street. But getting half way, he noticed the same silver Mercedes he'd seen parked there yesterday. And inside, the same guy, who he'd thought might be waiting for his girlfriend or grandmother, playing with his phone. Today, he was wearing a black woollen beanie with a peak.

Lesson one – remember: acknowledging something as a coincidence is a sure sign you don't know what's really going on.

It was time to get acquainted, Decker thought.

Tugging down the black man's baseball cap, Decker crept up behind the car, hands in pockets, head lowered.

The guy was still looking at his phone when Decker opened the door and smacked him over the head with the butt of the SIG. He slumped unconscious over the steering wheel. Close up, he looked younger than he'd first thought, Decker noted – 25 tops.

Decker set him back against the seat and checked his pockets and took his mobile and car keys and disarmed him of a flick knife. The guy was still unconscious when Decker crossed the road and rang the last called number on his phone.

'What is it?' a man said in a thick eastern European accent the other end.

Decker entered the building and walked up the stairs to the flat, saying nothing.

On the other end of the phone: 'Stop fucking around. What is it?'

Decker pulled out the SIG and kicked the flat door open.

A man – shaved head, tattoos – was standing in the middle of the room, sledgehammer in one hand, phone in the other, dust in his hair, veins bulging on his arms. Around him, the flat was a tip: sofa and chairs tipped up; linings ripped out; wall cavities smashed; plaster everywhere.

Chucking the phone away and picking up the sledgehammer in both hands, the man turned round and said, 'What the fuck?'

Decker shot him twice in the chest.

Opening the cupboard next door, Decker prized off the wall panel and felt round the water tank. The cavity was empty. The briefcase was gone. He checked round the bedroom and under the bed. His rucksack was gone as well.

Someone had come and gone before these clowns had got here, he thought.

Decker took some cash off the dead guy in the sitting room, crossed the street, holding the SIG under his jacket, and opened the passenger door of the car opposite.

Coming round, the young guy was stroking his head. Decker pointed the SIG at him and chucked the car keys on his lap and said, 'Now drive.

19

Decker refilled the magazine of the SIG with shells from his pocket. The driver looked at him. 'Where are we going?'

Decker returned the magazine and racked the slide. 'Just keep driving.'

They headed along Victoria Embankment, the young guy accelerating through the gears. Decker looked towards the river and tried to think. Only Corpus, his organisation, knew he was in that flat, he thought. But why would they take the case without telling him? What were they setting him up for?

He checked his watch, the time ticking down until his meeting in Covent Garden. Without the case, he was as good as dead. He was going to have to think of something, and quick.

Decker directed the guy driving towards a multi-storey car park he knew north of the river. It was tucked round the back of offices and an industrial estate. It never got too busy, especially after work, and had minimal security.

Stopping at the barriers, the guy lowered his window and took a ticket from the machine and headed up the ramp way. 'To the top,' Decker said.

Two men in suits were climbing into an Audi when they reached the top level. Scanning the area, Decker noted there was only half a dozen other cars on the whole level, so nice and quiet. He pointed to a space in the far corner. And the guy drove into the space and turned off the engine.

Decker checked the time on his watch: 17:03. Two hours left.

The guy looked round and said, 'Listen, mate, if it's all right with you, I'll just leave you to it now. Yeah … like nothing happened?'

Decker checked his wing mirror and waited for the suits in the Audi to disappear down the ramp way, then began removing his jacket, one arm at a time.

The young guy looked at him and said, 'What are you doing?'

Decker said, 'Give me your coat?'

'What?'

'Take off your coat.'

'Why?'

'Just do it.'

The young guy did as he was told and handed Decker his coat, a donkey-style jacket with PVC shoulder patches. Decker then gave him his in exchange.

'Now give me the keys,' Decker said.

The young guy gave him the keys. 'Where are you going?' he said.

Decker got out the car and put on the young's guy jacket, then walked round to the rear of the car and opened the boot. The young guy watched him over his shoulder.

Decker looked into the boot and then lifted the false bottom where the spare tyre was stored and pulled out a set of jump leads. Then he walked round to the driver's side and opened the door.

The young guy saw the jump leads and said, 'Whoa, what are you doing, mate?'

Decker said, 'Get out the car.'

The young guy held up his hands, 'Please, listen to me,' he said, palms spread, 'I don't know anything. You can take the car.'

'Get out,' Decker said, and he grabbed his arm and hauled him out the car.

The guy said, 'Mate, what's going on?'

Decker led him round to the boot of the car. 'Get in,' he said.

'You're joking, right?'

Decker flashed the SIG.

'Please, mate. Seriously, I don't know anything about this. I was just told to keep an eye on you. That's it.'

'Get in.' Decker spoke softly.

The man climbed in. Decker instructed him to tie up his legs with the jump leads then Decker took his hands, pulled them behind his back, and tied them up too. He ripped the guy's T-shirt and used it as a gag. He observed the guy was sweating. He took his peaked beanie hat and chucked the black man's baseball cap into the boot with him.

'I'll be back in an hour,' Decker said, then closed the boot and

activated the central locking and headed down the stairs.
****

Decker boarded a packed Underground train and stood near the doors. He was wearing the young guy's donkey jacket, collars up and peaked beanie.

He exited at Holborn and bought an A-Z street map at a kiosk, then crossed the road at the lights and headed down Parker Street. From there, he walked to the top of Long Acre and round the back of Covent Garden, where he stood at the top of side streets, checking possible access points and scanning rooftops and other vantage points and making a note of it all in the A-Z.

*

The light was fading. Two Asians were handing out free newspapers outside Holborn station.

Decker bought a black Samsonite briefcase from a luggage shop. It was a good enough match to the one he'd taken off the dead guy in Paris, he thought. He had it wrapped in a white plastic carrier bag and descended the escalator with it under his arm and boarded another packed train.

It was nearly dark when he exited the Underground 20 minutes later.

Decker entered the multi-storey through a side door and used the stairs. Walking towards the car, he activated the central locking. The taillights winked in the gloom. He opened the boot, undid the jump leads round the man's arms and legs, and removed the gag from his mouth, and said, 'Get out.'

The young guy got out looking barely conscious, but then suddenly produced a screwdriver from behind his back, raised his arm and came at him.

Decker moved out the way, grabbed the guy's arm holding the screwdriver then kicked his legs out from him. The guy fell over backwards. Decker put a foot on the guy's neck, took the screwdriver out of his hand and chucked it across the car park. The guy spat at him. Decker pushed him into the front of the car, and said, 'Start the car.'

The guy had blood running from the corner of his mouth as he started the car. He turned on the car's headlights and wiped his mouth with his sleeve, backed up the car and headed down the ramp-way.

They left the multi-storey and joined the traffic. Decker looked at the A-Z, which was covered in his notes, and played the scene through in his mind. He would get the guy dressed up as him to deliver the case. It was unlikely in a crowded Covent Garden that they would know it wasn't him. Just as they wouldn't know it wasn't the real case. This would give him a chance to see who was out there. And what he was up against. By the time they found out it wasn't him, and the case wasn't the case they were after, he'd have a new target, and the young guy could go back to watching someone else.

Decker looked at the guy driving and noticed his hands were shaking on the steering wheel and there was sweat on his forehead.

'What's your name?' Decker said.

The guy hesitated then said, 'Kyle.'

'Just do as I say, Kyle. And it'll be all right. Okay?'

The guy hesitated again then said, 'Okay.'

They stopped at traffic lights and Decker noticed the family in the car next to them and the little boy in the backseat looking at him through the window. For a second, Decker felt like the little boy knew all about him and what he was doing. It reminded Decker of how he'd felt seeing children with their parents at school. How he pretended he hadn't seen them. Pretended their world of families didn't exist and that he was somehow invisible – like now.

Next to him, Kyle said, 'That's not the real case, is it?

Decker looked up at the traffic lights, saying nothing.

Kyle said, 'You couldn't find it, could you? It wasn't in the flat. I'm telling you, there's someone out there you don't want to fuck with.'

Decker looked between his wing mirror and the lights.

The lights changed.

Kyle pulled away, saying. 'Seriously mate, this is fucking out of control. They'll kill us. You don't know what you're up against.'

Decker said, 'Get into the right hand lane. Take the next right.'

'Why don't I take you to the airport? How about that?'

Decker said, 'Just drive, Kyle.'

Kyle ran his hand through his hair and then gripped the steering wheel and said, 'What are you going to do – shoot them all? This isn't Paris, you know. There's cameras everywhere.'

Decker looked at Kyle. 'What do you know about Paris?'

'Things. It was you, wasn't it?'

Decker looked ahead, then checked behind them, and said, 'Turn left here.'

They turned down a narrow alley. Chain-linked fence, bollards, industrial units, the gleam of train lines in the distance.

Decker said, 'Stop the car.'

Kyle said, 'Please. I won't say anything. Just let me go.'

'Stop the car.'

Kyle pulled up alongside the kerb.

'Turn off the engine.' Decker turned and pointed the SIG at Kyle. 'What do you know about Paris?' he said.

'Nothing … honest … just what I heard.'

'What did you hear, Kyle?'

'That you took something that didn't belong to you. And that you're going to pay for it.'

'Who do you work for, Kyle?'

'I don't know his name.'

Decker lifted the gun level with Kyle's face and could see his pupils dilate.

'Schiller … Peter Schiller,' he said, his mouth trembling, 'that's all I know.'

Decker lowered the gun.

Kyle said, 'I'm telling you, he's a fucking crazy bastard.'

Decker said, 'Who else?'

'That's all I know, I swear to you man.'

'Keep your voice down, Kyle.'

'He's going to kill you. I swear to you. He's a psycho.'

'Yeah, you told me.' Decker checked his watch. It was time. Besides, he knew he wasn't going to get any more sense out of Kyle. 'Let's go,' he said.

Kyle grabbed Decker by the arm as he was about to get out, and said, 'Listen, mate. I know a place you can stay – real safe, like. What do you say?'

Decker removed Kyle's hand, and said, 'Move', then got out of the car.

Decker kept several paces behind Kyle, holding his gun under his jacket, and scanning the area around him. He directed him through a maze of backstreets that he'd plotted out on the map and memorised. Occasionally, Kyle slowed down and Decker had to nudge him in the back.

Soon, the lights of Covent Garden appeared at the end of an alley.

Decker observed people loitering outside shops and restaurants.

A busker was playing *Love is all around* by the Kinks. A crowd was gathered in the square watching a juggler on stilts.

Decker turned to Kyle and said, 'Put on your cap.'

He did as he was told, putting on the baseball cap.

Decker said, 'Pull it right down. And hide your hair.'

Kyle pulled the cap right down and tucked his hair in at the sides.

'Now take this.' Decker handed Kyle the Samsonite case, then looked out across the crowd, seeing couples holding hands, families reading menus outside restaurants, a circle of tourists gawping at a man posed as a statue.

'It's not going to work,' Kyle said.

'I need you to stay calm, Kyle,' Decker said still scanning the crowd. He picked out two people on rooftops, one using binoculars, the other speaking into a radio mike, then a man smoking a cigarette outside a café and two guys, hands in pockets, mingled in the crowd – five in total. Decker checked his watch: 20:00.

Then he looked at the crowd again. And there he was – the familiar face. Mr Charles was walking through the crowd, looking left to right. Who else were they going to send?

'He's here,' Decker said. 'Tall, grey hair, black overcoat, at eleven o'clock. Do you see him?'

'And you think I am just going to walk up to him.'

'Just give him the case.'

'Fuck it. I'm not going anywhere.'

Decker stuck the SIG into Kyle's stomach, pinning him back against the wall. To passers-by you wouldn't have known there was a gun involved.

'Walk slowly across the square,' Decker said. 'Keep your head down. And pass him the case.'

Kyle looked at Decker, and said, 'Are you sure?'

'Just take it easy. Don't rush. And pass him the case.'

Kyle started walking and Decker took out a mobile and memory-dialled the only saved number. After two rings, he observed Mr Charles fumbling in his pocket and answering his phone.

Decker said, 'Baseball cap, black jacket, at four o'clock,' and hung up.

The information was relayed on radio mics round the square on the tap on Mr Charles's phone, just as Decker knew it would.

Kyle started walking slowly at first then, hesitating and glancing back over his shoulder, broke into a run. It was about the worst thing he could have done.

'Don't run,' Decker said to himself.

The three men on the ground started moving in on him. A plainclothes on a rooftop mounted a rifle to his shoulder.

Decker saw Mr Charles change directly, barging through the crowds.

Tracking his movements, Decker moved round the edge of the square to stay with him.

Kyle stripped off his hat and jacket and started waving his arms.

'No,' Decker said.

A single shot from the Northeast rooftop caught him in the shoulder. There was cheering and clapping from the crowd for the man on stilts.

Decker said, 'Shit,' under his breath, although it looked like they had shot to wound.

The guys on the ground closed in around Kyle, breaking his fall. A couple of bystanders turned to look at what was going on, but they couldn't see much. There were four men round him now; they had a jacket over his shoulders. They were holding him up under the arms. Perhaps he looked just very drunk.

A black Ford Orion screeched to a halt at the top of Bedford Street. Decker saw the group of men hurrying towards it. No one paid them much attention.

Across the square, Decker saw Mr Charles enter Passenger's Road at the Southeast corner of Covent Garden, hands in pockets, walking quickly.

20

A black van was parked half way down the road, engine running.

Mr Charles was approaching the van when he saw Decker standing in the middle of the road.

'Martin,' he said.

Decker saw Mr Charles's eyes move from him to something in the distance. But before Decker could react, he heard the racking of a gun slide.

'That's it,' a voice said behind him. 'Nice and easy.'

Decker half-turned, saw two men behind him, wearing black Kevlar vests and paramilitary balaclavas, and pointing Glock 17s at him. A manner about them that told Decker they weren't amateurs.

The same man said, 'Put your gun down,' his aimed fixed on his chest.

Decker placed his gun on the tarmac.

'Now get in the van,' he said, motioning with his gun.

Decker got into the van's carpeted interior. A muted TV was playing the news in the corner. Cameras were built into the upholstery. A screen separated off the driver's cab. He saw Mr Charles speaking to one of the gunman outside then Mr Charles got in and sat beside him. The gunman slid the doors shut and tapped the roof with his fist. The other gunman got in beside the driver and the van pulled away and accelerated to the end of the road.

As they turned at the end of the road Mr Charles' phone started to ring. Decker saw the driver looked at them both in his rear-view mirror. Mr Charles answered his phone and, listening for not more than 20 seconds, said, 'Okay, I understand,' then hung up.

Mr Charles looked at Decker and said, 'Apparently, it wasn't you.'

Decker shook his head. 'No.'

Turning to the window, Mr Charles said, 'Why did you come back?'

They were driving down the Strand, everywhere a blaze of colour with lights streaming from shop fronts and billboards with phosphorescence brilliance.

Decker said, 'Where did I have to go?'

'They think you're rogue, Martin.' He kept his face turned to the window. 'They can only see one way out of this.'

Decker observed his own reflection in the glass and said, 'What do you think?'

'That I have known you for a long time.' Mr Charles turned towards Decker. 'There was nothing I could do. You understand that, don't you?'

Decker didn't understand, but played along anyway. 'I understand,' he said.

Mr Charles turned the other way again. 'They are closing us down, Martin.'

Decker looked at the driver and the gunman at the front of the vehicle, then at the doors either side of him.

Mr Charles said, 'There's nothing you can do now, Martin.'

They were passing through Aldwych, a sleekness to the evening, like a screen image.

Decker said, 'Where are they taking us?'

Still turned to the window, Mr Charles said, 'You know my father used to go to church every Sunday. Yet, he never talked about religion. But looking back, I guessed he must have believed in something. There was a time I thought about going to church myself, but somehow I never got round to it.'

'Maybe there's still time,' Decker said, glancing over his shoulder now.

'It would be nice to think so, wouldn't it?'

Decker looked round again and noticed the driver looking at him in the rear-view mirror.

They were crossing Blackfriars Bridge.

Mr Charles said, 'I know it wasn't easy for you, what happened. Most people would have come apart...'Mr Charles turned to look at Decker. 'You never questioned it, did you?'

'What was there to question?'

'Perhaps you knew. Deep down.'

'Knew what?'

'That the truth has many faces, Martin.'

'The case,' Decker said. 'It wasn't there.'

Turned to the window, Mr Charles said, 'I'm afraid I don't think that's going to make any difference now.'

They headed down a narrow side-street, accelerating. The vehicle's tyres screeched round the corners.

Stopping at a set of solid metal gates, the driver stuck his arm out the window and punched a code into a keypad mounted on a brick column. The gates opened and they drove forward into a forecourt surrounded by tall buildings, and as they did so, an emergency light snapped on. Decker saw three men standing there in the dark, hands clasped out front, automatics equipped with sound moderators at the ready.

They stopped alongside them. The driver and the gunman got out.

Mr Charles said, 'There's a stray dog, Martin,'

But before Decker had a chance to ask him what he meant, the gunman opened the sliding door and waved Decker out with the gun.

Mr Charles said, 'I'm sorry, Martin.'

Decker looked at Mr Charles and said, 'Sorry for what?'

'That it had to end like this?'

The gunman signalled for Decker to move aside. Decker did as he was instructed, hands on head. He stepped out onto the tarmac and one of the men fired his gun three times – muffled, sound-suppressed reports, in the hollow building space.

The top of Mr Charles's skull blew out, his body bucked into the corner, blood flooding the seat. Before Decker could react, the man turned his gun on him, saying, 'Keep your hands on your head and kneel down.'

At that moment two cars drove in, doors opened, and four men got out. One of the men stuck a gun into Decker's face.

Decker dropped to his knees, holding his hands above his head, as another of the men cuffed his hands behind his back and put a hood over his head. Decker could then hear what sounded like Mr Charles' body being bagged up and the interior of the vehicle being wiped down, the men working quickly.

The van drove away first – Decker could tell that much from the sound of the diesel engine – then the two saloons. As the sound of the vehicles receded, Decker became aware of the whirring sound of the closing gates, then the clunk as they closed.

Decker looked round himself in the hood, wondering if he was alone or not. The bright outside light was just discernible through the hood but nothing else. Maybe there was someone there, he couldn't be sure. He moved his hands in the cuffs behind his back. He felt the damp tarmac soaking through the knees of his trousers and could hear the sound of running water, a drain nearby maybe.

They are closing us down, Martin.

Then the outside light clicked off; just the sound of running water. He pictured a manhole cover somewhere and saw himself prizing it open with tied hands and dropping into the stream of water.

He stood up slowly and edged forward. Then he heard the sound of a car accelerating down the narrow alleyway towards him and started running.

The outside light clicked on. The gates whirred into life. Headlights shone across the forecourt. Doors opened. Footsteps.

He felt someone grab his arm. He kicked out and connected with someone's stomach. He heard swearing. Then someone grabbed him from behind, pulling him up, and he received a large thump over the back of his neck. The pain vibrated through his body and he felt his legs go under him. He wasn't sure if someone caught him or if he hit the ground.

He blacked out.

21

Decker felt a sense of time passing.

Then he hit his head against something hard and sat up.

There was a coursing pain down his neck. He tried turning round, but couldn't see. There was a ceiling close to his head, a cold surface behind him. They were moving ... in the back of some kind of vehicle.

He realised the hood was still over his head and his hands were still cuffed.

He stood up, swaying, and felt along the side of the vehicle for a way out. The area was about the size of a small transit. At the rear of the vehicle, he felt around the door, found what must have been the handle and tried moving it, but it wouldn't budge. He gave the door a kick, then barged it with his shoulder but didn't have any strength. His head was spinning. They must have drugged him with something, he thought.

He sat down again and listened closely to the vehicle's engine. They seemed to be negotiating roundabouts and slowing down for zebra crossings, which meant they were probably still in a built-up area. Decker could also identify the sound of buses, so they were possibly still on the outskirts of London somewhere, which meant he'd been passed out for less than an hour. Therefore the time would be around 2200 hours.

Decker started to build a picture ...to get a sense of his situation.

He listened to the sound of an ambulance recede into the distance. Before long, they stopped at what must have been a set of traffic lights. They were stood there for at least a minute so it must have been at least a three-way system. When they pulled away, the road surface sounded different. Clipping chevrons and cat's eyes, their speed increased. Decker reckoned they had joined an A road.

They were now travelling at about 50 miles per hour, keeping to the speed limit. Every now and then, he felt the vehicle slowing for a speed camera. Decker guessed they were on the A3, heading south, knowing that particular road to be punctuated by regular cameras.

They were on the same road for about 30 minutes, Decker only just managing to keep himself awake. Then he heard the vehicle's indicator and, slowing down, they veered to the left and turned off at a junction.

After that, the roads became increasingly minor. Decker was thrown from side to side as they went through a series of sharp corners. Soon, the gradient of the road steepened. They splashed through puddles and hit potholes. The road was like this for several miles. Eventually they stopped in front of what Decker imagined was a set of house gates. He heard the whirring of the gate's electric motor as they opened. Then they set off down a long drive.

There was a slight incline to the road, several gentle corners ... after a few minutes, the sound of loose gravel. They slowed right down. The engine echoed between what must have been buildings. Then they stopped.

Decker heard two doors open and close, then footsteps receding over the loose gravel. He waited, expecting the footsteps to return. They didn't.

It started getting cold. Decker heard the hoot of an owl, the swishing sound of treetops in the breeze. He reckoned they were somewhere on the North Downs, judging by the distance they'd travelled from London. The time, he estimated, was around midnight.

After about ten minutes, Decker heard the sound of footsteps return, then the vehicle's central locking activated. He turned his head as the rear door opened and someone said, 'Get out. You're coming inside.'

Two men helped him out. He didn't resist this time. He felt unsteady on his feet and wondered what they'd drugged him with. The two men flanked him on either side, each holding one of his arms, and they entered a building. They walked up some steps and along a corridor. There was an odour of floor polish. Their footsteps echoed. Every now and then, they walked over a rug. After about 30 paces, they went down a narrow set of stairs, turning all the time. The temperature dropped, the ceiling felt closer overhead. At the bottom of the steps, they walked along another corridor. This time, the surface was stone. There was a dank smell. Before long, they stopped at a door. A four-digit code was entered on a keypad. The door clicked open and they went into a room. The lights were brighter.

The two men sat him down on a chair and removed his hood and Decker turned his head away from the light, half-blinded by the glare, and just caught the outline of someone closing the door behind them, but that was it, the bright lights making him wince, his head rocking from side to side, the drug still working in his system.

22

Snapping his arms in the restraints, Decker woke up and winced into the light again. There was dribble running down his chin. He turned his head round the room. Bare stone walls, concrete floor, exposed wooden beams. A rack of spotlights trained towards the chair. The light burnt into his retinas.

He shifted in the chair, realising he wasn't tied to it. That only his hands were tied. The chair was metal with a foam seat like something you'd find in a village hall. He saw a camera mounted on the wall above the door, a red LED light flashing on the front.

It felt like a private residence, which meant his visit here wasn't being made public. He tried to work out what time it would be. He remembered seeing 19:43 on the TV in the van when driving through Aldwych with Mr Charles. Then he went back over the evening's events – Covent Garden, the taxi ride, Mr Charles getting shot, the journey out here – and estimated it to be around two o'clock.

He glanced up at the camera again and imagined himself somewhere on a monitor screen in black and white and a guy running searches on him and slowly putting a profile together. But he knew there was nothing he could do about that for now. The good news was they wanted him alive.

Decker studied the bare walls, the even symmetry of the mortar joints, and thought about the process of laying them stone by stone, working off a level line, building the room up layer by layer.

Time passed. Dust circled in the spotlights.

After a while, Decker's heavy eyelids closed and his head hung forward as he nodded off to sleep again.

*

When he woke up, he jolted backwards in the chair and nearly fell off.

He looked round the room – bare stone walls, lights, camera – and noted nothing had changed.

He stood up, with hands tied behind his back, and walked across to the room's only door and looked round its edges, then turned round and looked back at the chair in the middle of the room under the lights.

As he stood there, he heard a bleeping sound and looked up. He saw the red LED light flickering on the camera.

A voice said, 'Please remain in the chair.'

Decker continued to stare at the camera for a moment, imagining a guy the other end watching him.

The voice repeated itself, 'Please remain in the chair.' The voice was flat and anodyne, fed through some kind of voice coder.

Decker walked back to the chair, knowing the time for disobeying orders would come soon enough.

Several hours passed.

To stay focused, Decker thought about the position of the room in relationship to the rest of the house, building floor plans in his mind as he reconstructed the walk back through the house. Turn right out the door, walk 30 paces along a corridor, then up a narrow, winding staircase. At the top of the stairs, turn left, walk along another corridor, then down some steps, and through a door outside where a security light would come on and he'd expect to find a forecourt, outbuildings and one or more vehicles. And he'd hot-wire one of the vehicles and maybe find some spare fuel and supplies in the sheds.

Then Decker imagined himself driving back down the driveway and would have kept driving like this all the way back to London if the bleeping sound hadn't interrupted him again, and a voice said, 'What is your name?'

Decker looked up at the camera. The red light blinked hypnotically.

'Please answer the question,' the anodyne voice said. 'What is your name?'

Decker knew the opening questions in an interrogation were usually designed to establish rapport between source and interrogator, and that most of the questions they'd already know the answers to, so there wasn't much to be gained by offering any resistance. Not at this stage.

'Martin Decker,' he said.

'Have you ever gone by any other names?'

'Yeah. Many.'

'Who do you work for?'

'I'm not told.'

He also knew questions would be short and direct, nothing tricksy, no compound questions that might result in ambiguous answers or require additional enquiry, nothing to break the rhythm or flow. The camera would be doing the real work at this stage, observing his reactions, facial expressions, pupil dilation, levels of perspiration and changes in speech tones, trying to assess his state of his mind.

The voice said, 'Who is your handler?'

'The guy you had killed. Remember.'

'And what was his name?'

Decker got an image of the blood-soaked van. 'Mr Charles.'

'How long was he your handler?'

'For a long time.'

'How long, approximately?' The tone remained calm and even-tempered, intended to strengthen rapport and levels of cooperation.

'About ten years.'

'So Mr Charles is no longer your handler?'

'What do you think?'

'So who is your handler now?'

Decker hesitated. 'No one.'

The camera light stabilised briefly. They were looking for a slip, a reveal … some facial expression or other mannerism.

The voice said, 'Can you tell us why you're here, Martin?'

'Because you brought me here.'

'And why did we bring you here?'

'I don't know. You tell me.'

'Are you in contact with your organisation?'

'Not that I know of.'

'Then whose orders are you following?'

'There are no orders.'

The camera lens zoomed.

'What is your current assignment?'

'There is no assignment.'

'What does the name Daniel Howell mean to you?'

'Not much.'

'Have you ever had any contact with Howell?

'I followed him for a while.'

'What happened?'

'He disappeared.'

The LED light blinked a little quicker.

'Where did he go?'

'I've no idea.'

'Was Howell ever a target?'

'I don't know.'

'Was he in danger?'

'You'd have to ask him.'

'Do you know how we can reach him?'

'Nope.'

There was silence.

Decker looked up at the camera and waited.

Dust circled in the spotlights.

Several minutes passed, then hours.

Decker knew this was only the beginning.

At some point, he fell asleep again.

23

When Decker woke up again he saw two men walking across the room towards him. Both of them were wearing paramilitary balaclavas and carrying batons. Sitting up in the chair, the light shone in Decker's eyes and he put up his hand.

One of the balaclavas smacked him across his shoulders with his baton. He tried shielding himself. A succession of blows followed from both men. He crumpled to the floor. One of the men kicked him in the stomach then they hauled him up into the chair again. At which point, another man came into the room, wearing a white ski mask and black shirt with sleeves rolled up. He produced a syringe, tapped the side, and released a squirt of liquid into the air. With the men holding him down, Decker felt the needle go into his arm.

Decker looked up, his vision tunnelling. The three men left the room. Decker felt blood running down his cheek. The red light pulsed on the camera. The lens appeared to zoom in on his face. And he thought he could see his reflection in the lens and then someone the other side sitting in a room.

Then a single bleep sounded in the room and the voice said, 'Can you tell us why you think you're here, Martin?'

Decker noticed the insertion of the word 'think' and knew they were giving him the chance to give a different explanation of events, without him feeling he was betraying his earlier version.

'Because you brought me here,' he said. He wasn't going to be led down that path.

'Why did we bring you here?'

'I don't remember.'

'Was it because of your last assignment?'

'I don't know.'

'Do you remember what your last assignment was?'

'Yeah.'

'What was it?'

'To follow Howell.'

'That was all?'

'Yeah.'

'Who gave you the orders to follow him?'

'Mr Charles.'

'Did he say why?'

'No.'

'What happened?'

'Howell disappeared.'

'How can you be so sure? Did you speak to him?'

Decker's head rocked forward, a string of saliva hanging from his mouth, his injected arm beginning to twitch.

The voice said, 'Has Howell been in contact, Martin?

Decker lifted his head. The light shone in his eyes.

'Martin, has Howell been in contact with you?'

Then his head went again and his eyes fluttered closed.

*

When Decker came to again, he was shivering. He lifted his head, winced in the bright light and wondered how long he had been asleep. It felt like it could have been anything from a few minutes to several days. He tried to remember events leading up to falling unconscious, whether the injection had come first or the beating. The chronology of events was going. Was this his second day here or his first? Had Mr Charles really been shot or had he dreamt it?

The door clicked open. The two balaclava-clad men entered the room. Decker tried standing up but they grabbed his arms and cuffed them to the chair. The masked man walked in after them, syringe in hand, giving a squirt of liquid in the air. Decker wrestled in the chair. The masked man injected his arm. A heavy liquid spread through his bloodstream. Then he felt metal probes being clipped to his arms.

Decker lifted his head. His eyes rolled. The room was getting smaller like it was disappearing down a tunnel.

The voice said, 'Whose orders are you following?'

Decker tried to speak but nothing happened. Bloodied saliva dribbled down his chin. He felt a tingling in his arms and legs and then a sudden jolt of electricity.

The voice repeated itself, 'Whose orders are you following?'

Decker felt his head sway; the room pitched from side to side. 'No one's,' he said.

A second whack of electricity buckled Decker in the chair.

'Who sent you?'

'You brought me here.'

'Who are *we*?'

'I don't know.'

'Who do you work for?'

Decker saw the two balaclava-clad men standing in front of him with their batons held across their chest as if on parade. His vision blurred. He wondered if this was happening now or before.

'Corpus Industries,' he said. He knew this was a concession on his behalf but you had to try to manage your breaking points. Because you know it's inevitable, given the right conditions, that they will come. In the end, it's more a question of *how* you break.

'And who is your contact there?'

'He's dead.'

'What is your relationship to Howell?'

'I followed him.' Decker tried desperately now to keep his mind clear, least something come to him at the last second that he couldn't control.

The voice said, 'Why did you follow him?'

'I don't know.'

'What did you find out?

'Nothing. He runs.'

Another thump of electricity; Decker arched in the chair. When his body went limp, one of the balaclavas stepped towards him and whacked him across the stomach.

The voice said, 'What else?'

The words "stray dog" came into Decker's head. He could see Mr Charles saying the words in the taxi. But he knew for some reason he mustn't say the words. Images flashed up in his head of his room in The Compound: the cracked concrete of the courtyard; the wire fence; and the woods beyond.

'I ... I don't ...' His tongue felt like it was curled up in the corner of his mouth like a trodden snail. Blood and saliva ran down his chin. '... remember,' he slurred.

'What do you remember, Martin?'

Decker's head fell forward.

The voice said, 'Answer the question, Martin. What do you remember?'

Decker experienced a hissing sound in his ears.

The voice said, 'Were you working for Howell?'

'No.'

'Was there a target?'

'I don't know.'

'Was Howell the target, Martin?'

Decker lifted his head and looked into the camera lens and saw his reflection and what he thought was the man on the other side of the camera. Then the room tunnelled and he felt his head go. He saw four green lights on a black background. And he wasn't sure if his eyes were open anymore or if he was seeing these things in his head. Voices jabbered. Was he passing out?

*

When Decker opened his eyes he was lying on the floor by the chair. He was alone again. Time had moved on. There were no electric probes. No balaclavas.

Had he dreamt it?

He sat up and wondered if it was the same day as before or another day entirely, but he couldn't remember when *before* was. He tried working backwards, remembering his first night here – the interrogation, and before that the van with Mr Charles – and tried to calculate how many days had passed since then.

He sat there and looked round the room – the bare stone walls, the camera … It felt like he'd been unconscious for some time. He stood up and sat down on the chair.

When he did, the voice said, 'What is your name?'

Decker looked up at the camera. 'I told you. Martin Decker.'

'Was your name ever Daniel Howell?'

'No.'

'How do you know?'

'I would remember.'

'What were your orders?

'To follow Howell.'

'Was Howell the target?'

'I don't know.' The questions coming quicker now, designed to confuse him and bring about a slip.

'Do you think he was?'

'Maybe.'

'Are you in contact with Howell?'

'No.'

'Where do you think he went?'

'I've no idea.'

'Do you think he's dead?'

'Maybe.'

There was a pause. Decker got the feeling there was a change of personnel, though the voice remained the same:

'Does anyone know you're here, Martin?'

'I doubt it.'

'Would Howell know you're here?'

'No. He disappeared.'

'Did you speak to him before he disappeared?'

'What do you think?'

'Did Mr Charles?'

'I wouldn't know.'

'Was Mr Charles in contact with Howell at any time?'

'I don't know. You should have asked him.'

There was silence.

A minute or two passed.

Then Decker heard footsteps and the door opened. The two balaclavas entered the room, carrying batons, and walked over to where he was sitting. Then the man in black shirt and ski mask appeared, eyeing up a loaded syringe.

*

When Decker came round, he squinted in the bright lights.

He wondered how long he had been out for and how much time had passed since he'd last thought this.

His tongue stuck to the roof of his mouth as he swallowed. He could feel his lips were cracked and his heart was working harder than normal.

He stood up. But as soon as he did, his vision fissured. The walls around him appeared 20 metres further away than they really were.

He tried taking a step. But the floor seemed to tip up. For a moment, the camera appeared to extend towards him, the red LED light filling one of his eyes.

He took another step and all of a sudden he was face to face with the wall, like he'd been standing there all this time.

He felt nauseous. His diaphragm tightened. An acidic fluid rose in his stomach.

Stumbling against the wall, he tried to hold on. But the wall felt soft and malleable and seemed to give way under him. He had the sensation he was falling. He vomited several times with little more than bile in his stomach.

Doubled up on the floor with saliva hanging from his mouth, Decker heard the bleep of the camera. He looked up at the red light and drew the back of his hand across his mouth.

The voice said, 'Please remain in the chair.'

24

Decker was slumped in the chair when he next opened his eyes. The two balaclavas were crossing the room. One of them pointed a Heckler and Koch USP 9mm in his face while the other slipped a hood over his head. Then they stood him up and walked him out of the room.

Decker heard the door slam shut behind him. They stood for a moment. There was the sound of a key in a mortice lock opposite. Then one of the men pushed him through a doorway and he fell against a wall. As he lay there, they removed his cuffs and took off his hood and then one of them said, 'Get cleaned up,' closing the door and then locking it again.

Decker stood up in what was a very small room with crumbling brick walls and no window. A light bulb hung on a flex from the ceiling. In one corner was a toilet and washbasin. On a table there were some clothes, a bottle of water and army ration pack.

Decker picked up the bottle of water, broke the seal and took a drink. Water ran down his chin. He started coughing.

Someone started banging on the door. 'Hurry up in there.'

Decker got undressed and washed, then changed into the clothes provided and ate the bar of chocolate from the ration pack and took another drink of water.

One of the balaclavas opened the door and gestured at him with the Heckler and Koch. They put on his hood and cuffs again and walked him up some stairs and along a corridor. Decker noted the wooden flooring and smell of floor polish again. At the end of the corridor, they went up more stairs, carpeted this time, then turned right and stopped. They stood for a second then a door opened.

Decker felt and heard a dog sniffing at his leg. He heard voices in the background. Then they led him into the room and his hood was removed – but no bright lights this time. They were stood in a large dimly lit room, like a study in a stately home, with oil paintings on the walls, an open fireplace, and thick tasselled curtains drawn across bay windows. Decker saw a man sitting in a leather-backed chair behind a desk. A laptop was open on the desk. A desk light provided the only light in the room. The man was in his mid-60s, had short-cropped greying hair, a compact frame, and had his sleeves rolled up to his elbows. His legs were crossed and his hands were bridged on his lap.

Decker looked over his shoulder. The three balaclavas were standing against the wall at the back of the room. A large dog, some kind of pointer, was curled up on a rug in a corner.

'Sorry for the discomfort,' the man in front of him said. 'Did you eat?'

Decker looked at the man, and said, 'What do you want?'

The man smiled. 'I will come to that. Sit down.'

Decker sat down, looking over his shoulder again.

The man behind the desk made a signal. The balaclavas began filing out the room. The dog lifted his head and watched them depart. The door was pulled shut, making a heavy clicking sound.

Decker watched as the man opposite him stood up, opened a desk drawer and took out a remote control. He pointed it across the room, pressed a button, and a projector appeared from the ceiling and beamed a square of light onto the far wall. Then he pressed another button and an image of Decker appeared on the wall.

Decker looked at himself on the screen. In the picture he was walking down a street in Paris. It was raining. He had his hands in pockets. He was looking across the road. It was near the Sorbonne. He was on his way to kill someone.

The man said, 'My name is Sachs. And I'm going to call you, Michael … if that's all right?'

Decker shrugged.

'If what you tell us is true, Michael,' Sachs said, 'you are without a handler. You are what we call a stray dog.'

Decker looked at Sachs, remembering Mr Charles saying these words in the van just before bullets tore into his chest and he spat blood across the windows.

'Are you familiar with this expression?' Sachs said.

Decker didn't offer a response. He was thinking about Mr Charles and how he'd been like a father to him and now was dead.

Sachs walked round to the front of the desk. 'Well, I will tell you. A stray dog is someone living on the outside, hand to mouth. They belong to no one. They have become feral, unwanted ...' Sachs turned and looked at the picture on the screen, '... someone like yourself, Michael.'

Sachs changed slides. Decker recognised the man he'd shot in Paris.

Sachs said, 'I expect you recognise him. Well, his name's Zishan. And he was involved in intelligence-sharing.' He changed slides again. This time it was a photograph of Mr Charles.

'You need no introduction.'

Sachs changed slides again. It was a picture of Alharbi.

'This is Hatton Alharbi, Zishan's contact.'

Changing slides again, Sachs said, 'And what do they have in common?' he walked towards the image on the wall. It was a photograph of Howell.

'This man ...' he looked up at the image as he spoke, '... is Daniel Howell. I believe you were shadowing him.'

Sachs looked at Decker.

Decker said, 'So what?'

'Well, Howell has gone missing.'

Decker said, 'And you think I killed him?'

Sachs smiled. 'No.'

'But you want me to?'

'I want to offer you a job.'

'It's the same thing.'

Sachs smiled again. 'Howell has something that belongs to us. We want it back. I believe you can help us with this.'

Decker realised they were finally getting to why he was here.

Sachs changed slides. This time it was a picture of Annie. She was sitting in a restaurant. She was smiling. Decker was sitting opposite her in the picture; it was their last dinner together.

Sachs walked across the room and put his hand on Decker's shoulder. 'Like you, Michael, Howell has become a stray dog. Unfortunately, I cannot help him now. But I can help you.' He stroked his shoulder. 'I can bring you back, Michael. Give you a new life.'

Decker said, 'I'm not interested.'

'Think of it as just another job. You were paid to kill Zishan and take care of the case. Now I'm paying you to remove Howell and get it back. You remember the case from Paris?'

Decker felt his jaw muscle flex as Sachs continued to rest his hand on his shoulder.

'You see it belongs to us,' Sachs said. 'And we don't have it … which makes you somewhat responsible. We want you to find it for us. What do you say?'

Decker had nothing to say.

Sachs walked towards the image of Annie. 'She's pretty, isn't she? You must miss her.'

Decker looked at the picture of Annie but couldn't think about whether he missed her or not at that moment. He glanced across at the windows on the other side of the room, with the heavy curtains and ornate tassels hanging off cords. Outside, he imagined a sloping roof, a drop of two floors, and gravel below.

'Get someone else,' Decker said.

'Why would I want to do that? You are the perfect candidate.'

Decker's eyes returned to the window. With his hands cuffed, he knew he would have to rely on luck how he fell. From there, even more luck to find cover. He imagined a heavy landing, perhaps more broken ribs or a fractured collarbone, tripping and stumbling as he fled across a quad, two balaclavas by this time already at the window, tapping out shards of glass with their Heckler and Kochs, time on their side. Then the thick bead of a foresight trained to the widest part of his moving figure to make a hit most likely, somewhere around the middle of his spine. The first shot exploding through his shoulder, bringing him to the ground; barely a moving target now, dragging himself across the grass like a deer that's been rear-ended by a car, shots two and three finding his chest and stomach.

Decker glanced back at the photo of Annie and imagined the small article in a Paris newspaper reporting the tragic death of a young woman drowning in the Seine or in a car accident on the ring road.

He said, 'What do you want me to do?'

Sachs walked back behind the desk, switched off the projector and sat down. 'We believe Howell has the briefcase. We want it back. Then we want Howell out the picture. Of course, all this must go under the radar. But that's what you're here for. Few people are further under the radar than you are at this moment, Michael.'

Decker knew now why he was in a private residence. He said, 'And if he's already dead?'

'We don't think he is. Howell's too smart for that.'

'And how will I find him?'

Sachs smiled. 'You'll find a way.'

Decker didn't smile back. 'The case,' he said. 'What is it?'

'Let's just say it's another stray dog, shall we?'

Decker looked into Sachs' eyes so he wouldn't forget him.

Sachs smiled again. 'It's just another job, Michael. That's all. You'll be paid and given a new life. Don't complicate it. Think of us as the new Mr Charles.'

Decker's eyes narrowed at the mention of his name.

Sachs said, 'I'm sorry. I realise the two of you were close.' And he dropped his gaze for a second as he brushed his finger across the laptop's touch pad to stop it from hibernating. 'Does all this make sense?' he said.

Decker nodded.

'Good.' Sachs gave a signal and the two balaclavas came back into the room. 'You have seven days,' he said. 'You'll be given a place to stay.'

Decker felt the balaclavas grab hold of his arms. 'Money?' Decker said.

'When the case is recovered.'

'My way out?'

'We'll make arrangements when the time comes.' Sachs bridged his hands as he had done at the start of their conversation. 'Anything else?'

Decker shook his head.

'Good. Your name is Michael from now.'

25

Blindfolded, Decker registered the gear changes down the long drive, simulating the corners in his mind, imagining lines of tree and cultivated fields, trying to commit it all to memory.

He wondered what time it was, whether it was the day or night. The walk from the house to the car had told him it was cool and damp, probably early morning, pre-dawn, but he couldn't be sure.

Decker continued to monitor the changes in road surfaces, the shifts in speed, the number of turns, the durations of straight, knowing it might prove useful later.

Then somewhere near the end of the A3, if his calculations were correct, the vehicle pulled up – a lay-by or empty slip road; loose grit on the tarmac; the sound of traffic in the distance.

The doors opened and two people got in. Struggling, Decker felt the prick of a needle in his arm and a heavy liquid flood his system. Then the doors closed. He slumped into a corner. The van pulled away.

He became aware of a metallic taste in his mouth and a melting sensation running down the back of his neck. Sweat prickled across his forehead. He turned his head, his muscles starting to spasm, and snapped his arms in their cuffs. Then his body started to convulse and he slipped down the side of the van, banging his head against the wheel arch, and lost consciousness.

*

Decker felt a lurching movement when he came round. He opened his eyes to sunlight.

Sitting up, there was a pain in his neck. His blindfold and his cuffs were gone. He rubbed his neck. He noticed a panel of glass in front of him, behind it a man driving, and now looking at him in his rear-view mirror. He was in a taxi.

'Heavy night was it?' the cabbie said, catching his eye in the mirror.

Decker made no reply. He observed a wide street, tall Georgian buildings and red buses. They were in London, just off Trafalgar square. He checked his watch: 10:18. Then he said, 'Where are we going?'

The driver chuckled. 'Isn't that your job? Wow! It must have been a good night. You don't remember anything, do you?'

Decker read the driver's identity card, displayed below the rear-view, and matched it to the man driving – bald, middle-aged, picture of his kids clipped to the sunscreen – then noticed the £11 on the meter which Decker estimated in the current traffic to be about ten minutes' worth of driving.

'Not much,' Decker said, electing to play along.

'Your friend said something about a promotion.'

'Did he?'

'You don't think you got into a taxi on your own, do you?' The driver looked up to his rear-view mirror again, grinning.

Decker said, 'I guess not.' He noticed the cabbie turn into the Charing Cross Road and head north. Someone must have given him directions, he thought.

Just before Goodge Street station, Decker said, 'Can you take the next left.'

The driver flicked a glance up to his rear-view and said, 'You sure? Your mate said Fitzwilliam Grove.'

'Change of plan,' Decker said.

'Okay. You're the boss.' The cabbie turned left.

Decker, looking round, noticed a bike behind them. Taking no chances, he said, 'Now take the next right.'

The cabbie said, 'Sure you're feeling all right, mate?'

'Getting there.'

The driver took the next right and Decker noticed the bike carry on past. 'Okay. Drop me off here.'

The driver pulled up to the kerb. Decker got out, leant down to the driver's window and said, 'Whereabouts in Fitzwilliam Grove did they say to drop me?'

The cabbie looked a little surprised. 'No12. Why?'

Decker nodded. 'I think my colleagues were playing a bit of joke on me. You see, I don't live anywhere near there.'

'Oh, I see.'

'But if they happen to ask ...'

The cabbie nodded. 'I've got you – I dropped you back at that address.'

Decker crossed the road as the cab drove off.

Soon, he was passing through a department store, picking a jacket off a peg and ripping out its security tag. He stood on the store's escalator putting it on. Then, pulling up the hood, he left the store and descended the steps to the underground.

Standing on the Tube, Decker scanned the carriageways in both directions, looking for the pair of eyes or a certain tilt to the head that looked out of place; knowing they would be expecting him.

Getting off at Baker Street, Decker entered a grubby-looking internet café and typed the address the taxi driver had given him into Google maps. Zooming in on Street View, he surveyed the house, which was middle terrace over three floors, and noted a block of flats nearby from where he could conduct some initial surveillance. He knew he had to find Howell, and fast. If they'd already killed Mr Charles over this then he'd be next. And if that meant playing along with Sachs, perhaps it wasn't such a bad option. But it would be on his terms.

It was just beginning to drizzle when Decker left the internet café. He skirted round Euston Road, crisscrossing backroads towards Regent's Park. Along the way, he entered a camera shop and bought a pair of binoculars.

He found the block of flats without any problem. It was just opposite where he was meant to be staying. A young woman, in duffel coat, leggings, UGG boots, was walking up the steps laden with bags of shopping. Decker closed in behind her and helped her with the door, making a comment about the weather and letting himself in at the same time.

He climbed the building's five flights of stairs and swung through a window onto the fire escape. From there, he climbed over a parapet wall and walked across a flat roof and scanned the adjacent street through the binoculars ... tracking along the fronts of houses and locatingNo12 ... then scanning rooftops and the resident's park and following a couple sharing an umbrella.

A few minutes passed. He was looking along the line of parked cars when he noticed a windscreen wiper move, sweeping once then twice, clearing the drizzle, before being turned off. Decker trained the binoculars on the car when he saw the door to No12 open opposite. He zoomed in on the house now and observed a man letting himself out, looking left then right before trotting down the steps. The man was tall, rugby player size, black leather jacket with large front pockets, receding hairline and crooked nose. He crossed the road, shrugging at the guy waiting in the car. Decker lowered the binoculars and watched him with the naked eye. The waiting car drove off while the rugby player guy continued along the pavement. Decker knew this was his cue.

*

The rugby player guy was pulling on a baseball cap when Decker barged into him coming round a corner.

The man swayed backwards. 'What the fuck!' he said.

Decker thrust his elbow into the man's face and then drove the heel of his hand up through his nose causing his cap to fly off.

Decker checked the windows above him before kicking the rugby player in the stomach and sending him rolling down some steps leading to a basement flat.

The rugby player was attempting to stand up when Decker joined him at the bottom of the steps. Decker shoved him backwards against the wall and the man collapsed on top of a clay flowerpot, breaking whatever plant was growing there, and slumped unconscious.

Blood ran from the guy's nose as Decker emptied his pockets – gun, phone and wallet. He pocketed the gun and phone as well as a wad of cash from his wallet then walked back up the steps, picking up the rugby player's cap for him and tossing it over the railings.

Reaching the main road, Decker stepped on a bus. Blood dripped off his hand, whether his or the rugby player's he wasn't sure. He wiped it on the seat and looked out the window.

*

About 20 minutes later, Decker got off the bus on the Marylebone Road. As he was crossing the road, the rugby player's phone started to ring in his jacket pocket.

Decker answered it with, 'Hello.'

Sachs said, 'What's going on, Michael?'

'Get rid of the extra personnel. I work alone.'

'We need you to stay in contact, Michael.'

'Get the money to me by tomorrow. And I will get you what you want.'

'That's not what we agreed.'

'That's right. It's not.'

Decker hung up the phone and dropped it in a bin.

*

It was getting dark when Decker booked into a hotel.

He stood under the shower with his eyes closed. Then, tying a towel round his waist, he sat on the edge of the bed and counted up the money he'd taken from the rugby player, £80 in all. That gave him enough for a hotel and some food. Then if Sachs played along, he'd have enough for another few weeks.

Next, Decker checked over the gun he'd acquired – a compact Glock 19 9mm, with a Gemtech Trinity silencer – releasing the magazine, drawing back the slide and peering through the ejection port.

Putting the gun under the pillow, Decker then lay on the bed and watched a property programme about a couple looking to buy a house in the country. The woman was overweight and the man was pencil thin. They both kept referring to everything as a 'space'. And both seemed a little hard to please. Then he fell asleep for half an hour. When he woke up, a quiz show was on TV. He stared at the screen for a minute, not really watching, then switched it off from the remote, got up, and helped himself to a bottle of water from the fridge. Then he did 50 press-ups on the floor and washed his face at the sink.

It was gone 2100 hours when Decker got dressed and took the lift downstairs. He crossed the foyer where a group of tourists were standing with their luggage.

Putting on a cap, Decker scanned in each direction as he left the building. He walked to the end of the road, turned the corner, and read a menu outside a restaurant while he checked to see if anyone was following him.

He continued east, checking road signs, memorising his route.

He waited at traffic lights to cross Wardour Street. The drizzle swirled. Two men were getting out of a taxi. One of them was texting on an iPhone.

Decker checked over his shoulder as he crossed the road.

He entered Soho and walked into a Chinese restaurant where a waiter showed him to a window table. He ordered dim sum and Oolong tea. An Asian couple were eating at the table next to him. The woman was pouring beer for the man. Through the window, Decker could see young men entering the pub across the road. The waiter brought over his food and Decker ate with chopsticks, drank the tea and kept an eye on the pub opposite. He finished off the meal with four slices of orange, left a tip, and exited the restaurant with a toothpick between his teeth.

Walking across the road, picking orange pith from his teeth with the toothpick, Decker went into the pub opposite and scanned the room. A bouncer on the door, 16 men, three women, two barmen working the taps, three exits, two at the front, one at the rear.

Decker walked to the bar, continuing to scan the room, and work the toothpick between his teeth. Half-way across the room, it was then he noticed Howell's boyfriend, Will Fenton, exiting a "Staff only" marked door. Dressed in jeans and zip-up hoodie with a cigarette behind his ear, he walked across the pub towards the exit. Decker turned and followed him.

Fenton was lighting his cigarette at the front of the pub when Decker put his arm round him and drove his fist into his solar plexus.

26

Fenton spat the cigarette out onto the pavement and gasped for breath. Decker held him upright against the wall and said, 'Where's Howell?'

Fenton wheezed, reddening in the face. 'Why don't you leave me alone?'

Decker smacked him in the stomach again. 'Where is he?'

'I don't know,' eyes watering. 'Really, I don't know.'

Decker grabbed Fenton's right hand and started to crush his fingers. Fenton squealed. Several passers-by looked round. Decker glared at them and turned Fenton in the opposite direction.

Fenton said, 'He's gone away.'

'Where to?'

'I don't know. Honestly.'

'When did he leave?'

'That day … when you came.'

'Where did he go?'

'I don't know. He didn't tell me.'

Decker increased the pressure on his fingers.

'Please, I don't know anything. He disappeared.'

'When did you last see him?'

'A week ago. '

'What did he say?'

'Nothing.'

'When are you next seeing him?'

Fenton hesitated.

Decker stamped on his foot.

Fenton grimaced. 'I don't know. He said he'd ring.'

'When?'

'Soon. Tonight, maybe.'

'Maybe?' crushing his fingers some more.

'Yes, tonight. He's back tonight.'

'Where are you meeting him?'

'I don't know.'

Decker twisted Fenton's fingers right back.

'I swear. There's nothing's fixed. Please.'

Decker looked up and saw someone had gone over to speak to the doorman. They were looking in their direction. The doorman, a big, bulky black guy, was puffing himself up. Over he came, flared nostrils. 'You!' he said, pointing at Decker. 'Get lost.'

Decker dropped his head, eyes below the peak of his cap. Fenton stepped away.

The doorman said, 'You all right?' to Fenton.

Fenton said, 'Yeah, fine. Everything's fine.'

The doorman turned to Decker again, giving him a shove, saying, 'Didn't you hear me?'

Decker didn't move, keeping his head lowered and face hidden.

The doorman said, 'Something wrong with you?' He shoved him again.

Fenton said, 'It's fine, really. We were just talking.'

'Funny talking'

'Really. He's an old friend.'

'Could have fooled me.'

Fenton stepped between the doorman and Decker and said to the doorman, 'I'm coming back inside in a minute. Really, it's all all right.'

'Are you sure?' the doorman said. 'Who is this guy?'

'No one,' said Fenton. 'We're fine, really.'

The doorman shrugged then said to Decker. 'I'll be watching you, all right?'

Decker didn't respond.

The doorman walked back to the door.

Decker turned to Fenton, and in a lowered voice said, 'We're leaving.'

Fenton said, 'I can't. I've got to go to work.'

'Say you've got to go. Make an excuse.'

'Why?'

'Because I say so.'

Fenton gave a nod then walked back into the bar.

111

Less than a minute later, Fenton reappeared.

Decker was waiting for him round the corner.

'Where are we going?' Fenton asked.

'Keep walking.' Decker scanned the street in both directions. 'Do you have a key to Howell's place?'

'No. What's this about?' Fenton turned round.

'Keep looking straight ahead. I need to speak to him.'

'I thought you told me he was dead?'

Decker made no response.

Fenton said, 'Who are you, anyway?'

Decker said, 'What time do you normally finish work?'

'In about an hour. Around ten. Why?'

'You've got Howell's number?'

'Yeah,' Fenton said. 'But like I said, I haven't seen him recently.'

'Send him a message.'

'What … now?'

'Yes, now.'

'And say what?'

'That you want to meet.'

'Why? He'll be suspicious.'

Decker grabbed Fenton round the neck, 'Send the message.'

'Okay, Okay,' holding up his hands.

Fenton began texting.

Decker said, 'Make it good. Do you understand?'

'What do you mean?'

'Make sure he comes.'

'What are you going to do?'

'You don't need to know. Turn left.'

They passed an oriental food shop; an elderly Chinese man sat outside smoking a cigarette and watching raindrops drip off the metal awning. Living in another time, another life, it seemed to Decker.

Decker said to Fenton, 'There is a café 50 metres on the right. Go in, order two coffees, and join me at one of the tables. Do you understand?'

'Okay. And if he rings?'

'Answer it.'

Decker sat down at a table by the door and watched Fenton at the counter ordering two coffees. Paying the girl, he dropped some money and had to pick it up.

Fenton sat down, coffee sloshing on the table, hands shaking.

Decker drew his cup towards him and stirred in a sachet of sugar. 'Put your phone on the table,' he said, keeping his eyes below the peak of his cap.

Fenton did as he was instructed. 'What happens if he doesn't call?' he said.

Decker checked his watch. It was just past ten. 'I'll let you know,' he said. Decker took a sip of coffee. It wasn't bad.

Fenton juddered his leg under the table. 'Can I go out for a cigarette?' he said.

Decker lifted his head enough to make eye contact with Fenton.

'Okay, okay,' Fenton said. 'I understand.' He ruffled his hair a couple of times and looked over his shoulder.

Decker said, 'Keep still.'

Fenton held his head with one hand, and said 'What's this about?'

'Howell,' Decker said.

The phone bleeped with a message. Fenton jumped in his chair and grabbed the phone.

Decker replaced his cup in its saucer. 'Take it easy,' he said, watching Fenton putting in his password and opening the message.

'He wants to know when I'm free. What shall I say?'

'What you normally say – that you're free. And you want to meet.'

Fenton typed out a message. Decker checked the message before he sent it.

Fenton said, 'What are you going to do?'

Decker emptied another sachet of sugar into his cup, taking his time, not rushing it so all the sugar dissolved.

Fenton watched him stir it in, and said, 'You like a lot of sugar, don't you?'

Decker kept stirring.

The phone bleeped again. Fenton grabbed the phone and opened the message.

'He wants to meet now,' he said.

'Tell him you're still in Soho. You want to eat out. Suggest you meet at The Albacore.'

'What's that?'

'A restaurant. He'll know.'

Fenton stared at him.

Decker said, 'Do it now.'

Decker drank the remaining coffee and returned the cup to its saucer. It was warm and sweet. Fenton sent another message.

A message came back almost instantly. Fenton read the message to himself and looked at Decker.

'He's coming,' he said.

'How long?'

'Fifteen minutes.'

Decker stood up. 'Let's go.'

It had started drizzling again. Leaving the café, Fenton put up his hood and got out a cigarette. Decker told him to wait and to keep walking. Fenton did as he was told, returning the cigarette to the packet.

Decker walked behind him, giving him directions, eyes lowered, as if he was speaking to the ground.

They turned down a narrow alley and walked into a porn shop. Decker stood next to Fenton at the back of the shop and pretended to look through a rack of DVDs and said, 'Give me your phone.'

Fenton passed him his phone and Decker slipped it into his pocket.

'I want you to stand outside The Albacore and wait for Howell. It's about 100 metres from here, left at the end of the road, then right. Smoke a cigarette when you get there. When he arrives, act as normal. Do you understand?'

'Then what?'

'Just do what I've told you. Nothing else matters. Do you understand?'

'Yeah.'

Fenton turned left out of the shop.

A minute later, Decker did the same, crossing the road, and scanning in both directions. He expected Howell to be early and just as cautious.

Decker walked the length of a narrow street behind the backs of shops and restaurants. At the end of the street he had a view of The Albacore, a well-lit glass fronted restaurant with black awning, no more than 30 metres away.

Decker leant against the wall, drew out the Glock and racked the slide.

A minute passed.

Fenton approached along the main road, hood up, hands in pockets.

Decker checked up and down the street for any sign of movement.

Fenton stopped outside The Albacore and lit a cigarette.

Drizzle floated through streetlights. Decker watched people walk past. Fenton puffed on his cigarette, one hand in his pocket, shoulders hunched.

Decker wondered if Howell was already in the neighbourhood, wondered if he was watching the two of them now. The seconds ticked past.

Fenton dropped his cigarette on the pavement, turned a white plimsoll on it, and put both hands in his pockets now.

Decker wondered how long Fenton was going to last, whether he was going to make a run for it. There was always that chance. He looked on edge, strung out. More so than usual, he thought. Decker suspected it was because he wasn't telling him something.

Decker observed two men in suits leave the restaurant and stand under the awning and light cigarettes. Decker checked his watch. The fifteen minutes were nearly up.

Fenton walked to the kerb, hands in pockets and looked in both directions. Decker observed his eyes flicking from side to side, like an animal about to break cover. Then further down the street, Decker saw a man approaching under an umbrella; the umbrella was tilted at an angle so you couldn't see his face.

Decker flattened himself against the wall, holding the Glock inside his jacket, and slowed down his breathing.

A delivery van drove past, spraying water, and the man lifted his umbrella enough to have a look at the van, and enough for Decker to identify his face.

It was Howell.

27

Howell walked up to Fenton, lifting the umbrella to reveal who he was, and their eyes locked. Fenton didn't need to speak for Howell to get wind that something wasn't right. Backing up, he dropped his umbrella and started to run.

Decker broke cover, weaving between cars, and went after him.

Passers-by stopped and stared.

Howell hurdled over a pile of bin bags and turned down a side-street.

Decker followed, nearly knocking over a woman speaking on a phone.

They came to a main road, Howell cutting diagonally across the lanes of traffic, vaulting the safety rails and splashing through a puddle.

Decker had to wait for a gap in the traffic, stopping in the middle of the road, cars blasting their horns. He saw Howell already at the end of the street, disappearing round a corner. Decker ran to catch up him but when he reached the same spot, he couldn't see him anywhere.

He clutched his sides, breathing heavily. He saw a bus splashing through potholes, pull in opposite and two girls get off and linked arms. The drizzle swirled though streetlights.

Decker stood there a moment longer, remembering Fenton's mobile and removing it from his pocket. Looking at the lit screen, he thought about phoning Howell for a second but then gave up on the idea. If Howell wanted to make contact he would in his own time. Phoning him wasn't going to help.

Decker turned back. The time: 23:23.

*

Twenty minutes later, at 23:43, Decker scanned parked cars and shop fronts across the street from the hotel where he was staying. Satisfied no one was waiting for him he crossed the street and entered the hotel.

He rode the lift to the fifth floor, noticing water dripping off his wet clothes onto the floor. He walked down the corridor to his room, swiped his card and went in.

Removing his wet clothes, he sat on the bed and flicked through channels on the TV. He drank two whisky miniatures from the fridge to warm up. Then he lay down with the lights off but his eyes open and pictured Howell standing on the street under the umbrella, then dropping his umbrella, and chasing after him.

The rain kept falling outside. At some point, his thoughts became dreams…

*

He saw the bullet passing through Mr Charles's head, skull fragments thwacking against glass; heard him saying, 'they are closing us down,' as bullets racked into his chest.

Then a pigeon took off from aluminium railings.

Then he was back at Sachs' house, sitting on the chair under the lights. His hands cuffed behind him, sweat dripping off his forehead, an electric shock ripping through him. The voice saying, 'Who are you?'

Then he was curled up on the floor, head in his hands, the balaclavas beating him with batons.

Then he was looking at Sachs behind his desk, telling him, 'You are what we call a stray dog.' Then turning round, he found he was alone in the room. No Sachs, no dog. The windows open, the curtains sucked out in a draught.

Then he was looking at a photo album on the floor; a picture of a churchyard. Then he was standing in the churchyard, looking at a headstone, with the names of his parents, James and Annabel, engraved on the stone.

Then he was shooting the guy in the Kensington apartment, blood soaking through his white Lacoste shirt.

Then it was raining and Zishan's arm was snagging in the door of the BMW as his blood diluted on the pavement.

Another surge of electricity. 'Who were you before?'

Mr Charles's head dashed against the interior of the van.

His grandmother waving him off from her porch as he left in a taxi for school.

Then a bell was ringing. And he was looking round a room which he realised was a lift. And the ringing was getting louder.

And louder.

*

Decker's eyes flicked open in the dark, realising the ringing was coming from the room he was in. He sat up and saw Fenton's mobile lit up on the table beside him.

'There is a café on Chandos called Dave's,' Howell said. 'They put a chalk board outside on the pavement.'

Decker grabbed the pen on the table.

'It's opposite the post office.'

Decker started writing on the back of a postcard.

'At 8:30, walk past the café. You'll get further instructions.'

28

Grey dawn light. Decker, pulling up his hood, headed down the steps to the underground. The time: 7:33.

He boarded a Northern Line train, scanning the carriage, and stood by the door.

He didn't expect Howell. Not yet.

He got off at Leicester Square, walked down Cranbourne Street and turned right down Garrick Street. Three suits hurried past him carrying Café Nero cups.

On New Road, he went into a Costa and came out carrying a coffee, more to blend in than to drink.

He came out onto Charing Cross Road, walked down to Trafalgar Square then turned left and walked up Adelaide Street. Saw the café on Chandos where Howell had asked to meet, stopped and looked in a shop window, drinking his coffee. Over his shoulder, he saw a motorcycle courier sat on a bike speaking on his phone. A second later, two men in high visibility jackets left the café.

Decker approached the café as the courier came off his phone, put on his helmet and sped off down the road. Watching after him, Decker noticed a man step out from a doorway. He was wearing a puffer jacket, slouch beanie and fingerless wool gloves. Catching Decker's eye, he crossed the road and headed towards Trafalgar Square. Decker followed him, keeping a distance of about 50 metres.

Approaching the square, the man stopped and lit a cigarette. He leant against the wall, lifting his head and gazed up at Nelson's column. He put his foot up against the wall and smoked.

Decker mingled with a crowd of tourists, listening to the guide explaining the history of the four plinths, when he observed the man put out his cigarette and walk up the steps to the National Gallery.

Decker fell in behind him and followed him into the gallery.

Once inside, the man walked into the gift shop.

Decker waited in the lobby and watched the man pick a book off a shelf and go straight to the till with it and pay for it in cash.

Leaving the shop, the man crossed the gallery foyer, carrying the book in a bag, and headed down the steps to the gents. Moments later, Decker came down the same steps, stopping outside the gents and drawing the slide of the Glock and tucking the gun into his waistband.

The man was washing his hands at the sink when Decker entered. The bag was sitting on the side of the sink. Decker came and stood beside the man. No eye contact was made. The man finished washing his hands and turned on the hand dryer. In the mirror, Decker watched him rotating his hands under the hot air. Then, without picking up the bag, the man left the gents.

Decker checked around himself. He was alone. He picked up the bag and looked inside. There was a book on Cezanne and a free audio set.

Putting on the headset, Decker walked back up the steps to the gallery. On the audio, a woman's voice began speaking about the gallery's history. Decker found his way to the exhibition room containing pictures by Cezanne. Once in the room, he walked round the walls of paintings, reading the names of the painters as he went. He came to a Cezanne, stopped and read the blurb about the picture. The woman on the audio was talking about a different painting, some religious 18th century work. All of a sudden, her voice began to break up. There was a second or two of white noise and then no sound at all. Then a man's voice came over the headset:

'Don't turn round.'

It was Howell.

'Keep looking at the picture in front of you. Your name is Martin Decker. You are a contract killer and you have been sent to kill me.'

Decker said, 'Where are you?'

'Keep looking at the picture, Martin. Your handler's name was Mr Charles. The agency that hired you had Mr Charles killed and will kill you once you have fulfilled your contract.'

Decker caught a reflection of someone wearing a headset behind him.

The voice said, 'Check the bag, Martin. Your answer is in there.'

Decker's eyes flicked to the bag. He pulled out the book and opened the front cover. Inside was a photograph. It was the photograph of his parents skiing. The flat, he thought; the cupboard behind the boiler; the deadman's briefcase; the missing bag.

So it was Howell.

Decker turned the photograph over. On the back Howell had written the words "Stray dog".

Decker spun round, scanning the room but seeing only a blur of paintings. Then he experienced a flashback, so vivid it was like it was happening now, of him sitting on the floor at his grandmother's house, turning the pages of a family photo album, a little boy again; boxes about the room, full of his parent's belongings; people in suits talking in the next room. It was the day of his parent's funeral.

Over the headset, the voice said, 'Leave the gallery and get on a number 43 bus heading south.'

There was a second or two of white noise again, then the originally audio resumed about religious paintings.

Exiting the gallery, Decker stripped off the headset and tossed it in a bin along with the book about Cezanne. He crossed Trafalgar Square and boarded a number 43. Sitting down, Decker noticed a man stand up at the back of the bus and walk down the aisle towards him. He was wearing sunglasses and a fur trapper hat. The man sat down next to him. It was Howell.

'Hello, Martin,' he said.

Decker kept looking straight ahead. 'The photograph?' he said.

'From the flat.'

'You knew then.'

'Yes.'

'And the case?'

'We had to get it out.'

'They killed Mr Charles,' Decker said.

'There was nothing we could do.'

Decker pulled out the Glock and stuck it into Howell's stomach. 'We will get off at the next stop,' he said. 'You will walk in front of me.'

'Put the gun away, Martin.' Howell looked straight down the aisle of the bus. 'You need to listen.'

Decker felt his jaw muscle flex as he gripped the gun.

Howell said, 'If I don't walk off this bus, they will kill you too.'

At the back of the bus, two teenage girls were playing snatches of music aloud on their phone.

'*Getting jiggy with it*

Na nananananana nana
Getting jiggy with it ...'

'Listen to me, Martin,' Howell said. 'This goes deeper than you think.'

Decker, with the gun still on Howell, said, 'We get off at the next stop.'

'Your father was involved, Martin. Listen to me.'

Decker felt his finger closing on the trigger, imagining Howell's blood sprayed across the window of the bus, his guts spilt onto the seat, and people screaming around him. It would be one hell of a mess, he thought.

'Your father worked for the agency,' Howell said. 'Twenty-five years ago, your father was killed by the same man that hired you. His name is Jonathan Sachs. He worked with your father on a project called Stray Dog. Your father was Sachs' supervisor. They were trying to expose a mole in the organisation. Only Sachs was the mole. There were four of them working on Stray Dog. The other man was Charles Sackerville – or Mr Charles, as you knew him. You need to listen to me, Martin. Time is not on our side. Put the gun away.'

Decker lifted the Glock up under Howell's rib cage, his eyes narrowing as he readied himself for the spray of blood.

'The gun, Martin. Killing me will just get you killed quicker.'

'We'll see.'

'Martin, you've no idea. Sachs won't stop. There are things he wants to hide. Things he wants buried. Think back, Martin.'

The memory returned to Decker's mind, flickering like a badly tuned TV. He was a little boy again, sitting on the floor at his granny's, the photo album of his father's on his lap, a man in a suit had come into the room. There were loose photos on the floor. Decker had been pulling them out of the album pockets ...

Howell said, 'He'll find you, Martin.'

The girls at the back of the bus began to sing over the top of Beyoncé's *Crazy In Love* ... '*Uh oh, uh oh, uh oh, oh no no ...*'

Decker said. 'It was an accident.'

'No, Martin. There are no accidents. You should know that.'

Decker slackened his grip on the gun. The memory came again. The man who had come into the room was saying, 'What have you got there?' extending his arm, taking the album, and Decker holding onto one of the loose photos, the one of his parents skiing.

Howell said, 'For 20 years Sachs has been covering his tracks – first your father, then Mr Charles, now you.'

Decker shook his head, his mind computing the following sequence of events: wait for the bus to start pulling in; two chest shots; stand up; walk down the aisle; exit the bus.

'Listen to me, Martin,' Howell said. 'There's someone else. I need more time.'

Decker looked at Howell. 'You don't have time.'

'There were four of them: Sachs; Mr Charles; your father; and the person giving the orders. We need to find him.'

'No. We don't.'

'Martin, he killed your parents.'

Stay on foot. Eurostar that night. Stay over in Paris. Head south in the morning.

'How do you think Mr Charles knew about you all those years ago? He watched out for you, Martin.'

The bus starting pulling in, Howell saying, 'I think you've known all along. There are no accidents. No coincidences.'

Decker recognised Mr Charles in his voice ... *Remember: acknowledging something as a coincidence is a sure sign you don't know what's really going on.* He felt the default setting in him clicking into place that he was powerless to override. His grip on the gun went slack, his arm dropping to his side.

Howell said, 'When I stand up, Martin, you will not move. You will stay on board for another two stops. You will not attempt to follow me. You will forget I was here. Do you understand?'

Decker didn't move, didn't speak.

Howell stood up, saying 'Stay away from everywhere you know. I will contact you at the address on the card.' He handed Decker a card. 'It will be safe for now.'

Decker looked at the card ... a hand-written URL and password.

Howell stepped off the bus and Decker watched him pull down the ear flaps of his hat and disappear round a corner.

29

Decker entered an internet café off Charing Cross Road and checked the URL Howell had given him. It took him to a secure bulletin board. At the top of the page there was a photo of his father and a short profile about him. It mentioned the various locations he'd worked and contained photographs of dams and office blocks he'd been involved with. Jonathon Sachs and Charles Sackerville appeared in some of the photographs.

Further down the page, there were also photos and profiles of the men Decker had killed in Paris: Zishan Badar and Algerian, Omar 'B'.

Decker spent some time reading about how Omar 'B' had won a scholarship to a French university, completed a Masters in Engineering and then become involved with extremist groups. "To the world outside," the article went, "a polite, intelligent young man, well-liked by his peers and professors. To others, a fanatic, a killer." Omar 'B' was rumoured to be part of the motorbike killings in France. Decker wondered what Sachs had promised him: information … money?

Next, Decker read about Zishan Badar. Listed as a government agent, Badar posed as a businessman running Zishan Enterprises, an international property company that really traded in intelligence and weapons technology. There was a company website and Wikipedia entry. On the website, Decker found the name Hatton Alharbi on the board of directors. Decker then stopped and googled Alharbi. He found a portfolio of property listed under his name as well as a desalination plant in the Middle East. He followed other links, turning up journal articles about water provision to arid regions, newspaper and magazine columns on property prices, the global economy, plus a tennis club membership in Chelsea. Then he hit upon a photograph of

Alharbi at some industry dinner party. He was accepting some award. Sitting at one of the tables was Jonathon Sachs.

Lastly, there was a picture of the contract in Paris – the overcoat-wearing gunman at the window. The same guy that Fenton had met at the museum and that Kyle had talked about, Peter Schiller: ex-army, ex-security services, a table tennis champion in his teens and graduate of care homes and orphanages.

While none of this proved that Sachs had killed his father, or that Howell could be trusted, Decker knew now that this ran deeper than a missing briefcase and whatever it might contain.

Decker left the internet café. The wind was getting up, dry leaves skating across pavements. He continued along the road, narrowing his eyes against the wind and scoping his surroundings. He turned left under a glass walkway, took the steps down to Tottenham Court Road station and boarded a Central Line train.

Changing at Oxford Street, Decker got off at Victoria, crossed the station concourse and paid for a train ticket in cash, leaving tomorrow.

Exiting the station, he continued on foot, picking up cash from a Western Union courtesy of Sachs, taking all the usual precautions to ensure he wasn't being followed.

Next, he went into a bookshop and bought two Ordnance Survey maps covering the North and South Downs. Then he went into a mobile phone shop where he bought a pay-as-you-go phone. Afterwards he stopped in a camping shop where he bought a rucksack, compass, and hat. For all purchases he paid in cash. His last stop was a Tesco Express where he grabbed sandwiches, chocolate and bottles of beer.

At 19:15, Decker stepped off a Northern Line train and walked up an escalator. Leaving the station, he turned left, cutting across a park and out the other side where he knew of another quiet hotel to spend the night.

It was getting dark. Decker approached the hotel from the other side of the road. A couple left through the glass doors arm in arm. A police siren wailed in the distance. Checking round himself, Decker crossed the road and entered the hotel.

In his room, Decker laid out the maps, clothes, and compass on the bed. Next, he unpacked the mobile, inserted the SIM card and placed it on the bed as well. Then he dismantled and reassembled the Glock and put that on the bed too. Then one by one, he put these items into the rucksack. It was like being in the army again, he thought.

Decker sat on the bed and ate the sandwiches. He flicked through channels on TV. He watched a nature programme about whales. He swigged from a bottle of beer. He remembered eating whale in Japan and it being very nice. It took him a moment to remember why he was in Japan. It had been a missing person case. The guy's body had been found on a mountain. There was no sign of a struggle, no injuries. The guy was reported to have died of natural causes, whatever that meant. Decker had caught up with his killer two days later. He tracked his hire car to a remote house in Hakone. He was staying with a woman. The next morning, the woman left early for work. The man appeared an hour later at the front door. He was wearing a ski jacket and fur-lined snow boots. He was going for a walk. Decker was hidden up the slope behind conifers. The first shot entered just above the man's right eye, the second through his heart. Decker rolled him down the bank through the snow, but he got snagged up between fir trees and Decker had to climb down and kick him free. He'd taken the train back to Tokyo that day. The body, as far as he knew, was never recovered.

Decker thought about whales again, then about fishing. He remembered a picture on his grandmother's piano. In the picture, he was sitting on his father's knee. He was four at the time. His father was holding a fish. A fishing rod and landing net were lying on the grass in the foreground. Three years later, he'd started fishing at his grandmother's house, like his dad had before him. He remembered the first carp he'd caught, a 5.5lb common, on 3lb main line and luncheon meat straight on the hook. He'd caught it right up against the branches of an overhanging oak tree at seven o'clock in the morning. He'd thought he'd hooked a monster. It surged right across the lake and seemed to take hours to land.

He hadn't gone fishing in a long time, Decker thought, and decided he would go fishing again when all this was over.

Draining the bottle of beer, Decker heard the hotel bedside phone start to ring. He looked at the phone on the bedside table as it rang. His lip curled in irritation. Then he reached across, picked up the receiver and waited. Had he forgotten to pick up his towel? Or pay a deposit?

'Hello, this is the front desk,' a man's voice said the other end, 'sorry to disturb you but we have someone here who wishes to speak to you. He won't give a name and doesn't want to speak on the phone. What would you like me to do?'

Decker's eyes moved to the door.

The guy on the phone said, 'He says he's a friend and that you would be expecting him.'

Decker was pulling the slide on the Glock, and putting on his jacket, and slipping his arms through the straps of the rucksack he'd packed earlier.

'Hello... Hello ... Are you there?'

The receiver lay on the bed.

30

Decker was walking down the corridor, tucking the Glock into his waistband. He knew the back of the hotel was his best way out – the front was lit up like a Christmas tree.

He followed the corridor round a corner when he heard the lift ping open. He backed off and flattened himself against the wall. In the mirror on the opposite wall, he saw a man in a grubby navy overcoat appear from the lift. It was Schiller.

Schiller moved along the corridor towards him, checking room numbers. Decker backed off round the corner and knocked on the nearest door. A woman in a dressing gown answered. 'Yeah … can I help?' Decker punched her in the face. She went out cold. Decker saw a half-naked man in the background stumbling out of bed. Walking through the room, Decker pushed him against the wall. The man fell on the floor and then reverse-crawled into the bathroom. Decker left him to it and climbed out of the window onto the ledge.

A breeze whistled round the building. Decker moved along the ledge, four stories up, and then lowered himself onto a flat roof. He jumped the parapet wall and swung himself over railings down to a lower level.

Two pigeons clattered from a cage of electrical units. Decker ran to the far wall, looked over the edge, and spotted fire exit steps below. He jumped onto the nearest platform, ran down the steps and came into a courtyard.

He saw a CCTV camera mounted above double gates. He was out of shot as long as he stayed close to the wall, he thought. He pulled the Glock and edged round the outside of the building.

Reaching the gates, a security light clicked on and flooded the courtyard. Decker tried the gates but couldn't get them open. He looked round the courtyard for an alternative exit. He observed bolted storage units with aluminium roller doors, then a row of wheelie bins alongside, and wondered if he could use one to get over the wall. As he was thinking this, he heard the sound of keys in a lock.

He squatted down behind a bollard. A fat man left the building with a bundle of keys attached to his waist. He was wearing a blue parka anorak with fur collar. The fat man walked over to one of the storage units, his keys jingling round his waist, and lifted the roller blind and disappeared inside.

Decker moved into position to climb the wall when he saw a woman leave the building. He darted behind the wheelie bin and crouched down. He heard the sound of the woman's heels on concrete and then the aluminium roller blind. He peeked round the corner of the bin. The woman was in her late 20s, blonde hair tied up in a pony-tail, wearing a skirt and jacket uniform, and carrying a brown leather shoulder bag. She was checking her mobile as she crossed the courtyard.

'Goodnight Vernon,' she called out.

The fat man, shutting the blind, said, 'Is it that time already?'

The woman smiled. 'Yeah, afraid so.'

'Better get back to work, then,' he said. 'See you tomorrow.'

'No, you won't. I'm off tomorrow.'

'Oh, are you,' the fat man said. 'All right for some, eh.'

The woman smiled as she walked over to one of the cars, pressing a key fob to activate its central locking. The car's indicators flashed. The woman opened the door and put her bag on the passenger seat and climbed in. The fat man waved to her and disappeared back into the building.

The woman started the car, headlights lighting up the courtyard, and drove forward. Decker crept out from behind the bins and followed behind.

The car stopped at the security gates, activating the underground automated system. And as the doors were opening, Decker walked round to the passenger side of the car.

The door wasn't locked. Getting in and closing the door behind him, Decker put his hand over the woman's mouth before she could scream.

The gates clicked open.

Decker said, 'Drive on.'

The woman stalled the car; they jolted forward. Decker saw the

129

woman's hands were shaking as she reached for the gear stick.

Decker said, 'Take your time. Nothing is going to happen to you.'

The woman said, 'What do you want?'

'Just drive the car.'

The woman pulled out onto the road. 'Where am I going?'

Decker scanned the street. 'Where do you normally go?'

'Home.'

'Then do that.'

They stopped at the traffic lights at the front of the hotel. Schiller was standing on the pavement, speaking on his mobile. Decker put his elbow up on the windowsill to cover his face. Schiller was looking up at the hotel. The traffic lights seemed to take ages to change colour. The woman's arms were shaking as she held the steering wheel. Her face was drained of colour. If she stalled now, Decker thought, that would be it. He said to her, 'Keep breathing. Nothing is going to happen to you.'

The woman looked round, 'What do you mean?'

'It's going to be okay. Slow your breathing down. Take a deep breath.'

The lights changed. The woman pulled away, grinding on a gear change, and saying, 'I'm sorry.'

Decker nodded. 'You're doing well.'

Decker noticed she had kicked off her shoes, was wearing tights.

He checked behind them, and said, 'How long?'

'What do you mean?'

'To your house?'

'About 30 minutes,' glancing at him. 'What's going to happen?'

'Nothing. Keep driving.'

'Please … what do you want?'

Decker's eyes narrowed as he focused on road signs. 'Nothing, I'm not going to hurt you.'

'Why are you here?' Again she glanced at him.

Decker noted she spoke English with a slight accent, eastern European, hard to say exactly where.

Decker checked his watch: 23:46. 'You work at the hotel?'

'Yeah.'

'You drive everyday?'

'No, only when I work late. What's this about?'

Checking the interior of the car now, 'Who do you live with?'

'Why?'

'Just answer the question.' Decker opened the glove box and rifled through CD cases.

'I live on my own. What has that got to do with anything?'

'Describe your building.'

'What?' She turned her head. 'What are you talking about?' Her hair fell forward across her cheek. She blinked like she couldn't understand English anymore.

'Describe the building you live in. Is it a block of flats or a house?'

'I live in a house. Why?'

'Terrace?'

'Yes ... no ... it's detached ... semi-detached.'

'Floors?'

'Three. No, four. I don't know. I can't remember.'

'That's okay. What about flats?'

'What?'

'How many flats are there?'

'Eight, I think. Why do you want to know?'

'Do you speak to your neighbours?'

'What do you mean?'

'It's a simple question. Do you speak to your neighbours?'

'Yes, occasionally ... when I see them. We're not like friends or anything.'

'Okay, good.'

The woman turned towards Decker. 'For what?'

Decker looked puzzled.

The woman said, 'Good for what? You said, "Okay, good." Good for what?'

Decker said, 'I need somewhere to stay. That's all. You've nothing to worry about.'

'Really?'

An oncoming vehicle blasted its horn as the woman drifted across the road.

'Keep your eyes on the road,' Decker said, helping her with the steering wheel, then said, 'Are you expecting anyone tonight?'

The woman shot a glance at him. 'Are you going to kill me?'

'No.' He hadn't anticipated all these questions and was beginning to regret involving her now. He could have waited and climbed the fence, he thought. But his instinct told him the woman would be useful. He needed somewhere to hide, someone to get him out. Hotels were out the question now.

Decker said, 'Do you have a boyfriend?'

The woman hesitated. 'What?'

'A boyfriend ... or housemate?'

'Why?'

'Just answer the question.' She was pretty, Decker thought. A woman like that would have someone.

'No.'

'Are you sure?'

'Yes, I'm sure.'

Either she was lying, thought Decker, or she had just broken up with someone.

'Family?'

'Look, I can give you money. Not much. But I have some savings.'

'I don't want your money. Any family?'

'No, not here. They're abroad. I'm not English. You're scaring me.'

'I need to stay tonight. That's all. Do as I say and nothing will happen to you. Do you understand?'

'Who are you?' Tears were running down her face. 'What do you want?'

'You don't need to know. I'm not a threat.'

'Why me?'

'You were there. Now describe the area you live in?'

The woman wiped her eyes with her hand and then clutched the steering wheel again. 'How?' she said.

'What's on your street?'

'Houses ...' she began, glancing at him, looking flustered, tears filling her eyes again.

Decker said, 'Any public buildings or open spaces?'

'There is a church at the end of the street ... a sport's field and playground at the back.'

'Good. What else?'

'Nothing I can think of.'

'What about bus stops, train stations?'

'No.'

'Any tall buildings?'

'No.'

They stopped at traffic lights. The woman had stopped crying now. Decker looked at the road. Streetlights punctuated the road. He observed a man walking a small dog; a polystyrene takeaway container slid along the pavement in the wind.

The lights changed. The woman pulled away and Decker noticed the woman's hands on the steering wheel and the silver bracelet with the small charm round her wrist. Her wrists seemed very small and slender and Decker couldn't help staring at them for a moment, thinking how he'd never looked at a woman's wrists like this before.

The woman said, 'Are you in trouble with the police?'

'Not exactly.'

'Is someone following you?'

'How much further is it?' Decker said, checking the wing mirror.

The woman glanced at him and said, 'Are you going to rape me? Please tell me now if you are. I want to know.'

Decker shook his head.

The woman half smiled. 'Thank you.' She brushed hair out of her eyes. Decker looked at the road. They didn't speak again.

*

Slowing down, the woman turned into a narrow residential street. As she had described, there was a playing field and kids' playground at the back, then a church at the end of the street.

The woman parked the car and Decker told her to turn off the ignition. They sat in silence for a moment. Decker checked the wing mirror for anyone coming. Then he heard woman's phone buzz with a message.

'Check your phone,' he said, not looking round.

The woman hesitated.

'Do it now,' he said.

The woman reached into her bag and took out her phone and read the message. 'From my brother,' she said.

'Where is he?'

'Not here. Back at home, in my country. I told you.'

'Give it to me.'

The woman handed him the phone.

Decker said, 'If someone sees us just smile, wish them a goodnight or whatever you normally do. Remember everything is as normal. I am a cousin staying for a couple of nights before I move into my new flat. Do you understand?'

'Okay, I understand.'

Decker looked in the wing mirror, and said. 'Okay. We go in

together.'

31

Once inside the woman's flat, Decker drew the blinds and took note of the layout: single room with separate bathroom and kitchen; one rear-facing window, one at the side.

The woman said, 'It's like you've done this before.'

Decker said, 'What do you normally do when you get home?

'What do you mean?'

'Do you watch television, play music?'

'I put the TV on, I suppose.'

'Turn it on, then.'

The woman remoted the TV. 'What do you want to watch?' she said.

'What you normally watch.'

She flicked through the channels to some American comedy.

Decker went into the kitchen and opened the fridge; he could hear the sound of canned laughter next door. 'Have you eaten?' he said.

'No.'

'Do you usually eat?'

'Yeah, but I'm not hungry.'

'I'll make something. Sit down.'

Decker got down a pan and fried some eggs. He knew how important it was to keep eating even when you may not feel like it. It kept you focused, alert. He knew also, they may not always get a chance like this.

He put two slices of bread in the toaster and turned on the kettle, saying. 'Do you have any coffee?'

There was no answer. Decker walked into the main room. The woman was sitting on the sofa, bent over, crying. Decker noticed her silver bracelet had slipped down her arm.

Seeing him there, she sat up and wiped her eyes. 'What is it?' she said.

Decker said. 'Do you have any coffee?'

'No. I only drink tea.'

Decker went back into the kitchen and made tea instead.

Neither of them said a word as they ate. The woman ate everything on her plate. When she finished, she asked Decker if she could get a cigarette from her bag. Decker nodded and the woman stood up and retrieved a packet of Camels from her bag and took a glass ashtray off the table.

Sitting back down again, she put the ashtray on her knees and lit a cigarette. The ashtray had a picture of mountains set in the solid bottom, the sort of ashtray sold at tourist shops all round the world. Perhaps it was her home country in the picture, Decker thought, a joke present from a relation maybe. Or maybe she'd brought it herself as memento of a fun day with friends before setting off to the UK. There was an italicised name, *Krkonoše*, written on the bottom, which Decker was pretty sure was somewhere in the Czech Republic. The woman curled her hair behind her ear as she smoked and Decker watched her.

Seeing him looking at her, the woman said, 'I'm sorry. Do you want one?' and offered him the packet.

Decker looked at the packet and the woman's fingers holding the packet and the silver bracelet round her wrist and for a moment didn't know what to do. It was like she was offering him more than a cigarette. He'd given up. He didn't know what made him reach forward and take one. Or perhaps he did. Perhaps it was something to do with her and how for a second she made him feel like someone who'd lived a different life to the one he had.

Decker put the cigarette between his lips and the woman held the lighter for him. It was like no other cigarette he'd had before.

The woman changed channels on the TV. Decker stood by the window and peeked through a gap in the blinds, the cigarette smoking between his fingers.

The woman said, 'By the way, my name's Evie.'

Decker looked round. 'No names,' he said.

'Sorry?'

'We don't need to have names.'

Evie nodded, tears sitting in her eyes.

Decker wished she hadn't said anything. 'Evie'... it was stuck in his head now. It was pretty; it suited her. And he knew from now on he would always think of her as Evie.

Evie said, 'How long is this going to last?'

'I don't know.'

'Am I going to die?'

'No, not yet.'

Evie dragged on her cigarette. 'Was that a joke?'

Decker heard the sound of keys in a lock, then the front door opening downstairs. He drew the Glock and flattened himself against the wall, signalling to Evie to get down.

She said, 'It's just my neighbour.'

Decker put his finger to his lips and listened at the door. The TV blared in the background. There were voices on the stairs. Evie looked at Decker pointing the gun at the door. The voices carried on past the door. Decker walked to the window.

'They live upstairs,' Evie said. 'Jesus! Who were you expecting?'

Decker looked through a crack in the blinds again. A cat was walking along the pavement. 'Tomorrow,' he said. 'We're leaving. We can't stay here.'

'*We?*'Evie said. 'I can't. I've got to go to work,'

'You have the day off.'

'How do you know?'

'I heard you saying at the hotel.'

Evie gazed at him. 'But I may get called in to cover,' she said.

'I don't think so.'

'What about the day after?'

'What about it?'

'I have to go to work then.'

'You'll call in sick.'

'I can't.'

Decker turned from the window. Evie took in an audible intake of breath. Decker was pointing the gun at her. 'Yes, you can,' he said.

Evie looked at him. 'I'm sorry,' she said. 'Please. I'll do whatever you say.'

Evie's mobile started ringing.

Evie looked at Decker.

Decker took out the phone and looked at the screen, then said, 'Answer it,' and tossed it over.

Evie looked at the screen.

'It's a friend,' she said. 'What do I say?'

'That you're having a quiet night in. Make no plans.'

137

Decker sat by the window; he held the gun on his lap. Evie answered the phone. As she spoke, Decker looked across the room where there were pictures and photographs of family and friends on a chest of drawers. He didn't look want to look too closely; it was best not to know. More things to think about later on. He already knew her name. That was enough. He observed a tennis racket in a corner, a pink hairdryer on a table, a pile of magazines on a chair. It felt like a long time since he had been in someone's home. He drew on the cigarette. It must have been over two years since he'd last smoked a cigarette but it felt like not a day had passed. How could that be?

Nat King Cole started singing *Route 66* on the TV.

'If you ever plan to motor west,
Travel my way, take the highway, that's the best ...'

Decker glanced at the screen. It was a car advert. Evie was saying on the phone, 'Maybe ... I don't know yet ... No, I'm not sure.' She stood up. 'Yes, I'm fine ... just busy, I guess ...'

Decker looked at Evie, signalling to her to end the conversation. She was rolling her bottom lip, blinking hard, struggling.

She said, 'Not yet ... no ... I'm a bit tired actually.' She saw Decker still looking at her. 'Okay,' she said. 'Look, I better go. I'll give you a ring soon.'

Evie hung up. There were tears in her eyes again, her hands shaking. Decker took the phone out of her hand.

Evie wiped her eyes then blew her nose with a tissue.

'I'm going to make another cup of tea,' Decker said. 'Would you like one?'

Evie nodded.

Filling the kettle, Decker watched her out the corner of his eye. She was staring at the TV, rubbing her eyes. She was about 27, he thought, and stronger than she looked; living alone in a foreign country, with a job, a flat. Soon, he knew, she would begin to rationalise the situation and make a plan. He would have to be careful.

The kettle boiled and he poured the water into their cups.

'Here you go,' he said. He put her cup down next to her.

'Thanks.' She lit another cigarette and looked at the TV.

Decker knew she wouldn't be taking anything, still in shock. He wondered how long it would take Schiller to track them down. If it was him, how long would he need? Maybe 24 hours, maybe just the night. Then he thought about Sachs, Mr Charles and his father working together. He wondered who their commander was, the man Howell was yet to find – the man who had ordered 'Stray Dog'. He thought about Howell; wondered whether he could trust him; thought about Alharbi and Sachs in the photo at the party. Had Howell been working on Alharbi and found out something he shouldn't have? Had Sachs pulled the plug on him? Had Sachs killed his parents?

Decker stood up and walked across the room. Evie watched him over the back of the sofa. Decker checked the window beside her bed. It looked over a back garden. There was the sport's field she had mentioned. He turned and looked at Evie.

'Can I use your laptop?' he said.

Evie nodded. 'It's over there.'

Decker looked up various locations on Google Maps, tracking the roads from the ground, making mental notes of place names. He moved his lips when he read something on screen. Every now and then, he scratched his neck. He thought about checking the bulletin board but didn't want to risk it. Evie sat on the sofa, lighting another cigarette, and stared at the TV. Without looking up, Decker asked her, 'What time to you go to bed normally?'

'About 12.'

'It's 12:30. Get ready.'

'What do you mean?'

'What I said.'

'Where are you going to sleep?'

'On the sofa.'

Evie didn't move.

'Get into bed and try to sleep,' Decker said, looking at her. 'You'll be perfectly safe.'

Evie nodded, but still didn't move.

'Go on,' he said.

Evie stood up, walked across to her bed and, without undressing, got under the duvet.

Later, Decker closed the lid of the laptop and turned off the lights. He checked the windows and Evie. She was turned towards the wall. She didn't move but Decker doubted she was asleep.

He lay down on the sofa and pulled the blanket over him. He lay there with his eyes open in the dark. Light seeped through the blind from the street lights. He could make out a photo frame and pot plant on the windowsill. The green lights of the router flickered in the corner of the room. There was a smell in the room that he wasn't used to, unlike any hotel room – the smell of a woman, of a home. Decker found it easier than normal to close his eyes.

*

Decker was asleep when Evie got out of bed. She'd walked into the sitting room and was behind the sofa. It was hard to say at exactly which point he became aware that she was there.

Evie felt over the table-top for her phone. It wasn't there. She curled her hair behind her ear and bit into her bottom lip. She was carrying her shoes. She began to unlock the door.

Decker sat up, sliding the rack of the Glock and, swinging his arm over the top of the sofa, grabbed Evie's arm. Evie screamed.

Decker jumped over the top of the sofa and covered her mouth with his hand. Evie kicked out, as if pedalling an imaginary bicycle, and bit into his arm.

Decker let her go and Evie lurched at the door again. This time, Decker grabbed her by the waist, picked her up and chucked her over the sofa. She landed on the floor the other side and stopped screaming.

Decker listened at the door. He heard nothing. He looked at Evie curled up on the floor, her legs pulled up under her chest, sobbing quietly.

Decker checked the windows. Nothing had changed. He couldn't hear anything. Evie was still lying on the floor. He walked over and shook her shoulder.

'Go back to bed,' he said.

32

It was still dark outside. There was a light on in the kitchen, the sound of frying, the TV's volume turned right down. Decker stood beside Evie's bed, and said, 'Wake up.'

Evie sat up in bed, looking black-eyed from lack of sleep.

'We're leaving in half an hour.' He walked back into the kitchen where four eggs were frying in a pan. He set slices of toast on two plates, buttered them, and then slipped the eggs onto the toast. He ground salt and pepper over the yokes and carried both plates next door.

Evie was pulling on a roll-neck jumper over skinny blue jeans.

'Are you hungry?' he said.

Evie shook her head. Decker began eating.

Standing, Evie lit a cigarette and folded her arms. Behind her, BBC24 was on the TV.

'There's a cup of tea,' Decker said.

Evie said nothing.

Decker put a forkful of egg into his mouth. As he chewed, he looked at the TV. 'You should eat,' he said. The commentary on the TV was barely audible.

Evie didn't look round; smoke curled from her cigarette. Decker took another mouthful of egg and wiped his mouth with his hand.

Evie dragged on her cigarette and exhaled smoke towards the ceiling. 'Where are we going?' she said.

'South.' Decker kept his eyes on the TV, loading his fork with more egg when all of a sudden he stopped what he was doing and just stared at the TV.

A news reporter was standing outside a terrace house in London doing a piece to camera. The street was cordoned off, police standing like sentries at the door, white-suited forensics swarming the house. They replayed footage from earlier that morning: same street; a black body bag being stretchered out the house.

Evie looked at Decker and said, 'Is that what this is about?'

Decker made no response. He turned up the volume a couple of notches. The guy for BBC24 was interviewing someone from the police. A man believed to be working for government intelligence agencies had been found dead in his flat. The police were not ruling anything out. Circumstances surrounding his death were far from clear. Work colleagues had grown concerned after the man was absent from work for over a week. The body was discovered in a holdall in the cupboard.

Decker put his knife and fork together on the plate, his eyes fixed on the TV.

Evie looked at the man and said. 'You know him?'

Decker said, 'Get changed. Pack a bag. You'll need some warm things.'

The reporter was now in conversation with the news desk. They were talking about possible causes of death … there were rumours of strangulation, poison … Police were looking at CCTV footage … There was talk of a tip-off … Two mobile phones and several SIM cards were found in the man's flat … The man's name was Daniel Howell … News reports confirmed that he was working for government intelligence services and had been recently seconded to London … He was 33 and a keen runner.

Decker turned the TV off from the remote. Evie hadn't moved, the cigarette smoking between her fingers. She now put it out on the plate. Decker knew what she was thinking. He also knew a lot more dangerous people would be thinking the same thing. They didn't have much time.

'Pack you bag,' he said.

'I won't say anything, I promise,' Evie said. 'You can take my car. I don't mind.'

'We're leaving in five minutes. Get ready.'

'I can't do this.'

Decker produced a roll of £50 notes. 'I'll pay you £500 now and £500 later. All you have to do is drive me out of London. Okay?'

Evie shook her head. 'I don't want your money.'

'That's up to you. You're still driving. Get ready.'

Evie walked next door. Decker stood by the window and parted the blinds. He observed Evie's car, a second-hand red Peugeot 205, about 50 metres down the road. He looked for someone sitting in a parked car or someone with an earpiece at the end of the street. Everywhere looked clear.

Evie returned with an overnight bag.

Decker put a cigarette in his mouth, checked the Glock, then put his arms through the straps of his rucksack and nodded at Evie. They left the flat together.

*

They headed west along the Marylebone Road. Decker slouched in the passenger seat, baseball cap and sunglasses; Evie drove, hair tied back, jumper sleeves pulled up. Street cleaners were sweeping up leaves outside Regent's Park. The traffic was stop-and-start with the lights. The sun shone between buildings; the temperature was up a couple of degrees from yesterday. It was mid-October.

When a pair of unmarked police cars sirened passed, Decker lifted his arm to cover his face. He wondered how far the police had got with the CCTV … and whether the agency would leak an e-fit of him. Make him the scapegoat. He heard Mr Charles saying, *They're closing us down*, and wondered how much Mr Charles had known that night – whether he knew Sachs was going to send him out after Howell, and Howell was going to tell him about his father, leaving him to take revenge for his parent's death. Had Mr Charles planned it to happen like this? After all, he had trained him.

Decker's mind wandered back to The Compound, the trees swaying in the wind and Mr Charles standing by the window, saying:

Remember, Martin: Half-truths, and even untruths, can end up becoming reality. Therefore, knowing what is going on is less important than reacting to it. Because, when it comes to it, no one really knows what is going on.

Decker wondered how many assignments had been leading up to this one; wondered even if they'd only ever been one assignment.

Acknowledging something as a coincidence is a sure sign you don't know what's really going on.

Decker looked at the dashboard clock: 7:46.

They broke clear of the traffic on the Marylebone flyover and Evie pulled into the inside lane and accelerated. Decker observed the speed limit of 40mph and told her to slow down. She moved back into the middle lane and slowed down.

The sun glinted on the glass-fronted office blocks. Decker opened an Ordnance Survey map on his lap and began making notes.

Leaving the A40, they headed down the slip road, followed the road past Westfield shopping centre and came to Shepherd's Bush.

Stopping at the traffic lights, Decker observed people crossing the road to the tube station. He still had the Ordnance Survey map open on his lap. He had circled various locations, made notes and drawn arrows. He looked across at Evie. She was gripping the steering wheel with both hands and biting her bottom lip again. Something she had probably been doing since she was a little girl, he thought. But still, there was something strong about her, he reckoned: life hadn't always been easy; he knew she wasn't going to panic or scream again.

They lights changed and they pulled away. Decker observed Evie curl back loose strands of hair behind her ear between gear changes.

A little further down the road, they both noticed the petrol light begin to flash on the dashboard. Decker spotted a service station ahead of them and, angling the wing mirror, checked behind them.

'Pull in,' he said, 'at the garage.'

Decker kept his eye on the mirror as Evie pulled into the garage.

Cars continued along the road, no one pulling in after them.

Evie got out and started filling the car. Decker stared across the forecourt. Occasionally, he looked in the wing mirror.

Evie replaced the nozzle, leant into the car, and said, 'Do you want anything?'

Decker shook his head and handed her some cash. 'Make it quick.'

Decker watched her take her place in the queue. When she reached the font, the Asian guy on the till looked out the window at Evie's car to check the pump number. Evie half turned her head at the same time and Decker thought, *Don't turn round.* The Asian guy confirmed the pump number on the till and then read the amount. Evie pointed to the shelf behind him. The Asian guy took down a packet of cigarettes.

As she was walking back through the shop, Decker saw Evie drop the packet of cigarettes. A man entering the shop at that moment waited for her to pick up it up. Evie said something. The man laughed and held the door open for her.

When she got into the car and shut the door, Decker said. 'What did you say to the man?'

'What man?'

'As you were leaving … he held the door open for you. What did you

144

say?' Decker watched the man in the shop, checking to see he wasn't about to make a call.

'Nothing, I made a joke about being clumsy.'

'Next time, don't speak to anyone.'

'I'm sorry. I thought I was supposed to be normal.'

'You are. Just don't engage where you don't have to.'

Evie's cheeks had gone red.

Decker turned and looked at her and said, 'Do you understand?'

'Yes,' she said, sounding angry now, which probably wasn't a bad thing, Decker thought. Anger showed she was reacting, on top of her fear, so less likely to give them away.

'Is this going to be as much fun all the time?' she added, and she started the car and pulled out of the garage.

She was adapting to the situation quickly, Decker thought. Humour was a common default. But it reminded him he'd need to be careful with her. Having her along was always going to be a risk. But he needed a car. And she would provide useful cover. Travelling as a couple would attract less attention than if he was alone.

Decker watched Evie light a cigarette and accelerate through the gears.

'Where now?' she said.

'Next left.'

'This reminds me of driving lessons. *At the next junction, take the...*'

That humour again, Decker thought.

Evie turned left. 'What do you do when you're not doing this?' she said.

Decker said, 'We don't have to talk.'

'It helps pass the time. Besides, I like to talk.'

'Keeping going straight,' Decker said.

'So, do you have a normal job?'

'Sometimes.'

'Like what?'

'The travel industry.'

'Seriously?'

'Seriously.'

'I can't imagine it – you being nice to customers.' She was smiling. 'Why did you leave?'

Decker said nothing.

'Because of the man who got killed? What was his name again?

Howell?' The smile had gone.

Decker turned and looked at her. 'Forget that name,' he said.

'Why? Did you kill him?'

'No.'

'But you know who did?'

Decker looked across at the wing mirror. 'Maybe.'

'But you've killed someone, haven't you? Other people?'

Decker said nothing.

Evie glanced at him. 'Why do you do this?'

'I'm paid to.'

'Is that the real reason?'

'It's one reason.'

'But there are others, right?'

'Possibly.' Decker looked straight ahead at the road. She'd probably decided she had nothing to lose now, he thought. He was right to think there was something strong about her.

Evie's eyes moved up to the rear-view mirror and then back to the road ahead. 'We sometimes get guests like you,' she said. 'They stay several nights but never say a word to you – not even a thank you.'

Decker said, 'I doubt it's personal.'

'I doubt it too. My dad never says very much. So I'm used to it.' That smile again, softer now. Stopping at traffic lights, Evie tapped ash off her cigarette into the car ashtray, then took one last puff and put it out. 'Do you have any family?' she said.

Decker didn't respond.

Evie went on, 'I have a mum and dad, a younger brother called Zenick, and a dog called Stipe…' She paused, smiled, and by way of explanation, said, 'It's the name of the lead singer of REM. My dad's a big fan.'

Decker noticed how her eyes shone when she smiled.

'I miss them a lot …' she said, '… my family that is. My dad's not well at the moment. He's got cancer. I will go back home soon to be with him.'

Decker said, 'Stay in the left lane. I don't need to know this.'

'I'm telling you anyway. I work at the hotel. I'm also studying for a Masters in Business Administration. I'm writing my dissertation at the moment on hospitality management. I've done 10,000 words; another 5000 to go.' Evie curled her hair back behind her ear and then closed the window. 'Whoever killed that man on the TV is after you now, isn't he?' she said.

Decker said, 'It looks that way.'

'But you are trying to get away. But sooner or later they are going to catch up with you. Then what are you going to do?'

33

The truth was Decker didn't know what he was going to do. But he didn't say that. He remembered the website address of the bulletin board Howell had given him, and wondered if he'd got a chance to leave a message there before he'd been killed.

They crossed the river at Hammersmith Bridge, a pair of rowing boats cutting through the misty water in the shadows of trees.

Coming to some shops, Decker said, 'Pull over on the left.'

Evie nodded, putting on the indicator, and pulled up next to the kerb.

Decker said, 'I've got to check something. I'll be a couple of minutes.'

Taking the car keys with him, Decker went into an internet café. At the till, an Asian guy was sat drinking a can of coke and reading the *Sun*. Decker paid him for an hour screen time, then sat down at a free computer and logged on.

Two bearded Africans chatted at a neighbouring computer as Decker waited for the bulletin board to load. Outside Evie was lighting a cigarette in the car.

The screen came up. There was a message from Howell. It was sent the day he was found dead. He said he'd found everything he needed, that the puzzle was complete. That they would meet soon.

Below, there was a file on Alharbi. It contained information about his relationship with Sachs. Alharbi provided safe houses and identities for people. The list contained drug dealers, exiled politicians and terrorists. Alharbi paid Sachs for his cooperation, while Sachs paid Alharbi for information and vice-versa, with Zishan also in the loop, working with contacts across Europe, Africa and Pakistan. Howell must have been working on Alharbi, Decker thought, when he'd uncovered information about Sachs, his handler – which left him isolated.

The message ended there. There was no mention of where they would meet or exactly what he knew. Decker assumed Howell was going to tell him at their meeting. That meeting wasn't going to happen now.

Decker was just about to log off when he noticed a second message appear on the screen.

This one wasn't from Howell.

"My name is Reeves. I can help. Please contact me as soon as you get this message." A number followed the message.

Decker looked up from the screen. He saw the Asian at the till stifle a burp in his fist and then turn the page of his newspaper. Across the road, Evie was still smoking in the car. Traffic passed along the road. Decker imagined a team of agents in a room of monitors: the IP address of his computer coming up on their screens; a location radioed through; car doors slamming.

He read the message again. Logged one minute ago. Who was Reeves?

He was still wondering when he opened the car door.

Evie smiled. 'Find what you were looking for?'

'Yeah. Let's go.'

Soon, they were belting down the inside lane of the A3. Decker was smoking a cigarette and thinking how someone must have accessed the bulletin board off Howell's computer after he was bagged up in the cupboard.

But who?

Decker shut his eyes. He remembered sitting in the back of the van, his arms cuffed and eyes blindfolded. He re-experienced the sound of the tarmac, the turns in the road, the bumps. He fast forwarded to somewhere on the North Downs – the snaking roads, the long driveway and gravel courtyard. He remembered the basement cell, the walk to Sachs' study. And could picture Sachs sitting in his chair, hands steepled, the short-cropped greying hair, his shirt sleeves rolled to his elbows; the balaclavas filing out the room.

You are what we call 'a stray dog'.

He pictured the images on screen of himself, Mr Charles, and Howell; the photograph of his parents in his dream.

Think of it as just another job.

Decker knew he must have inadvertently led Sachs to Howell. In his mind's eye, he went back still to the National Gallery; Trafalgar Square; the number 43 bus. Accessing memory-stills like a slide show as he had been trained. He tracked along the bus, looking for clues. He pictured the girls listening to their phone; an old man at the front of the bus, sleeping; on the lower deck, a black woman with carrier bags; a couple of school kids; a man, hood up, on his phone. Was that him? Rewind back to the gallery again: the gift shop; the room of paintings. He searched for a suitable face, someone out of place. He recalled tourists, a party of school kids, pensioners. Saw a woman sketching in a notebook; behind her, a guy, in a hooded top looking at his phone. How had he let this go? Decker crossed-checked the face with the guy's on the bus. Were they the same? He pictured Howell getting off the bus; the doors closing. And he remembered a car indicating behind them. He pictured the guy under the hood getting off at the next stop – the same guy that was in the gallery.

Decker opened his eyes, and said, 'Take the next exit.'

Evie said, 'Are you sure?'

'Yeah. I'm sure'

They joined the A29 heading south, the landscape becoming greener, the tarmac bordered by hedgerows and farmland.

Decker looked at the Ordnance Survey maps and compared them with what he saw outside. He tried to remember the timings between dual carriageways and B roads. On the map, he'd circled several possible locations for Sachs' house. He now numbered them in order of preference. He would concentrate on those areas first, he thought. Determining which house was Sachs' could take time. But he'd made a rough calculation of its size by piecing together his estimates of floor space during his stay. And going by the map, there weren't many houses of that size in the area.

They passed through an avenue of beech trees and got their first glimpse of the North Downs, a shadowy fold in the landscape where the wooded escarpment gave way to a patchwork of grassland and scrub.

Evie lit a cigarette and lowered her window.

They turned uphill, the road narrowing.

Decker's eyes moved between map and wing mirror.

Kicking up leaves, they snaked in and out of tree shade. Before long, Decker looked up from the map and told Evie to slow down, knowing he was getting near to his first location. Beech trees stood along the verges. Decker saw a field gateway ahead of them and told Evie to pull over. Evie did as she was instructed.

They sat for a moment without speaking. Then Decker got out the car, crossed the road and scanned the landscape through binoculars. He stood there for several minutes.

Returning to the car, he scribbled notes on the map, then told Evie to drive on.

Decker worked systematically round each area like this, Evie following his instructions without resistance, sometimes turning round in the middle of the road, or reversing back along a lane when they missed a turning, then waiting in the car while Decker scanned the landscape through binoculars. She no longer asked him questions – no longer complained. Though Decker knew she would be thinking about things and reminded himself he had to be careful with her.

Later that afternoon, after working round nearly all the circled areas on the map, Decker turned to Evie and said, 'Okay, pull in here.'

Evie pulled up on the verge and turned off the engine.

Decker got out of the car and leant on a gate. There was a pile of round straw bales left out in the field opposite. The field sloped down into a narrow valley where chalk track divided the fields. On the far slope, there was a plantation of maize and a strip of woodland.

Decker scanned the slope through binoculars. Pheasants paraded along the field edge. A 4x4 pickup was driving along a track. A breeze picked up in the trees. Decker lowered the binoculars. Something felt to fall in place.

Decker climbed back in the car. 'Okay,' he said. 'Keep going ... slowly.'

They turned down a single-track road, with passing spaces cut into the high banks. Evie accelerated through the dip in the road and then dropped through the gears as they headed up the other side. At the top of the slope, there were the beginnings of an estate wall.

Decker said, 'Okay. Slow down.'

They came to a gated entrance to a private property.

'Stop here,' he said.

Evie pulled up at the side of the road.

Decker opened the car door and looked over the roof of the car. He saw the gate was operated with a four-digit code ... and that there were no cameras. He walked round the car, saying, 'Stay here.'

He crossed the road, stood and looked down the driveway, opening up his mind again to the memory of that night.

The driveway cut across open fields, turning round the corner of a wood then snaking back the other way before straightening through an avenue of beech trees. At the end of the drive was a large house, nestled in the valley, backed by woodland. Decker looked at the house through the binoculars. There was a large gravel turning circle in front of the house, then in the field at the front a patch of grass cut shorter than the rest, probably for a helicopter. The house had three floors. Lights were on in several windows, shutters across others. There were outbuildings at the back of the house; a tractor; the tailgate of a pickup.

Decker raised the binoculars and scanned the wooded slope at the back of the house. There was a grass track running up through the middle of the wood. It stopped about half way up the slope. It was about 30 metres wide.

Just then, Evie sounded the car horn behind him. And he looked round and saw her waving her arms out the window at him. The 4x4 he'd seen in the valley was heading up the slope towards them.

34

Decker jogged across the road and got in the car. Evie pulled away as he was closing the door.

Glancing at Evie, Decker said, 'Thanks.'

Evie looked up at the rear-view mirror and said, 'What for?'

'The warning.'

Evie nodded, changing gears, a cigarette in her mouth. 'Where now?'

Decker glanced down at the map. 'Straight on. Follow the signs for Ash Down.'

Evie nodded, tapping ash off her cigarette out the window.

Decker noticed she was wearing her hair down today, the breeze blowing strands across her face. Every now and then, she hooked it back behind her ear, and when she did, he noticed the tiny mole on the narrow part of her ear, and how her eyes were green and caught the sunlight and glistened.

She was pretty, he thought, but he couldn't think about that now. He just wanted to help her if he could for what she was doing. He remembered the ashtray in the flat with the photograph on the bottom.

'Where are you from?' he said.

'You said you didn't need to know that stuff.'

'I don't.'

'Then let's not bother.'

Decker turned to the window and tried again. 'You said your father was ill.'

'Yeah.'

'I'm sorry.'

'It's not your fault.'

'Will you go back soon?'

'Yeah. At Christmas.'

Decker kept looking out the window, and said, 'Do you need money?'

Evie's mouth fell open. 'What?'

'Money for the flight; for your father.'

'Pardon?'

'I need you to drive me out here tonight,' Decker said, turning to look at her, 'and to stay one more night.'

'You said just to drive you out of London.'

'I'll pay you.'

'I don't want your money.'

'It will help you get home.'

'I can get home without it. I work, remember.'

'Think of this as work.'

Evie glared at him. 'Is that what you do – think of it as work?'

'I will pay you another £500,' Decker said.

Putting out her cigarette, Evie said. 'I don't have a choice, do I?'

'You have a choice.'

'Really?' Evie wiped a tear off her cheek with her hand and looked at the road ahead.

They passed through an avenue of trees coming down a hill and Decker looked down at the map and then up at the road ahead. Along the next straight he saw a pub covered in wisteria, its chimney smoking. There was a car park and a garden at the rear. He had the pub marked on the map. He said, 'Pull in at the pub.'

Evie flicked on the indicator and pulled into the empty car park. Dust clouded round the vehicle. She stopped up against a fence, pulled up the handbrake and turned off the engine. She left her hands on the steering wheel and looked across the field in front of them.

Removing an envelope from his jacket pocket, Decker said, 'Here's the £500.'

Evie said, 'I don't want it.'

'Take it. You don't have to like it. Just drive me to the house later. Okay?'

Evie turned and looked at him. 'And tonight?'

'That's up to you?' Decker knew it would make him stand out less if she was with him. A single man appeared suspicious. The truth was he needed her help but couldn't expect her to do anything she didn't want to now.

Decker watched Evie open the envelope and finger the wad of £50s.

'It's a lot,' she said.

'It's £500. I will give you another £500 later.'

Evie looked across the fields again. 'Okay,' she said. 'Just work.'

'That's all it is.'

Evie nodded. 'What do you want me to do?'

'We're a couple … escaping from London for a few nights. Everything is normal. We'll book a room. Eat. Then go for a drive. In the morning we'll leave.'

Evie smiled. 'We're a couple?

'Yeah.'

*

The landlady, a middle-aged woman with large breasts and a tattoo on her upper arm, wrote down Decker's details. 'We only have a twin room left,' she said. 'Is that okay?'

'That's fine.' Decker paid in cash, and held Evie's hand as they walked up the stairs. They followed the corridor round to the right, under low wooden beams and entered the room at the end. Decker locked the door behind them.

From the window, there was a view of the downs. Cattle bellowed in the field opposite. Decker stood at the window for a moment and looked at the view. The cows were standing round a water trough. Along the fence-line were clumps of bramble and elder. It took Decker's mind back to his parents, their cottage on the downs, and the churchyard where they were buried, and the fact that he hadn't visited in a while. He thought: there was something else he could do when this was over.

Decker drew the curtains and opened his bag on the bed. Evie was sitting in the room's only chair and watched him. He removed the Glock, released its magazine, and pulled back the slide and checked the ejection port. Then he put back the magazine and retrieved the sound moderator from the bag and screwed it on. Then he laid the gun on the bed.

'After we've eaten,' he said, 'you will drive me out to the house. I will need an hour there. You will need to wait. If you are disturbed, drive on and come back. In the morning, you will return to London.'

Evie looked at the gun on the bed. 'How will you get back?'

'I won't be coming back.'

'How do you mean?'

'Just what I say.' Decker took out one of the maps and spread it open on the bed.

Evie looked at him. 'How long have you been doing this?' she said.

'Doing what?'

'This.'

Decker traced his finger across the map. 'Does it matter?'

'I suppose not.' Evie pulled out a cigarette.

Decker looked up. 'It's no smoking.'

'Is it?' Opening the window, Evie lit the cigarette. She turned her head to the window and pulled up her knees to her chest.

She said, 'You're going to kill someone, aren't you?'

Decker looked at the maps, saying nothing. The smell of tobacco permeated the room along with the fresh downland air.

Evie said, 'Actually, I don't want to know.' She pushed back her hair, leaving the cigarette in her mouth. 'But thanks for the money. It will help.'

Decker said, 'Don't mention it.'

Evie turned to the window. 'You never said anything about your family.'

Decker continued studying the map.

Evie said, 'I suppose you don't get time to see them doing this.'

Without looking up, Decker said, 'They're dead.'

Evie looked at him across the room. 'I'm sorry,' she said.

Decker scribbled something on the map. 'Get ready,' he said. 'We're eating in a minute.'

Evie took a final drag on her cigarette. 'What about friends? Or someone close?'

Decker drew a line across the map, marking out his route for tonight. 'As you said, I don't get time,' he said.

'You're all alone, then.'

Still drawing the line, Decker said, 'Aren't we all?'

Evie shook her head. 'Is that what you really think?'

Decker realised it was mistake talking like this. Talking like this never got you anywhere, he thought. And here he was on the verge of swapping his life story. 'Yeah,' he said. 'That's what I really think.'

Evie shook her head. 'I disagree. People have each other.'

Decker folded the maps. He wasn't going to be drawn.

35

The landlady smiled when she saw them come downstairs. Decker held Evie's hand as they walked into the dining area. There were two other couples eating, middle-aged and overweight. A fire crackled and flickered in a brick-lined fireplace. Two men were drinking at the bar. Decker ordered steak and chips, Evie chicken.

At 20:22 they crossed the car park and climbed into the Peugeot. Neither of them said a word. Evie pulled out of the car park, full beam lighting up the wooded slope, while Decker checked behind them. It was a two-and-a-half mile drive.

Just past the gated entrance, Evie pulled up on the side of the road and Decker turned to her and said, 'You know what you've got to do?'

Evie nodded. 'Drive to the end of this road. Wait with my lights off. And you'll find me.'

Decker checked his watch. 'What time do you make it?'

Evie checked her mobile. 'Eight-thirty.'

'If I'm not back by ten o'clock, just leave. Okay? Spend the night at a friend's or at a hotel. But don't attempt to come looking for me. Do you understand?'

Evie nodded. 'Okay.'

Decker got out of the car, crossed the road and climbed over a fence into the wood. He didn't look back but heard Evie pulling away in the car. He joined up with a ride that ran through the trees and started running. Pigeons broke roost and clattered from trees.

He passed pheasant hoppers and straw bales then came to a gateway and, crouching, scanned in each direction. A belt of maize about 30 metres wide ran along the edge of the wood. Maize plants swayed in the breeze; the moon was nearly full. Giving himself the all-clear,

Decker set off along the field edge and ran all the way to the end of the wood, then climbed through strands of barbed wire into the adjacent field planted with kale, and headed down the slope, the wet kale soaking through his trousers.

At the end of the field, he stopped in a gateway and looked through the aluminium rails. He observed the house about 500 metres away; an apron of light on a shingle drive; a Range Rover parked out front.

He checked the time on his watch, estimating his return journey to be about 20 minutes. That gave him just over half an hour snooping around the house. He started to climb the gate when he heard a diesel engine straining up the slope. He quickly swung himself over the gate and rolled into the ditch.

Two headlights flashed across the field. Decker heard the vehicle stop; then a metallic clinking, a gate latch perhaps, and the vehicle start up again, headlights raking across the slope in the opposite direction.

He waited a minute, the sound of the truck receding into the distance, then continued along the hedge line to the end of the field where he joined up with a track. He ran now, following the track round the side of the house and into the horseshoe-shaped wood at the back where he picked his way through fallen trees, with sticks cracking underfoot, until he came to a gun ride and stopped.

Decker scanned in both directions and caught his breath. Moonlight shone into the clearing. A deer high-seat was positioned half way up the slope. He estimated he had approximately 100 metres of open ground to cover before the gardens. From there he could use thick yew hedges as cover to approach the house.

Decker took out the binoculars and surveyed different parts of the house – rooftops, windows, doors – searching out exit points and camera positions. Then he spotted an open window and tracked down to an adjoining flat roof and then a water butt on the ground. He could climb up from there, he thought.

An owl shrieked overhead. Decker moved out from behind the trees. But just as he was coming out from their shadows an outside light snapped on and he dropped to the ground.

He saw a man leave the house and light a cigarette in the courtyard. Lying in the grass, Decker put the binoculars on him. Quilted Barbour jacket, walkie-talkie, a bulge under his arm – security. Another man joined him, same set up. They chatted and smoked. Decker thought he recognised them as the men in balaclavas. After a few minutes, both men stamped out their cigarettes and returned inside.

Decker waited for the security light to click off, then ran across the open ground towards the house. He stopped briefly behind a cedar tree then ran down the length of the yew hedge to less than 50 metres from the house where he stopped again.

Decker looked round the side of the hedge. Topiary trees cast shadows on the lawn in the moonlight. He took a couple of deep breaths and ran across to the first tree, stopped briefly, then ran to the next. He was half way across the first section of lawn when he heard the crunch of gravel again.

The outside light snapped on again.

Decker squatted down behind a stone statue of a naked woman. One of the security guards left the house and went into an outbuilding. Decker kept very still. The man reappeared carrying a toolbox. He was crossing the courtyard when a rustling sound in the bushes behind him – a rabbit maybe – made him stop and look round.

Decker watched him.

The man turned his head, scanning the darkness. Clutching the Glock, Decker fixed his eyes on him and didn't move.

The man scratched his unshaven chin, giving it a second longer, and then continued back to the house.

Decker released his grip on the Glock, waited a minute, and then ran across the remaining section of lawn.

Reaching the house, he clambered on top of the water butt and scaled up the wall using the drainpipe. He traversed across a narrow apex, leapt across to a flat roof, and used another drainpipe to pull himself up. With his back pressed against the flint-studded wall, he stood on a narrow ledge, two floors up.

Below him, the security light clicked off. He felt for the bottom of the window and, getting his fingers under the lower sash, opened it and pulled himself through. Lowering the window behind him, Decker walked along a corridor that had dark claret coloured carpets and wood-panelled walls. The smell was familiar, as was the feel of the carpets. He came to the top of a staircase where he heard voices and saw light coming from a half-open door below.

Heading down the staircase, he noticed massive oil paintings hanging on the walls, most of them featuring horses. He reached the half-open door, flattened himself against the wall, and peered round the corner. Inside was a small sitting room with a set of double doors open at one end. Through these doors, Decker could see through to another room where people were sitting round a dining-room table. Sachs was sitting at one end. A child was sitting on his knee. The child's mother was standing beside them, hands on hips, smiling. She was no more than 30. The child looked like Sachs' grandchild.

Sachs kissed the child goodnight and handed him back to his mother. The mother walked round the table carrying the child. Other adults said goodnight to the child. The woman then walked towards the double doors.

Decker got behind the door and the woman walked right past him as she left the room and walked upstairs. When she was out of sight, Decker stepped out from behind the door and checked his watch. He had less than 20 minutes left.

He entered the room. Through a gap in the doors of the next room he could just see Sachs pouring himself a glass of wine. The scene wasn't what Decker had expected. Family complicated things. Better he knew nothing about his target.

Decker pulled the Glock, extended his arms, and walked through the sitting room: an open fire burning, another horse painting; family photographs on the mantelpiece; lights off ... just the light of the fire.

Decker, wearing a black beanie and hooded Gore-Tex coat, hadn't planned it like this. Had just come to look round the house and here he was, ready to kill. Sometimes an opportunity presents itself. And you have to take it.

He was aware of the drawbacks. Shooting Sachs like this may mean never finding out what happened to his parents, Mr Charles and Howell.

But he may not get another chance.

Sachs was standing, raising his glass to make a toast. The others, sitting, held up their glasses.

Step out from the door and drop him, Decker thought. At this range, there would be no mistake.

He raised his arms as he approached the door, getting ready for the shot.

Sachs was making a speech, making the others laugh. Decker saw a young man at the other end of the table that looked like Sachs' son, the father of the child. The family resemblance was clear. He was sitting next to what must have been his mother, Sachs' wife.

Decker realised he was going to have to shoot Sachs in front of his family.

This would be a first.

Sachs raised his glass and said, 'Cheers.'

The others round the table did the same. 'Cheers.'

One happy family.

Decker put pressure on the trigger, thinking, they would barely have time to react before he was out of the house.

There was laughter round the table. Decker felt his jaw muscle flex, his eyes narrow, double handing the Glock, his breathing coming under control. But just as he was about to fire, he heard footsteps and dropped his arms. Moving across the room, he ducked behind a sofa. Was it the woman back already?

But the footsteps were different.

They went into the sitting room and stopped at the double doors. Round the side of the sofa, Decker recognised the security guard's boots and combat trousers. He stood in the doorway for a moment. Then Sachs appeared beside him. The security guy whispered something in his ear. And Sachs nodded, then turning back to the room, excused himself and followed the security guard out of the room. As they went past, Decker heard Sachs say, 'Has he got it?'

They headed down some back stairs, Sachs putting on a jacket and making a call on his mobile. Decker followed them. At the bottom of the stairs, he saw Sachs and the security guard go through a back door out into a courtyard.

Decker stepped into the room next to the door, which was some kind of utility room full of racks of boots, outdoor jackets, cartridge belts and washing machines. Through a window he saw a man outside leaning, arms folded, against the bonnet of a car. He was wearing jeans, black Reebok trainers and a hooded fleece. He straightened up when he saw Sachs approach.

Sachs was saying, 'Who the hell has it then?'

The man standing by the car lowered his head, holding his arms behind his back ready for the beasting.

Ex-military by the look of it.

'I don't understand,' Sachs said, raising his hands. 'How can it not be there?'

'There was nothing in the flat, sir,' the man said.

'And nothing on the laptop?'

'Nothing.'

'For Christ's sake,' Sachs said.

The guy by the car looked at the ground.

'Did you have your fucking eyes closed?'

'No, sir.'

'Look again.'

'Yes, sir.'

'Pull the fucking place apart if you have to.'

'Sir, the police are all over it.'

'I don't give a shit about the fucking police. Find out who's got that fucking hard drive and get it from them.'

'Yes, sir.'

Sachs took a call on his phone. The other two men stood in silence, waiting.

Finishing on his phone, Sachs said, 'Listen. Look at every move Howell made in the last two weeks. Go over those tapes again – who's come, who's gone. For fucksake, find out what fucking loo paper he wiped his arse with.'

'Yes, sir.'

Sachs shook his head, and then said, 'That gay cunt was up to something. Distract the police. Tell them it was a sex game or something. Put a fucking gimp suit in his cupboard. I don't give a shit what you do. That hard drive is somewhere. Just get it. You understand?'

'I understand.'

Sachs thrust his hands in his coat pockets. The man standing opposite him, hands still gripped behind his back, waited.

Sachs said, 'Listen, just have a look at the tapes again. They'll be a clue there somewhere. And try that neighbour again.'

'Yes, sir.'

'All right. Is there anything else?'

The man nodded. 'That guy hasn't been found yet?'

'What guy?'

'Following Howell. That you sent. The contract guy.'

'Let's not worry about him for now. If he's got any sense he's somewhere hot.' Sachs started walking back to the house. His security guy followed him inside.

Stepping through the door, Decker heard Sachs say, 'Keep an eye on him.'

36

The wind had picked up. Decker glanced over his shoulder as it gusted in the treetops, and then opened the car door.

Evie gasped. 'Jesus! You gave me a fright.'

'Let's go.'

Evie pulled out of the lay-by, headlights lighting up the tunnel of trees, saying, 'Everything okay?'

'Fine.'

'You were a few minutes late. I was beginning to think—'

'Everything's fine.'

Evie glanced at Decker but didn't say anymore.

Decker looked straight ahead. Roadside trees swayed in the wind. He saw images flash up in the dark of the wood-panelled corridor; the oil paintings; the family round the table; the raised glasses; Sachs standing; the movements of his mouth; the alignment of the front and rear sight on his head.

Adrenaline surged. He took deep breaths, knowing it would soon pass.

*

Evie dipped her lights as she pulled into the pub car park. Scanning the car park, Decker noticed a black VW Golf that wasn't there before, and said, 'Park over by the pub.'

'Why?'

'Just do it.'

Evie parked the car against the side of the pub and turned off the ignition. As she released her seat belt and went to get out, Decker stuck out his arm to block her in.

'What are you doing?' she said.

Decker looked across the car park.

'What's wrong?' Evie said.

Decker looked up at the pub, saying nothing. Evie followed his gaze. 'What is it?' she said.

Decker scanned the face of the building. He didn't know what it was. Just knew something wasn't right. And that was enough.

'Keep behind me,' he said. They climbed out the car and entered the pub.

The two men were still drinking at the bar, one of them, wearing a padded check shirt, was rolling a cigarette. The barman had one eye on the TV as they walked in. On the stereo, The Monkees were singing *Daydream Believer.*

'Oh, I could hide 'neath the wings of the bluebird as she sings ...'

Decker's eyes moved across the room.

Daniel Howell's boyfriend, Fenton, was sitting in the armchair by the fire. He was wearing a grubby baseball cap and resting a pint of beer on his leg. When he saw Decker, he sat up.

Decker's expression remained blank. He said to Evie, 'Let's have a drink.' He gestured to a corner table. Evie took the hint, went and sat down.

Decker ordered the drinks, ignoring Fenton. The barman, barrel-chested, goatee beard, pulled the pints. The man at the bar in the padded check shirt stuck his rollie behind his ear and looked at his smartphone.

Decker kept looking at the rows of bottles.

A young man and a woman, stayed one night, kept themselves to themselves, was all the description he wanted.

Now, Fenton was here.

Plans were changing all the time.

He had to change with them.

Decker set the drinks in front of Evie. She was mouthing the words to the song: *'Cheer up sleepy Jean. Oh what ...* 'Thank you,' she said.

Decker said, 'Wait there.' He walked past the fireplace, looking straight ahead. He entered the gents. Stood at the washbasin, ran the tap, and wondered what the fuck Fenton was doing here.

The door opened and Fenton walked in. Decker saw him in the mirror and turned off the tap. 'Are you alone?' he said.

Fenton nodded. Decker saw his eyes were bloodshot and darkly ringed.

'How long have you been here?' Decker said.

'Twenty minutes.'

'Who else knows you're here?'

Fenton grabbed Decker's arm. 'No one. Please, you've got to help me ...'

Decker removed his hand. 'Who sent you?'

'No one. Please, listen—'

'It was you on the bus, wasn't it?'

'Yes. But I can explain. Please.'

Walking to the door, Decker said. 'Wait outside in the carpark.'

Decker crossed the pub. The Doors singing *LA Woman* now:

Well, I just got into town about an hour ago

Took a look around, see which way the wind blow ...'

Evie said, 'Everything all right?'

'Yeah, everything's fine.'

Evie tipped up her glass. Decker did the same. Evie glanced about the room and said, 'Someone's here, aren't they?'

Decker said, 'Yeah. Someone is here.'

Through the window, Decker observed Fenton crossing the car park. He said, 'Keep drinking,' to Evie.

Evie tipped up her glass, and said, 'Who is it?'

Decker checked his watch. 'Turn away from the window. No one you know. Tell me about yourself. Your hobbies—'

'What?'

'Just do it.' Decker checked the window, scanning the surroundings.

Evie said, 'I like swimming—'

'Yeah. Do you swim every week?' Someone would know, Decker thought. Even if Fenton was telling the truth and no one had sent him, they would have had him followed. It was unlikely Fenton could have made it down here alone.

'Yes, if I can,' Evie said, hooking some hair back behind her ear and starting to engage, 'depends on work.'

Through the window Decker watched Fenton get into the VW. Pulling the door shut, the inside light went out and he sat there in the dark, huddled in his coat. Decker then turned and looked towards the bar. No one had moved. Where were they, he wondered?

Decker said, 'Why do you like swimming?'

Evie shrugged. 'I suppose to keep fit. But I find it relaxing too. Do you swim?'

'Not as a hobby.' Decker checked the window for any movement round the car park.

Evie smiled, that sparkle in her eyes again.

Decker said, 'Keep going.'

'Tell me what your hobbies are.' She took a sip of beer.

'Fishing.'

'Really? My brother fishes. When did you last go fishing?'

'Fifteen years ago.'

Evie laughed. 'It's not really a hobby then is it?'

Decker glanced at Evie for a second. 'Isn't it?'

'Not really. A hobby is something you do regularly.'

The landlord called last orders. Decker checked his watch and then nodded at Evie. 'I suppose. Let's go.'

Evie finished her drink.

Decker carried their two empty glasses to the bar. At the bottom of the stairs, Decker said, 'I left something in the car. I'll meet you upstairs.'

Evie hesitated. She touched her hair, curling it back. 'I'll come with you,' she said.

Decker stepped towards her and, pretending to kiss her, whispered in her ear, 'Pack up the room. Meet me out the front in ten minutes.'

Decker walked past the gents; exited the building out the back; walked round the side of the pub under the shelter of trees. He opened the passenger door of Fenton's car and got in.

Decker looked out across the car park and said, 'How did you find me?'

Fenton had his arms folded tightly across his chest. 'They know you're here.' He was shivering.

'Who knows?'

'They're everywhere, you know.' He began scratching his arm like something was crawling under his skin.

'Who is?'

'People.'

'What people?' Decker scanned the car park.

'This is your fault, you know. I didn't want any of this. Now Simon is dead and I'm going to be next.'

Decker looked up to the rear-view mirror. Chances were high that he wasn't wrong.

He said, 'No one is going to kill you.'

Fenton put his hands up to his head and pushed back his cap. There were cuts and bruising on his forehead.

'What happened?'

Fenton shut his eyes.

'Tell me what happened.'

Fenton rubbed his eyes with his hand and said, 'I can't go anywhere. They smashed up my flat.'

'What was taken?'

'Some memory sticks, my computer, some stuff.'

'Why were you on the bus?'

'I wanted to warn you. They were having Simon followed.'

Decker saw the two men that had been sitting at the bar leave the pub. The man wearing the padded check shirt lit his rollie on the way out. They stood there for a minute talking.

Fenton turned to the window.

Decker said, 'What are they looking for?'

Fenton looked blank.

Decker grabbed his jaw, turned his head, and said, 'What are they looking for?'

Fenton glanced down at his feet and then across at Decker.

Decker looked down into the footwell, and said, 'What is it?'

Fenton said nothing.

Decker said, 'Get it.'

Fenton removed a small case from under his seat. Decker recognised the case: Paris; Zishan; the deadman's briefcase. The case he had never delivered.

'Open it,' Decker said.

Fenton looked at the case like something precious from childhood. 'He gave it to me,' he said, tears filling his eyes. 'He trusted me.'

'Open it.'

'I never meant anything to happen to him.'

'I know. Open the case.'

Wiping tears off his face, Fenton opened the case. Inside was a black box – some kind of hard drive.

Decker said, 'You were with Howell.'

Fenton, shaking his head, said, 'I couldn't do anything ...'

'What did he say?' Decker glanced through the windows. There was high ground on the right, shelter from trees. He had sent Evie upstairs. Exit out the back; fields; stream; shelter under a bridge.

167

'You have to help me.' Fenton clutched at Decker's arm.

'What did he say?' Decker looked at the hard drive, which everyone was so keen to get their hands on. It was no bigger than a box of cigars

Fenton said, 'That you must give it to Reeves – that you can trust him. That it's all on the hard drive.'

Decker experienced a flash of memories: Hammersmith Bridge; the line of shops; the internet café; the Asian drinking the can of coke; the message reading: "My name is Reeves. You must trust me. Contact me as soon as you can." The bulletin board.

Fenton said, 'What's going to happen? Who are they? I didn't kill anyone.'

'Listen to me,' Decker said. 'You need to go away.'

Saying goodnight to his friend, the man wearing the check shirt climbed into a 4x4 truck. His friend went back into the pub. He turned in the car park, headlights sweeping through the trees. That was when Decker spotted the glint of a telescopic lens further up the slope. And when the first shot splintered the front windscreen.

Decker grabbed Fenton and pulled him down.

A second shot drilled through the foam of the headrest. Decker felt blood on his hands. There was a large hole in Fenton's neck. Decker could see the shattered windpipe and blood pulsing from the hole.

A third shot clipped the top of the dashboard. Fenton's body started to spasm. Decker reached over for the door handle.

Another bullet fizzed through the vehicle's interior.

Fenton's body went limp. Decker took the hard drive out of his hand and kicked the car door open and rolled across the tarmac.

A bullet whined through the trees over his head. Decker sat up behind the car. A rear window shattered, glass showering his head.

The 4x4 truck pulled out into the road, headlights boring through the trees, its driver oblivious to what was going on.

Decker took out the Glock and, on hands and knees, edged round the side of the car.

Another sound-moderated *snap* came from the trees. There was a loud puff of air beside him as the bullet found one of the rear tyres. The tyre hissed.

Just then, a light flashed on and a car engine started. Decker looked round. It was Evie. With tyres spinning on the loose stones, she reversed the Peugeot in an arc towards him, and shouted from the window, 'Get in.'

Decker got in, a shot clipping the door panel and wing mirror. Evie screamed. Decker held her head down and, through the window, shot the Glock three times towards the trees.

Evie pulled out into the road, tyres screeching.

'Jesus Christ!' she said. 'Call the police.' She clipped the kerb on the corner and swerved across the road.

Decker steadied the steering wheel. 'Watch the road.'

'Call the police,' Evie shouted.

Decker looked back over his shoulder to see if anyone was following them.

'Are you fucking crazy?' She changed gears, accelerating through an S-bend. 'Someone's dead! Jesus! Call the police.'

'No police.'

Evie veered across the road again, tyres juddering over the cat's eyes.

Decker said, 'Watch the road.'

Glancing at him, Evie said, 'Who was he?'

'No one.'

'No one?' she said, shaking her head. 'He's dead!'

Decker checked over his shoulder again. 'He shouldn't be.'

Evie smashed the top of the steering wheel with her hand. 'No one should be dead! What are you saying?'

'That it's not personal.'

'You're fucking crazy. You know that don't you. Jesus!'

Decker faced the front again, the road clear behind them. 'It's happened now.'

'You're bloody crazy. Don't you feel anything? Someone's dead!'

Decker adjusted what was left of the wing mirror, the glass shattered.

Head south, he thought, somewhere quiet. Hole up.

'You're as crazy as they are,' Evie said. 'Jesus!' She looked across at Decker. 'Look at you – there's blood all over you.'

'It'll wash off,' he said.

Evie started fiddling with something on her lap. Decker saw she had her phone. She must have got it out of his bag on the way out.

Decker said, 'What are you doing?'

'I'm calling the police.' She put the phone to her ear.

Decker grabbed the phone out of her hand, opened the window, and threw it into the hedge. Evie lunged at Decker, releasing the steering wheel. 'You crazy fucking idiot,' she said.

Decker slapped Evie across the face and pointed the gun at her.

'Drive the car,' he said.

Evie gripped the steering wheel and wiped tears off her face.

A lorry passed them on the other side of the road, blowing up verge-side leaves. And Decker checked the side-view mirror again.

Then he said, 'The police can't help us. We don't exist. The police can't help with things that don't exist.'

Evie glanced at him. 'What are you talking about? There's someone dead back there.'

'In 10 or 15 minutes a van will pull up in front of the pub. It will park at an angle to the car. Three or four men will get out of the van. The body will be covered with a black plastic sheet. The tarmac will be vacuumed for chards of glass. Any bloodstains will be sprayed. The car will be driven away with the body in it. The van will be last to leave. One man will remain behind to tie off any loose ends. The police, if they are called, will arrive ten or fifteen minutes later.'

Evie shook her head. 'Someone will have heard something.'

'Yeah, someone. Maybe there's even an eyewitness. But remember the car park is empty. The man left behind will ensure nothing is taken too seriously. The police get hundreds of calls like this every week. This will be no different.'

Evie appeared to think about this for a moment then said, 'What about my work? They'll wonder where I am.'

'You'll call in sick.'

37

Just after midnight, Evie pulled into a lay-by and Decker took over the driving. Lighting a cigarette, he re-joined the dual carriageway and headed south. Evie slept.

Just outside the village of Findon, Decker circled a roundabout twice before taking the last exit. Hedgeless fields opened up on either side to reveal the chalk escarpments of the South Downs. Every now and then, Decker checked the rear-view mirror. The road snaked and undulated. Somehow, for now, they were clear.

Decker drove from memory, the road bringing it back, with its wind-beaten hawthorns punctuating the hedgeless verges, and conveyor belt of tarmac. It had been ten years.

Glancing at Evie, Decker observed the play of shadows across her face. He knew things weren't going to get any easier with her here. But there was no going back now – for either of them.

The Peugeot zipped through a dip in the road and came up the other side.

At the top of the hill, Decker slammed on the brakes and stopped the car.

Exhaust fumes smoked over the rear of the vehicle.

Selecting reverse, Decker looked over his shoulder and started backing up. Evie opened her eyes.

'Where are we?' she said.

Decker stopped alongside a narrow track half way down the slope. There was a signpost on the corner. It read: "Chalkecoombe Ash 2 miles". Decker pointed to the sign for the benefit of Evie.

Evie read the sign.

Decker said, 'We're ten miles from the sea.'

Decker turned down the narrow road. It was just after one o'clock. The moon blazed above treetops. Slowing down, Decker turned through a gateway, switching off the headlights, and crossed over a cattle grid in the track.

Evie said, 'This is freaking me out. Where're we going?'

Decker said nothing; the car juddered down the unmade track. They passed through a conifer plantation. Piles of felled timber lay along the verges. A lake glistened in the distance. Further along the track, Decker saw the field barn he'd played in as a child. It was missing a few more sheets of corrugated iron but otherwise it looked much the same.

They came out of the plantation. Abandoned farm machinery lay swallowed up in brambles along the verges. Decker pulled up next to the barn and several sodden straw bales with grass growing out of them and turned off the ignition.

The engine ticked in the dark. An owl hooted.

Evie said, 'Jesus, where are we?'

'Do you have anything warm in the car?' Decker said.

'What do you mean?'

'Any blankets, sleeping bags. It's going to be cold.' Decker opened his door and got out.

Evie said, 'Where are you going?'

Decker walked round the car and checked the boot. It was empty. He said to Evie, 'Stay here. Put on your extra clothes. I'll be back soon.'

'Where are you going?'

'I won't be long.'

Decker walked along the track, passing an abandoned caravan and half-stripped car. He came to some outbuildings. Tarpaulin flapped on silage bays; the clinking sound of aluminium gates. He tried several of the buildings until he found an old horse blanket. He then headed back to the car.

Evie was smoking a cigarette when he got back to the car. Holding her knees to her chest, she was shivering. 'What's that?' she said.

'A horse blanket.'

'This is crazy,' she said, her teeth chattering. 'I can't do this anymore.'

'Put the blanket over you.'

Evie said, 'I won't say anything to anyone. I promise. Just let me go.'

Decker lay the blanket over her. 'Get some sleep,' he said.

'Please. You can have my car. I can walk.'

Decker got under the blanket his side.

Evie said, 'If it's the money, I don't care. You can have it back.'

Decker reclined his seat, pulled the blanket up to his chin, and shut his eyes.

Evie dragged on her cigarette, then, leaving the cigarette in her mouth, reached over and tried opening the door. Decker grabbed her arm.

Evie screamed. 'Let go of me,' she said.

Decker twisted her arm behind her back.

'That hurts. Let go! I need to pee, all right?'

Decker walked Evie to the edge of the trees. Undoing her jeans, Evie said, 'Turn round.' Decker turned round.

Back in the car, Decker covered them with the horse blanket again. It stank a bit but was thick and warm. They lay there in silence for a moment. A fox barked in the wood.

Evie said, 'What was that?'

'A fox. Try to sleep.'

Evie turned to the window.

The fox kept barking.

Evie said, 'What's it doing?'

'Just letting you know it's there. Go to sleep.' Decker closed his eyes.

Evie sat up, pushing aside the blanket. 'What's your plan? If I am staying, I want to know what the plan is.'

Decker kept his eyes closed.

'You don't have a plan, do you?'

Decker said, 'Go to sleep,' again.

'I know you don't like telling anyone anything,' Evie said. 'But you bought me into this, so now you have to tell me what's going on.'

'I need two more days. We need to keep moving.'

'That's it? That's your plan?'

'That's it.'

'You're crazy, you know that.'

'Go to sleep.'

'And then what? What happens after that?'

'Tomorrow, we will drive into town. I need to use the internet. And you'll contact your work.'

Evie sat quietly for a moment. The owl hooted. There was the sound of a breeze in the treetops.

Then she said, 'They'll come after us, won't they?'

Decker hesitated. 'Who?'

'The people who killed that man at the pub.'

Decker didn't respond.

Evie said, 'This doesn't have anything to do with me, you know!'

Decker had his eyes closed. 'Go to sleep,' he said.

Evie kept quiet this time.

Decker focused only on the importance of sleep at that moment, though he knew Evie was right, they would come after them, and they'd need to be ready when they did. But there was nothing he could do or say that would change that now.

Draw a circle. Put yourself inside this circle. And remember: this is your reality.

*

Decker woke at around five o'clock, covering Evie with his side of the blanket and getting out the car and walking over to a woodpile. He sat on the logs and lit a cigarette. It was still dark.

After a few minutes, Evie came over and joined him. Decker passed her his cigarette and Evie took a couple of drags before handing it back.

She said, 'I'm freezing.'

Decker said, 'We'll leave soon.'

Evie hugged herself from cold. Her eyes were red. She said, 'You don't sleep much, do you?

A crow cawed in the distance. Decker put out the cigarette on one of the logs, pocketed the butt and stood up. 'Come on,' he said. 'Let's go.'

They drove into a seaside town called Chalkecoombe Ash. It was overcast and grey, a stiff breeze coming off the coast, white-crested waves lining the bay. They parked in a multi-storey car park in the centre of town. Decker held Evie's arm as they left the building by a side entrance.

On the high street, the couple entered a Starbucks. A few minutes later, they left carrying lidded cups. Further down the street, Decker entered an internet café while Evie waited outside drinking her coffee.

He checked into the bulletin board. There was a message sent last night: "You are not alone. Please contact me as soon as you have read this message. I can help. Reeves."

A telephone number followed. Decker made a note of the number but didn't send a reply. Next, he looked at the BBC website. The story about Howell was still running. The police had found an array of bondage gear in his cupboard. Howell's sexual preferences were now in the spotlight. The focus had shifted onto his personal life. The suggestion was that his death was the result of a bizarre sex game gone wrong, and had nothing to do with his work. *The Guardian* was running the same story. There was a picture of Howell in running kit. They described him as a keen runner and fitness enthusiast, dubbing him "the marathon man". Decker recalled Sachs' conversation about distracting the police.

For a moment, Decker looked up from the computer and observed Evie outside. She was clutching her cup in both hands and blowing over the rim. She looked tired and agitated, as you do after two sleepless nights. He knew he couldn't keep dragging her around like this, but if he let her go, Sachs' men were sure to pick her up, which would lead back to him; yet having her around complicated things.

Then there was the problem of the hard drive. At least two people wanted it: Sachs and Reeves. They could be the same person of course but for now Decker was prepared to treat them as separate individuals. But could he trust either of them?

Decker googled Alharbi next, clicking on the link: "Property tycoon, Hatton Alharbi questioned by police in his involvement with spy killing."

It was only a short article. There was a CCTV image of Howell and Alharbi on the night of the killing. Howell was seen entering a Tube station. An image later there was a picture of Alharbi passing through the same entrance.

Evie was lighting a cigarette when Decker joined her outside. He whispered, 'Remember, we're a couple,' and he put his arm round her as they walked off. Further down the high street, they went into a Tesco Express and bought provisions to last them for a couple of days then walked back along the seafront.

Passing a hotel, Evie asked if she could stop and use the ladies. 'Please,' she said. 'I just want to wash.'

Decker nodded. 'Five minutes.'

Evie walked through the hotel entrance and Decker stood outside and watched her through the windows. Evie indicated where she was going and Decker watched her enter a downstairs ladies toilet. He checked his watch and then turned to the sea, watching the breakers, the seagulls.

Five minutes went past.

Decker entered the hotel, scanning the foyer. He knew he'd made a mistake letting her go. The reception was empty. He walked across towards the ladies toilets. He opened the door and walked in. A

175

window was open. He ran back into the foyer. He heard someone behind him say, 'Can I help, sir?' He ignored them. A set of glass doors led onto a patio. He climbed over the patio wall and dropped down into an alleyway. He ran to the end of the alleyway and found himself back on the high street.

He looked in both directions. At the end of the road, he saw Evie standing with two policemen. She was pointing over her shoulder as she spoke.

Decker lowered his head and walked into a shop. From inside the shop, he saw Evie get into the back of a squad car. A small crowd had gathered at the end of the road. The squad car pulled out into the road with its lights flashing but no siren.

Decker left the shop, knowing he had less time than before.

38

'It's good to hear from you, Martin. I'm glad you finally rang.'

Decker turned round in the telephone box, checking his watch. 'Leave the woman alone,' he said. 'Her name's Evie. She doesn't know anything.'

'I understand. We we'll do what we can for her. Where are you?'

'How did you know about the bulletin board?'

'It seems we have a mutual friend.'

'Howell wasn't a friend.'

'Martin, I can help you.'

'I doubt it.' Decker checked his watch again.

'You need to trust me.'

'Howell's boyfriend's dead,' Decker said.

'I know. He gave you something, didn't he?'

Decker didn't respond.

'Where is it, Martin?'

'Safe.'

'Tell me where you are. And we can get this over with.'

'Who are you?' Decker said.

'My name is Reeves.'

'That means nothing to me.'

'I knew your father.'

'So did Sachs.'

'Martin, you have to trust me.'

'So you said.'

'Whatever you're thinking, Martin, leave it alone. Get the hard drive to us and let us handle Sachs.'

Decker hung up the phone.

He crossed the road to the train station opposite. At a kiosk he stopped and bought a newspaper. He walked through the station concourse with the newspaper tucked under his arm. He stood under the departures board, checking train times. Then made his way to a platform where he boarded a train at 11:50.

*

Nearly 30 minutes later, Decker exited Brighton station with the hood up on his jacket. He headed out of town.

An hour later, he was seen walking round a garage forecourt, where he stopped beside a second-hand Nissan Almera, cupped his hands and looked through the windows. He walked round the car and inspected the tyres. Stuck to the glass was the sticker price of £750.

In the forecourt trailer, Decker paid in cash and left Brighton and headed west on the dual carriageway. He kept his speed to 70mph, occasionally using the outside lane to overtake lorries. Periodically, he checked his rear-view. At one point, he searched his pockets for cigarettes, but failing to find any, glanced across at the passenger seat and remembered Evie instead.

After about 20 minutes, he pulled off the main road and headed up a slip road towards a retail centre. Parking the Nissan, he entered a Sports Direct where he wasted no time once inside, putting a bivvy, sleeping bag and knife on the counter, and paying in cash. Next, he went into a Carphone Warehouse and bought a pay-as-you-go Nokia. In a matter of minutes, he was back on the main road again.

Before long, it started to rain. Turning on the windscreen wipers, Decker discovered the left-hand wiper wasn't working properly. At the next service station, he stopped and attempted to fix it.

He came off the A27, checking his rear-view on the slip road to see no one was following him, and headed north.

He accelerated through a dip in the road and came up the other side. To his right, a solitary oak tree stood in the middle of a ploughed field and shafts of sunlight splintered from a grey sky.

Coming over the brow of the hill, the road snaked back and forth. A light drizzle flecked the windscreen. He followed road signs for a village called Five Mile Ash, and before long a church tower became visible above hedgerows. Slowing down, he remembered lyrics from a song that Annie had often played:

There's just one place for a man to be when he's worried about his life ... I'm going home.'

Opposite the churchyard, Decker pulled up on a muddy verge and got out. Checking round himself, he put his hands in his pockets and crossed the road. Rooks flew from the trees and cattle bellowed in the fields. The place hadn't changed.

Decker followed the path round the back of the church and looked for somewhere to hide the hard drive. He came to a lean-to shed, cupped his hands and looked through the cracked window. Inside were a mower and several spades. He tried the door but it was locked.

He continued round the graveyard. Cows grazing in the adjacent field stuck their heads through the fence wire. Rooks took off from the field and landed again. He stopped and looked up at the church roof, the drizzle falling in his face, then, lowering his gaze, noticed a yew tree in the middle of the graveyard. He walked over and saw there was a hole in the trunk. He put his hand in the hole and it went right down. It would do, he thought.

He looked across the road to the row of cottages, saw no one was about and took out the plastic bag with the hard drive in and tied a knot in the bag. Needing something to hang it on, he took out the knife and stuck it through the bag and then pinned it to the inside of the trunk.

Decker left the churchyard, walked back along the road, and started the engine of the Nissan. He made a U-turn in the road and drove back the way he had come.

*

Taking the last exit on the Five Mile Ash roundabout, Decker joined the dual carriageway, and continued north.

The drizzle blew across the carriageway and he turned on the windscreen wipers. The left one still wasn't working properly and it began to squeak again. He turned on the radio and a DJ was interviewing an actor. The actor was talking about being made a father recently and how it had changed his life and made him appreciate why he was here. Then he talked about his parents and how important family was to him. He gave away more personal information in a minute than Decker had in most of his life. Decker tried other channels then turned off the radio.

He settled back in the chair, straightening his arms, and gripped the steering wheel. He felt like smoking a cigarette again, which made him think of Evie. He stared at the road ahead: the strip of tarmac; the grey clouds; the needle of the speedometer wavering around 60mph. He knew the police wouldn't have believed Evie's story and told her to go home and get some rest. And he didn't like to think who would be waiting for her there.

At the Bury roundabout, Decker pulled into a service station and sat in the car. He tipped back the seat and shut his eyes for a moment. When he opened them again, a woman was strapping a baby into a car seat in the car opposite him. She opened the boot of the car and then put a buggie inside. Decker watched her get into the driver's side, put on her seat belt, and drive off. Decker gave it a moment and then removed a photograph from his pocket. It was of a young couple skiing. He looked at the picture, turning it over where Howell had written the words "Stray dog". Decker spent about a minute looking at the photo before returning it to his pocket.

Remember: acknowledging something as a coincidence is a sure sign you don't know what's really going on.

*

It was still drizzling. Decker re-joined the dual carriageway, putting on his headlights.

Around Arundel, he noticed a Vauxhall Astra fall in behind him, several cars back. They must have got to the woman, he thought, for them to track him so quickly.

Heading north on the A29, Decker passed through several villages and kept to the speed limit. The Astra stayed with him. On the other side of Billingshurst, Decker joined the A24 and kept heading north.

From there, he checked his rear-view with greater frequency. The Astra hung back in the slow lane, overtaking when Decker did. Decker scratched his unshaven face and kept an eye on it.

It was still raining. The windscreen wipers were still squeaking.

He needed to be patient. Wait for the right opportunity, he thought.

Before long, Decker saw the lights of a service station ahead of him. It had a café and car park at its rear. Decker reckoned it was out of the way enough not to have any cameras. He pulled into the outside lane, flicking on his indicator. He looked up at his rear-view. The Astra's indicator came on.

Decker pulled into the car park and got out of the Nissan and made a quick scan for cameras or people sitting in cars. All was clear. He went into the café and ordered a coffee. He saw the Astra pull into the car park and park.

Decker opened a sachet of sugar, tipped it into his coffee and stirred.

The driver remained in his car and took out a newspaper. Decker kept an eye on him and sipped his coffee. Then after a few minutes, he walked down a corridor towards the gents. At the end of the corridor, there was a fire exit door propped open by a box of loo paper. Outside, someone was slinging bags of rubbish into a wheelie bin.

Decker left the café and walked round the back on the car park where he pushed through a Leylandii hedge and strolled straight up to the Astra.

The driver dropped his newspaper as Decker opened his door and pulled him out onto the tarmac. With his foot on the guy's neck, Decker said, 'Who sent you?'

The driver squirmed on the ground. 'You crazy fuck! Get off me!'

Decker took his foot of the guy's throat, allowing him to get up on his knees then drove the heel of his foot into the man's face. 'Who sent you?'

The driver spat a mouthful of blood onto the ground. 'Fuck you!'

Decker looked over the roof of the car, scanned the car park, then pulled the Glock out from under his jacket and stuck it into the guy's throat.

'Who's your contact?'

'What fucking contact?'

Decker slid the rack of the Glock.

'Okay, okay.'

'Names,' Decker said.

'Schiller. He calls himself, Schiller. That's all I know.'

'What were you instructions?'

'I'm just meant to follow you.'

'Why?'

'I don't know. Just follow him, that's all he said.'

'The woman – where is she?'

'What woman?'

Decker pressed the muzzle of the Glock against the man's forehead.

The man said, 'They have her … at the big house.'

Decker looked up as a couple were leaving the restaurant. He waited for them to get in their car and drive off then picked the man up and shoved him back into his car. Blood ran through the man's hair and down the side of his face.

Holding his door open, Decker said, 'Call Schiller and tell him you need picking up.'

'What are you talking about?'

Decker looked round again. Then, lowering the angle of the Glock, shot the man through the top half of his right leg.

The man squealed. Decker shut his door and crossed the car park. The squeals muted in the background.

Decker got into the Nissan and re-joined the carriageway, checking his mirrors. No one was behind him now. He pulled into the inside lane and accelerated up to 60mph. It was getting dark.

*

Later, with indicator flashing, Decker pulled across into the slip road and took the last exit on a roundabout. The road snaked up hill. Decker held the middle of the road, cutting out corners. Headlights lit up steep wooded slopes. Decker remembered the roads, remembered Evie next to him.

He knew they would be expecting him. But what choice did he have? He'd got her into this, he thought, now he had to get her out.

Decker slowed down as he passed the turning for Sachs' estate. He saw lights in the distance. He passed thirty miles per hour road signs and came into a village. There was a church on the left, a garage, some shops.

He drove passed the village square and turned left. Lines of parked cars either side of the road. He found a space and parked the Nissan. Switching off the engine, he sat for a moment. He looked at the village hall, the playing field with roped off cricket square, and the cul-de-sac of houses. He replaced the spent round in the Glock, stuffed the pay-as-you-go in the glove compartment, then got out of the car and opened the boot. He put on the rucksack, locked the car, and walked back out the village.

Alongside the churchyard, he jumped over a fence and crossed the field. Sheep bleated in the darkness. Climbing over a stile, he walked down a narrow lane, hearing a car in the distance, then climbed a gate and followed the edge of a ploughed field up a slope. He heard foxes barking in a gateway to a wood. The moon beamed through a ring of clouds. He went into the wood and followed the track.

Through the trees, Decker caught sight of Sachs' house. Coming to a clearing, he looked at the house through binoculars. There appeared to be more houselights on than before. He sat down against a tree, took out some food and began to eat. Between mouthfuls, he took sips of water. Afterwards, he shut his eyes for ten minutes and visualised the inside of Sachs' house, working his way along corridors, upstairs, towards Sachs' study. When he opened his eyes again, he stood up and hid the rucksack in a patch of brambles; then checking the time, headed down the slope towards the house.

39

'I should think there's a few million quid out here …'

A security guard stood at the front of the house speaking into a walkie-talkie. About a dozen cars were parked in the driveway: Range Rovers, Mercs, a Bentley. The estimate wasn't far away.

Lying on his front, Decker was peering round the corner of a stonewall watching him.

The security guard looked at each car in turn. His shoes crunched on the loose stones. His breath billowed in the cold air. He was wearing black leather gloves and as he walked he clapped his hands together to keep warm.

The security guard stood for a moment at the top of the driveway, looking down the long belt of tarmac towards the road. He clasped his hands behind his back. His walkie-talkie was clipped to the collar of his jacket, a red light flashing.

Decker looked across at the house. Through a downstairs window, he saw people dressed in black tie and waiters passing round canapés.

Just then, the front door came open and a man wearing a white apron left the house. The security guard glanced over his shoulder and, recognising him, waved. The man waved back, walking round the side of the house and disappearing through a side door.

The security guard looked back down the drive again as headlights blazed in the distance, sweeping across the fields and lighting up trees. A Range Rover appeared at the end of the drive. The security guard said something into his walkie-talkie that Decker didn't catch.

The Range Rover approached the house, its passenger window going down. It stopped briefly alongside the guard and there was brief exchange. Then the window went up again and the vehicle continued round the side of the house. Decker couldn't see who it was.

The security guard walked back across the car park, clapping his hands together again. The apron guy reappeared from the side door, carrying a box. The security walked over and talked to him. He made a fist with one hand and clasped it in the other as he talked. He was nearly a head taller than the apron guy.

As they chatted, Decker crept along the inside of the wall, following it all the way to the end, to where he'd seen the apron guy go. The door was left open. Decker went in and closed the door behind him.

He found himself in some kind of store room, full of boxes and pallets. A bulb on a flex hung from the ceiling. A set of stone steps led up to a door. Decker walked up the steps and tried the door but it was locked. He looked round for something to open it with when he noticed the key hanging from a nail on the wall.

Unlocking the door, Decker came out at the bottom of stairs in the main house. He could hear voices, laughter and music. He moved quietly up the stairs and came to a corridor with wood panelling. He recognised where he was now.

Decker took out the Glock and held it at his side as he followed the corridor to the end, to Sachs' study. The door was ajar. He pushed it open with his foot and entered, pointing the Glock round the room.

A desk lamp was on, a laptop open, Decker tracking round the room when a muffled bark came from the corner. He'd forgotten about the dog.

The dog sat up in its bed, ears back, eyes glistening in the dark.

'All right there,' Decker said, lowering the gun, but slowly.

The dog, extending its neck, sniffed the air, then stood up and walked towards him. Decker stood his ground and let the dog sniff his legs for a moment. Then he stroked the dog's head and the dog, wagging its tail, returned to its bed.

Decker walked round the desk and pressed the laptop's touch pad. A window appeared asking for a password. But he wasn't going to waste time guessing passwords and started opening the desk drawers and sifting through the paperwork. Most of it related to the running of the estate; and none of it was of any interest.

Decker looked round the room again, his eye stopping at a picture on the wall of a huntsman and foxhounds setting off down a country lane. He went over to the picture and stood in front of it for a moment. It was called *The Meet* and was done in thick oils and looked to be very old. From there, he walked over to a bookcase and started looking at the spines of hardbacks. The dog lifted its head and watched him.

Most of the books were biographies and history books. One book lay on its side on top of the row and Decker took it down. It was a book about the Cold War by someone called Giles Templar. He opened the book and saw the author's personal inscription inside addressed to Sachs.

Just then, a burst of laughter came from downstairs and Decker put down the book and went over and listened at the door. The noise receded. He checked the time on his watch then walked over to a filing cabinet. On top of the cabinet was a box file. He pulled it down. As he did so, a small black book fell onto the floor. Decker bent down and picked it up. It wasn't a book but a small photo album. He turned through the first few pages: shots of desert, sand dunes, HEP reservoirs, skyscrapers. Then a group picture of what looked like company employees. The pictures started to feel familiar. Decker flicked forward. He came across photos of a skiing holiday, couples standing on the mountainside, skis aslant. He didn't recognise the faces to begin with. Then he realised the pictures were of his father and Sachs and other work colleagues. Sachs must have dug them out after having his memory jogged about "Stray dog", Decker thought.

Decker turned forward and there was a picture missing. He looked at the empty pocket, then dug into his jacket pocket and took out the photo of his mother and father skiing. Decker slipped the photo into the transparent pocket. The picture fitted like the others. He removed it again and returned it to his pocket. Flicking forward, he saw more pictures of his father: one of him standing beside a helicopter; another with a group of Arabs in traditional dress; then another with his mother on a boat. Near the end of the album, there was a picture of Sachs, his father and a third man. Decker stared at this picture and was about to remove it when he heard footsteps on the stairs. He dropped the photo album, drew the Glock and pointed it at the door.

There was laughter outside the door. The dog stood up. Decker saw the photo album on the floor and kicked it under a chair.

Speaking on the phone, Sachs walked through the door, saying, 'How long ago? ... I understand—' saw the gun and Decker, dropped the phone and lifted his hands.

The dog trotted across the room towards him. Sachs ignored the dog.

Decker motioned Sachs across to a chair with the gun.

Sachs walked to the chair, sat down, and said, 'I didn't expect you so soon.' He was wearing black-tie and a maroon-coloured cummerbund. 'What do you want?'

Decker pointed the gun at his head.

'Stray dog. Remember?' he said.

Sachs nodded. 'I remember.'

'Do you remember the people you've killed as well?'

Sachs smiled. 'Do you I wonder.'

Decker narrowed his eyes. The bead of the Glock centred on Sachs' forehead. He should have shot him when he'd had the chance, he thought.

Sachs lost the smile. 'We have Evie, Martin. Put the gun down.'

Decker felt his jaw muscle twitch.

'Don't worry,' Sachs said. 'She's safe.'

Decker looked at Sachs, his eyes. He was in control, breathing steadily. He could be bluffing about the girl, but Decker doubted it.

Sachs glanced towards the door now, and said, 'Personally, I didn't think you were going to come back for her. But there you go. Others thought differently.'

There was a knock on the door. Decker moved the gun from Sachs to the door, ready to shoot whoever was coming in.

Evie came in first. Schiller was right behind her, holding a gun at the back of her head. Evie was crying.

Sachs said, 'Where's the hard drive, Martin?'

Decker put the gun back on Sachs, finger closing on the trigger. 'Tell him to let her go,' he said.

'I can't do that, Martin. You know that.'

'Tell him to let her go,' Decker repeated.

Sachs nodded in Schiller's direction. He released Evie. She fell on the floor.

Decker said, 'Now tell him to put his gun on the floor.'

Schiller didn't move, gun dangling at his side; dark bags under his eyes, blank expression on his face. Could have been watching paint dry.

Sachs said, 'Martin, what are you going to do? I have men waiting downstairs. You're not going anywhere.'

Decker kept the gun aimed at Sachs. 'Tell him,' he said

Sachs nodded at Schiller, who then placed his gun on the floor.

Decker said, 'Have someone drive a vehicle to the front of the building.'

187

Sachs smiled. 'I like you Martin. I always have. That's why I gave you a job. And you did well, you brought us Howell. He wasn't going to come out of hiding for just anyone, as you know. And we're grateful. But now we're here.'

Decker glanced between Schiller and Sachs.

Sachs said, 'The hard drive, Martin. Where is it?'

The doors opened; Decker spun round. The two security guards were standing in the doorway, handguns pointed at him. He moved his gun from one guard to the next. He spotted Schiller creeping forward.

Sachs stood up. 'Martin, the hard drive. It's that simple. Or I will kill both you and your girlfriend.'

The two security guards moved in on Decker, forcing him into the middle of the room. Schiller picked up his gun. Decker couldn't cover them all. He felt someone hit him round the neck. He collapsed to the floor.

*

When Decker came round the two guards were leading him outside into a courtyard; close behind them came Schiller with Evie. A Range Rover was parked in the courtyard. They stopped beside it while one of the guards opened a back door. Decker turned to Evie, and said, 'You okay?'And Evie nodded.

Then Sachs walked out into the courtyard, pulling the zip up on a green Gore-Tex jacket, the crunch of gravel underfoot echoing round the yard. And the guard pushed Decker into the back of the Range Rover, lowered his window, and Sachs walked over to the window and said, 'It's up to you, Martin.' His breath smoked in the cold night air. 'The hard drive ... where is it?

Behind him, Schiller stood holding Evie by her arm. Sachs now looked round and nodded at him. And Schiller took out his moderated H&K and put it against Evie's head.

Decker said, 'I don't know.'

'Come on, Martin, stop fucking us around.'

Evie began shaking. Schiller, gripping her arm, rested his finger against the trigger.

'It's in a churchyard,' he said.

Sachs smiled. 'Where?'

'I'll show you. Let her go.'

Sachs said, 'I will count to three. You understand that?'

Decker looked at Sachs, saying nothing.

Sachs nodded at Schiller.

Sachs said, 'One ...'

Tears ran down Evie's face, her hair bunching up where Schiller held the gun against her head.

'Two ...'

Decker said, 'All right.'

'All right what?'

'It's at a place called Five Mile Ash.'

Sachs signalled to the driver who started the engine of the Range Rover, then said to Decker through the window, 'You see. That wasn't so difficult, was it?'

Decker didn't respond, the driver closing his window.

Sachs then nodded at Schiller who pushed Evie into the back of the Range Rover alongside Decker. Then Schiller walked round to the passenger side and opened the door.

Sachs saying to him, 'When you've picked up the hard drive, drop these two off. I don't want to see them again. Understand?'

Schiller nodded

'Otherwise, it's as we agreed.'

Schiller nodded again and got into the Range Rover and shut the door and the tyres spun on the loose gravel.

40

Pulling out into the road, the driver in black beanie pressed a button on the sat-nav. A woman's voice told him to drive straight on. Schiller rested the Heckler and Koch on his lap and pulled up the collars of his jacket. The driver changed through the gears and flicked to full beam.

Clicking his tongue, Schiller said to the driver, 'Have you eaten tonight?'

The driver looked round, and said, 'Yeah. Why?'

'What'd you have?'

The driver paused. 'What are you, my wife?'

'No, seriously, what'd you have?'

'Chicken.'

'Good?'

'What?'

'Was it good?'

'Yeah. All right. Like chicken.'

Schiller nodded. 'You cook it yourself?'

'No. I ate in the pub.'

'So you ate out.'

'Yeah. What of it?'

Schiller turned to the window. 'Do you eat out a lot?'

'Not really. Twice a week.'

'That's a lot.'

'Is it? What's not a lot?'

Schiller shrugged. 'I don't know … once a month.'

The driver shook his head. 'What is this?'

Schiller said, 'I like to cook.' He looked over the seat at Decker. 'What about you, Martin? Do you like to cook?'

Decker said, 'When there's time.'

'That's nice. It's relaxing, isn't it? When I retire, I hope to move to France. You know, grow my own vegetables, keep a few chickens, eat big lunches like the locals.'

The driver said, 'Yeah. You'll get fat like them as well.'

Schiller shook his head. 'It's people like you who get fat. The French enjoy wonderful health, don't you think, Martin?

'So they say.'

'Yeah, that's what I want to do. Get myself a barn in the South of France somewhere, with a little plot of land. They say the light out there is fantastic—'

The driver said, 'You what?'

'The light ...' Schiller said, '... for painting. It's what I like to do – watercolours mostly.'

The driver chuckling, said, 'What ... you're fucking Vincent Van Gogh now?'

The security guard next to Decker started chuckling.

Lighting a cigarette, Schiller said, 'I don't expect you monkeys to understand.'

There was more laughter. As they were laughing, Decker noticed the security guard and the driver both had weapons holstered under their jackets. At the right moment, he should be able to take care of them. It was Schiller, with his gun on his lap, who would prove more difficult.

Schiller said, 'You need a hobby. For me, it's cooking and painting. What about you Martin? You got a hobby?'

Decker said, 'Not at the moment.'

'Oh, come on. I bet there's something. Every man has a hobby. You don't have to say. I understand; maybe a bit embarrassing in front of everyone.'

'Fishing,' Decker said, sensing something was going on here.

'There you go. I knew it. What's the point of living if you can't take a bit of pleasure now and then, eh?'

The driver said, 'You're full of shit, you know that?'

They stopped at a roundabout, sat-nav repeating the instructions to 'take the first exit' several times, and the driver telling it to 'shut the fuck up'.

Then they headed down a slip road to the dual carriageway, Schiller flicking his cigarette out the window and shutting it again; Decker catching Evie's eye and Evie offering him half a smile. She was holding her hands on her lap and seemed to be doing okay, he thought.

The driver joined the middle lane and turned on the radio. Schiller checked his watch and glanced out the window.

Every few minutes, the traffic cleared and the driver flicked to full beam, cat's eyes shining through an escarpment of trees.

After a few miles, the driver turned up the radio for the news; then turned it off when it was finished. At about the same moment, a mobile bleeped with a message.

Decker saw Schiller dig into his pocket and retrieve his mobile. He scrolled the messages and sent a reply.

Sat-nav informed the driver he needed to take the next exit. The driver looked at the GPS graphic.

Schiller said, 'How much longer?'

'Why?' the driver said. 'You got to get back and paint a picture?'

The guard in the back started chuckling again.

Flicking on the indicator, the driver pulled across the empty lanes.

Schiller said, 'What do you reckon, Martin, about an hour?'

Decker said, 'About that.'

Schiller said, 'That's what I was thinking.'

The driver pulled off the dual carriageway, clipping the chevrons.

Decker saw Schiller check his watch again.

The driver crossed a roundabout without slowing down, and Schiller starting to sing to himself:

Take it easy
Take it easy
Don't let the sound of your own wheels
Drive you crazy ...'

The driver shook his head, the guard in the back smiled to himself. They headed along a straight section of road through a wood. The driver overtook the car in front. After a few miles, Decker said, 'You'll need to turn left soon.' The driver caught his eye in the rear-view, then put on the indicator. Turning left, they passed through a small village, then out into open countryside.

The road narrowed; steep banks, high hedgerows. They passed several farms and Decker gave out more directions. Then the first signs for Five Mile Ash started appearing. They were about two miles away when, turning a corner, they came across a car stopped in the middle of the road. A man was squatting down beside the front tyre, looking to be changing it.

The driver of the Range Rover said, 'What the fuck's this?' and started slowing down.

Schiller leant round the side of the seat and pointed the Heckler and Koch at Decker and Evie and said, 'Keep very still now.'

The driver stopped the Range Rover, dipping the lights, and went to open his door.

Schiller fired twice.

Evie screamed and Decker pulled her into his arms.

The first shot went through the driver's ear. Blood splattered the windscreen and side window. The driver put his hand over the hole and let go of the door handle. Schiller put a second shot in his temple. In the back, the security guard was reaching for his gun when Schiller turned round and shot him through the head.

Two men walked towards the Range Rover. One of them opened the rear door next to Decker. The other one opened the driver's door.

Schiller turned to Evie and Decker, and said. 'We're going to change to the car in front, okay? Martin, you'll drive. We'll continue to the church and pick up the hard drive.' He was pointing the gun at him. 'Is that clear?'

Decker nodded.

'I will be right behind you. Let's go.'

Decker and Evie got out the car as the men covered the driver in a blanket, carried him out, and lay him in the back seat before starting to sponge down the windscreen and side window.

Schiller walked behind them to the car in front, a blue Ford Fiesta, then stood and watched as Decker got into the driver's seat and Evie got into the back. Schiller got into the passenger seat last and closed the door.

'I'm sorry about the mess,' he said, turning to look at Evie. Then, pointing the gun at Decker, said, 'Okay, start the car, Martin.'

Decker turned the ignition.

Schiller saying, 'And keep it steady.'

Decker let down the handbrake and pulled away. In the rear-view, he saw Evie on the backseat, clasping herself with her arms, and shaking. Behind them, the Range Rover was making a U-turn in the road.

Schiller rang a number on his mobile. Looking at Decker and pointing the gun at him at the same time, he said on the phone, 'Yes. All done,' and hung up.

Schiller then lit a cigarette and offered one to Evie, leaving one poking out of the packet.

Evie didn't react in anyway.

Schiller said, 'Are you sure?'

Evie still didn't say anything.

Decker said, 'She'll have one later.'

Schiller shrugged and put the packet away in his pocket.

The church appeared through the trees. There were lights in the windows, a dim glow behind stain glass.

Schiller said, 'Slow down.'

Decker slowed down.

'Okay. Pull up here.'

Decker stopped the car in a gateway and turned off the engine. A breeze gusted. Treetops swayed in the moonlight.

Schiller said, 'Who the fuck's in there at this time?' He leant closer to the windscreen and looked at the church. A ring of cloud haloed the moon above the spire, the lower slopes of the downs distinguishable in the background. 'For fucksake,' he said. 'What are they doing in there?'

Decker held the steering wheel and looked straight ahead. Out the corner of his eye, he saw Schiller's gun pointed at him and thought about making a grab for it, aware that he may not get a better chance.

All of a sudden, the church lights went out. There was the sound of a door closing; footsteps. A torch light juddered down the path.

'Come on, love,' Schiller said. 'Go to bed.'

A woman carrying a basket crossed the churchyard. There was the sound of the gate latch and then footsteps on the road. The torchlight came round the corner. Schiller put the gun at the back of Decker's head and said, 'Okay, no one is going to move.'

At the last moment, the torch light changed direction and pointed across the field. The woman with the basket climbed over a stile. They watched her walk across the field towards the cottages.

A minute passed.

An outside light came on; a dog barked. Schiller lowered the gun and reached inside his pocket. He produced several cable-ties.

'Here,' he said to Evie. 'Hold out your hands.' He tied up her hands and fastened them to the door handle. 'Any noise and I will shoot your boyfriend. We won't be long.' He looked at Decker, 'Okay. Get out.'

Decker got out and started down the road, Schiller keeping several paces behind him, with the gun held in the flap of his overcoat.

Decker reached the gate to the churchyard and lifted the latch and said, 'Was it the money?'

Schiller said, 'Keep going.'

Walking along the path, he asked, 'Wasn't Sachs paying you enough?'

'I'm a professional. Like you. I do what I'm paid to do.' Schiller looked up at the church windows and said, 'Let's get this over with, shall we? I hate fucking churches.'

'Whatever you say.' Decker walked round the back of the church, passed the lean-to, and followed the track.

Schiller said, 'I thought you said it was in a tree.'

'It is.' Decker stopped and pointed at the yew tree in the distance. 'Over there,' he said.

Schiller said, 'Okay. Go and get it, then. I'll wait here.'

'Who's paying you, Schiller?'

'No more questions. Go and get it.' Schiller withdrew the gun from his overcoat and, waist high, pointed it at Decker. In the moonlight, Decker noticed scratches on the sound moderator. 'Go on,' Schiller said. 'Off you go.'

Decker walked between the headstones. The grass was wet and came off on his shoes. He saw a rabbit bolt through the fence and across the field.

Reaching the tree, Decker looked back at Schiller. His breath smoked in the cold air. He stood with his back to the church, one hand in his overcoat pocket, the other holding the gun. Decker could make out the 9mm hole in the silencer. The distance between them was about 35 metres. Someone less able than Schiller and Decker would have taken his chances.

Decker reached inside the tree hole and felt his way to the handle of the knife.

Schiller said, 'Hurry up.'

Decker felt the plastic bag with his fingertips, the knotted end, the knife handle. He closed his hand over both the bag and the knife and started to withdraw his arm.

'Got it?' Schiller said, taking a step towards, now in full moonlight.

Decker saw Schiller's eyes narrow as he strained to see what was in his hand.

'Yeah,' Decker said. 'I've got it.' And he bought out the bag while tucking the knife up his sleeve. Decker knew Schiller wouldn't want to shoot him here. Better do it in the car – less conspicuous that way.

That's what he'd do anyway.

'Bring it here, then,' Schiller said.

Decker walked towards him.

About five metres away, Schiller said, 'That's far enough. Let's see it.'

Decker took the hard drive out the bag and held it up in the air.

Schiller stepped towards him, straining his eyes to see what it was.

At that moment, Decker heard the sound of an approaching car, but didn't move. He kept his eyes on Schiller all the time.

Schiller was first to flinch, turning his head in the direction of the car.

It was all the time Decker needed. Slipping the knife from his sleeve, he dived at Schiller and stuck the knife into his leg and swiped the gun from his hand.

Schiller staggered sideways, clutching his bleeding leg, and fell to the ground.

Decker picked up the gun and stuck it in the back of Schiller's head.

'I should fucking kill you,' he said.

The sound of the car was getting closer, the screech of tyres round corners. He heard Evie shouting out for him.

Decker said to Schiller, 'Give me the car keys.'

Schiller smiled as the car headlights swung through the trees.

Decker pulled Schiller up, keeping the gun on his head. 'The keys. Now!'

Schiller handed him the keys and Decker ran back down the church path.

Evie had got the door open, with her hands still tied to the handle. 'Hurry,' she shouted. 'They're coming.'

41

Headlights lit up the road. A Mercedes squealed round the corner. Decker was caught in the road, silhouetted by the headlights, gun dangling at this side.

The Mercedes stopped.

Decker lifted his hand to shield his eyes. Exhaust fumes curled over the rear of the vehicle. Evie turned to look at him. Decker saw a back door open in the Mercedes and a suede loafer step onto the tarmac.

Hatton Alharbi climbed out of the car. He was wearing a blazer and a striped shirt. A chunky sports watch glinted on his wrist. As he got out of the car, he looked up at the sky and smiled. 'Ah, the countryside,' he said.

Decker lifted the Heckler and Koch and pointed it at his head.

Alharbi held up his hands, saying. 'Please, no. Put the gun away.' A flashing white-toothed smile lit up his face. 'It's Martin, isn't it? My name is Hatton Alharbi.'

'I know who you are.'

'Please, the gun,' he repeated, his watch jangling round his wrist as he held up his hands. 'I can't talk like this.'

Decker looked at him down the sights of the Heckler and Koch.

Alharbi said, 'I am a peaceful man. Just tell me what you want.'

'Nothing,' Decker said.

'Please, I can pay you.'

'So can Sachs.'

'Sachs is going to kill you.' He gestured with his arms above his head. 'Please, Martin. I was a friend of Howell's.'

Decker heard a stone roll down the bank onto the road. He spun round, pointing the gun into the dark –Schiller. He should have killed him when he got the chance. What was happening to him?

He said to Alharbi, 'Move away from the car.'

Alharbi thrust his arms further in the air, saying, 'Nothing is going to happen to you, Martin. I just need the hard drive—'

Decker said, 'Do it now.'

Alharbi stepped away from the car, saying. 'Where is it, Martin?'

Decker started walking back towards Evie.

Alharbi said, 'I can take you anyway you want … the airport, Eurostar. Just you say.'

Decker saw someone move inside Alharbi's car. 'Tell your friend to stay right where he is,' stopping and pointing the gun at the window now.

Alharbi said something in French to the man in the car, dropping his hands as he spoke.

'Hands above your head,' Decker said, moving the gun back on him.

'Martin, please. This isn't very civilised.'

'Do it now.'

Alharbi lifted his hands above his head again and Decker continued towards Evie.

Alharbi said, 'Just tell me what you want. Money is not a problem.'

Decker cut the cable ties round Evie's wrist with the knife and passed her the keys. 'Start the car,' he said.

Evie climbed into the front seat and got the keys in the ignition.

Alharbi said, 'Where are you going?'

Evie started the Fiesta and revved the engine.

Decker walked round to the passenger seat, his gun trained on Alharbi all the time. He calculated two, possibly three in the car. One would have a shot at Evie, another at him.

'There is nowhere to hide, Martin,' Alharbi said.

Decker climbed into the car, keeping the gun on Alharbi through the window. 'Go,' he said to Evie.

Evie released the clutch, wheels spinning.

Two shots came in quick succession. The first shot grazed the roof of the car and the second took out the wing mirror.

Evie rounded a corner, clipping the verge.

Decker looked back and saw Schiller stagger into the road, clutching his leg, and then get into the Mercedes.

He looked at Evie, and said, 'Are you okay?'

Evie gave him a glance. 'Are you serious?'

Checking the road ahead, Decker said, 'Take the next right. Yeah, I'm serious.'

'You're crazy. You know that? Really. All of you are fucking crazy.' Evie tugged on the steering wheel and took the turning on the slide, the backend of the car kicking out, wheels spinning on the far verge.

As Evie straightened up the car, Decker looked over his shoulder again. The Mercedes was still with them. He put his hand out the window and broke off the wing mirror that was hanging loose. He didn't want to give the police an excuse to stop them later on if he could help it. He shut the window again and, checking the gun's magazine, said, 'It was dangerous to disappear.'

'What! And this fucking isn't?' Evie held her foot to the accelerator, the needle of the speedometer creeping up all the time. The car lurched from side to side.

Decker said, 'Where did you go?'

'What difference does that make?' Evie shook her head. 'So what's the plan this time?'

'I have another car. We'll pick it up. Then I need to make a phone call.'

'Great! Some plan. Then what?'

'I'll get you out of here.'

Evie laughed hysterically.

Decker looked up at a road sign and said, 'The next left.'

Evie braked hard, going into a slide again, the backend stepping out. 'You have no idea, do you?' she said, turning into the skid and holding the corner. 'Why don't you just say it? You don't fucking know.'

Decker put out his hands to steady himself as the car fishtailed.

Righting the car again and accelerating on the straight, Evie said, 'Men – Jesus! Why don't you just tell the fucking truth?'

Decker glanced back over his shoulder again. There was no sign of the Mercedes. He said, 'At the end of this road is the dual carriage. Turn left. How's your father doing?'

Evie turned and looked at him, shaking her head. 'My who?'

'Your father?'

'Now you suddenly care about my father. I mean, do you really fucking care?'

'Just a question. You said he was ill.'

'I don't think you care about anything. I don't think you have any idea what it's like to live a normal life.'

The dual carriageway loomed at the end of the road. Evie kept accelerating. Decker gripped the door handle in preparation.

Without slowing up, Evie spun the Fiesta out into the middle lane, tyres screeching, and accelerated again.

Decker said, 'When you get a chance, get over to the other side. We're going in the wrong direction.'

'Why didn't you just say?' Evie tugged on the steering wheel, cutting across the central reservation, divots of turf spitting over the windscreen, then pulled a 180 in the far carriageway to face in the right direction. Selecting first, she pulled away.

Decker looked behind them. Smell of tyre rubber came through the air con. There was still no sign of the Mercedes.

He said, 'Who taught you to drive?'

Evie shook her head, accelerating into top gear, and said, 'My father. You know … the one you suddenly care about.'

Evie took out a cigarette and lowered the window. Decker watched her light it. The tobacco crackled. The smell permeated the car. At that moment, he knew he had missed her.

Evie looked round. 'What is it?' she said.

'Nothing,' Decker said.

'Do you want one?'

Decker nodded.

Evie shook her head. 'Why don't you just say something? You never speak. Jesus! You're either pointing a gun at someone or just sitting there saying nothing. Try something in between for a change.'

*

Later, they pulled into the village where Decker had left the Nissan, Evie turning right by the village hall and Decker looking over his shoulder, knowing they didn't have long. The Fiesta, flecked with mud and missing its wing mirror now, would soon be traced.

Decker said, 'Pull up over there.'

Evie pulled over and cut the engine. Decker wrote something on a piece of paper. It was an address for a bulletin board he had once used with Annie. He handed it to Evie.

'You can contact me here,' he said. 'Check for my messages every day. And keep moving. It'll be over soon.'

Evie looked at the piece of paper, 'That's it?'

'Use different names. Have a story, a reason for being somewhere.'

Evie looked up. 'What sort of story?'

'You're visiting a sister who's just had a baby. You're a journalist researching a story. You're on a work trip – anything that's plausible and that you can stick to.'

Decker got out the car, opened the boot of the Nissan and removed the rucksack. He slipped his arms through the straps and secured the buckle across his chest. He walked back over to Evie and stood beside the driver's window.

Evie said, 'He's in hospital.'

Decker saw tears sitting in her eyes.

'My father's in hospital,' she said. 'You asked.'

Decker nodded.

Evie said, 'The cancer keeps coming back.'

Decker said, 'I'm sorry.'

'It's not your fault.' She sniffed and wiped her eyes. 'This is though.' And she smiled.

Decker looked over the roof of the car and said, 'Do you have a friend you can stay with?'

'Yeah. In Oxford.'

'Go there first.'

Evie nodded. 'What's going to happen?'

'I'll come and find you.'

Evie smiled again. 'Just remember, you still owe me some money.'

'I won't forget.'

'You'd better not!'

Decker checked along the road. 'Do you know how to get out of here?'

'I think so.' Evie reached in her pocket. 'Here, have these.' She gave him the packet of cigarettes. 'It's about time I gave up.' She turned the ignition

Decker crossed the road, hearing Evie turn the car behind him. Headlights lit up the trees; gears changed.

Decker hopped over a field stile and disappeared into the dark.

42

Standing in a gateway, Decker dialled Reeves' number on the pay-as-you. He pictured a bedside light going on; reading glasses; a man in pyjamas; a wife stirring next to him. He saw this man carrying the phone next door.

It took him ten rings to answer it.

'Who is this?'

Decker gave it a moment. 'I have the hard drive.'

There was a pause.

'Martin. I was getting worried.'

'That's nice.'

'Where are you?'

'Sussex.'

'Listen, get back to London. I will meet you there.'

'I can't do that.'

'Listen to me, Martin—'

'No,' he said. 'You listen. Look after Evie this time. And I will get you the hard drive.'

'What do you expect me to do?'

'She's flying home in a few days. Make sure she does. I want to know she's safe. When I do, then you'll get the hard drive. Do you understand?'

'And what are you going to do?'

'I'll be around.'

'Tell me where you are, Martin. You're taking a big risk.'

Decker looked across the valley where he could see Sachs' houselights glinting in the darkness and the moon ringed with clouds above the trees.

Reeves said, 'Whatever you're looking for, Martin, it isn't there. It's gone. Leave the past alone...'

'Make sure Evie is on the plane,' Decker said. 'That's all.' And he hung up the phone. Evie would be on the A3 by now, he thought, and it wouldn't take Reeves long to track her down. She'd make mistakes.

Decker walked deep into the wood and, using the bungee ropes, set up the bivvy between holly bushes – a fallen tree, covered with brambles, shielded him from the tack. He'd be hard to spot, even if someone was looking for him. He climbed into the bivvy, got into the sleeping bag, and shut his eyes. During the night it began to rain.

*

It was still raining when Decker woke up, pointing the Heckler and Koch through the entrance of the bivvy, breath steaming from his mouth, his face bearded and eyes bloodshot.

The rain fell through the trees. It was still dark.

Decker took down the bivvy and packed it into the rucksack. Then, shouldering the rucksack, he set off through the woods. Gradually, it stopped raining.

He sat down and leant up against a tree and watched the valley below. Dawn seeped through the trees. He ate two bread rolls and sipped from a bottle of water. He broke up a bar of chocolate and ate a piece at a time. He observed sunlight cut the slope in half and mist roll through the valley. He heard the crowing and rapid wing beats of pheasants.

Lighting a cigarette, Decker dismantled the H&K, removing the magazine, the sound moderator and the slide. Then reassembling the handgun, clicked the magazine back in place and tucked it into his backpack.

He checked the time on his watch: 6:45. He removed his hat, ran his hand through his hair, and put the hat back on. He took a last puff on the cigarette, pushed the butt into the ground, and then stood up and moved on.

Tracking along the edge of the wood, he came to a spot with a good view of the house and stopped, got out his binoculars and scanned the area. Cars still parked out front. The guests must have stayed over.

Through binoculars, Decker zoomed in on the house: curtains still drawn; no one about. Then he looked across the courtyard, the outbuildings, and farm cottages; focusing in on one of the cottages with a smoking chimney; two Springer spaniels running round outside, tails wagging. Then he spotted a 4x4 Toyota Hilux, its front door open and engine running and remembered the vehicle from his first visit with Evie.

To his right, Decker saw a man appear from an outbuilding. He was wearing shooting breeks, carrying a bag of corn on his shoulder. He dropped it into the back of the Hilux and called the dogs. The two spaniels ran over and jumped into the back and the man shut the tailgate, then got into the front and drove away.

They must be shooting today, Decker thought. And he remembered what Reeves had said about taking a big risk, about how it was better to leave the past alone. But did he have any other choice?

He lowered the binoculars and, leaning up against a tree, took out the photo of his parents skiing and looked at it for a moment. His training had taught to keep moving, to keep disappearing. As a result, he must have slept in over a hundred different rooms these last few years, just as he had called himself many different names. But there was something in him that hadn't changed, that he couldn't outrun. He carried it around wherever he went, so that in the end, every room was much the same. It was something his training could never erase. He should have come up with a name for it by now, because it had always been there, right from the start, this "stray dog" in him.

Decker took up the binoculars again and scanned the wood behind the house: mist-severed treetops; pheasants parading up a gun ride. He returned the binoculars to the house, to Sachs' study window. And he wondered if Sachs had received the news yet. No hard drive, two men dead. He wondered what Schiller had said to him. Perhaps Sachs was still waiting to hear. Or maybe Sachs was in on it too.

But he didn't spend long thinking about these things. He needed that photo album back. He needed to identify the man that ordered the killing of his parents.

Through the binoculars, Decker followed the Toyota as it climbed the track between plots of maize. Reaching the wood, the driver got out, put a bag of corn on his shoulder, and trailed a line of corn along the field edge. Decker moved the binoculars down the slope now, spotting a line of gun pegs, and studied the surrounding terrain to get an idea of where to position himself. Vehicles would gather in the valley below, he thought; beaters would push through the cover crops and into the wood. Judging by the position of the cover crops, the main shooting would be concentrated round the back of the house and the horseshoe of woods there.

Decker saw movement at the front of the house now and trained the binoculars on the front door. One of the guests, in shooting breeks and red-gartered socks, left the house, crossed the driveway and opened the passenger door of a Range Rover. Decker saw the man reach inside the vehicle, retrieve a case off the seat and carry it back into the house with him.

Scaling the house through the binoculars, Decker noticed a woman drawing curtains, a man speaking on a mobile and the two children from last night playing on a window seat.

Decker lowered the binoculars again, letting them hang round his neck, and checked the time. It was 8:16. Guns on pegs at nine, he reckoned, for the start of the shooting. This gave him an hour. He would wait for Sachs to get out the house first and then make his move.

Decker rubbed his hands together and puffed warm air into them.

*

When the first vehicles moved off, Decker crept to the edge of the wood, lay in the prone position and put the binoculars on them.

A convoy of 4x4s moved down the driveway. Though the binoculars, he moved from one vehicle to the next. It was difficult to make out the people inside.

The vehicles passed through a gateway into a field and followed a track across the field. Half way into the field, they stopped in convoy. The guests got out, shouldered cartridge bags and gun slips, and made their way across to designated pegs. Several other vehicles appeared from the other end of the valley and pulled up behind the gun line, dogs jumping from the backs and following their handlers to positions behind the guns. These, Decker knew, were known as the "pickers-up", whose job it was to retrieve any shot or wounded game. Then the tapping of sticks began as the beaters set off through cover crops, spaniels zigzagging out in front of them. Pigeons broke from the wood first and crossed high over the gun line and an early shot went off.

Decker trained the binoculars on the faces of guests, moving along the gun line, and spotted Sachs on the second peg. His wife was sitting on a shooting stick several paces behind him with two Labradors. Lowering the binoculars, Decker put the last square of chocolate in his mouth as the shooting began.

*

After the first drive, Decker observed a Subaru estate drive from the house across a field to where they were gathered. Two women started unloading trays of drinks from the back. The beaters came out of the end of the cover crop; a horn was blown to signal the end of the drive. The pickers-up began sweeping the lower slopes behind them, collecting birds. After scanning the scene one last time, Decker made his move.

From the other side of the valley, Decker quickly headed down the slope towards the house, traversing hedgerows and belts of woodland.

Nearing the house, he picked up a stick and walked along the track. He hadn't gone far when he saw a Land Rover crossing an adjacent field.

He moved along the hedge-line and, crouching, waited beside a gateway. Through the hedge, he saw the woman driving was speaking on a mobile. She stopped in the gateway just long enough for Decker to step onto the tow bar.

They followed the track round to the house and turned into the courtyard. Reaching into the back of the Land Rover, Decker grabbed a couple of loose pheasants and jumped off the back of the moving vehicle.

The Land Rover stopped and the woman got out. Two people were hanging pheasants in one of the outbuildings. Decker walked round the vehicle with the pheasants.

'From the first drive,' he said to the woman

The woman said, 'Oh, thanks. Just chuck them in the back.'

Decker dropped the pheasants into the back of the Land Rover from which he'd just got them. The woman didn't give him a second look, disappearing into the outbuilding where Decker could hear laughter.

Decker entered at the back of the house. He walked along the corridor and straight up the stairs. At the top of the stairs he pulled out the H&K and walked down the corridor towards Sachs' study.

He pushed on the door, looked for the dog, but its bed was empty. He walked to the chair, squatted down, and put his hand underneath. The photo album was still there. He started skimming through the pages, stopping on the photo of Sachs, his father and a third, as yet unidentified man. Then he tucked the album into his inside jacket pocket and started towards the door.

He was opening the door when he heard a child's voice.

A little boy was standing in the corridor. He was holding a red and yellow fire engine, driving it along a banister rail, making a *brrrrming* sound.

All of a sudden, Decker's vision fractured.

He saw himself sitting on his grandmother's study floor again. It was day of his parent's funeral. He was looking through a photo album. A man in a dark suit was speaking to him. He saw his lips moving but couldn't hear the words.

The boy said, 'What are you doing?'

Decker's vision came back. He hid the gun behind his back. 'Hello there,' he said. 'What's your name?' He looked along the corridor, over the banister, then at the boy again.

'Peter,' the boy said.

'Hello, Peter. That's a nice fire engine.'

'Where's grandpa?'

'They're having drinks outside.'

The boy put the side of his hand in his mouth. 'What are you doing?'

'I'm helping your grandpa.'

The boy said, 'What's that behind your back?'

'Nothing.' Decker stuffed the gun into the back of his trousers and showed the boy both his hands.

'See. Nothing.' He waved his hand. 'Where's your mummy and daddy?'

'Downstairs. What's your name?'

'My name's Michael,' Decker said. 'I'm a friend of your grandfather's.'

A woman's voice called up the stairs. 'Peter. Are you up there?'

Decker glanced over the banisters and saw a woman climbing the stairs. He squatted down by the boy. 'I've got to go. It's been nice meeting you.'

The boy took his hand out his mouth. Saliva hung from his lower lip.

'Peter,' the woman said, approaching along the corridor.

Decker walked past her, saying, 'Hello.'

The woman said, 'Hello.' Then called after him, 'Excuse me. Do I know you?'

Decker left through the back door and headed across the courtyard.

A man called out, 'Can I help?'

Decker looked round. He saw a man in wax-proof chaps and Gore-Tex jacket, carrying a roll of baler twine and putting his hand above his eyes to shield out the sun. Then a security guard walked through the back door of the house, followed by the woman on the stairs. Decker saw the woman from the game ladder was also standing in the open now, hands on hips and pointing in his direction.

Decker clambered through the rhododendrons round the courtyard. The security guard was on his walkie-talkie. Decker headed up the slope, hearing footsteps behind him. They weren't shooting, though, which meant they had been told not to, he thought.

Decker weaved through the trees, vaulted a fence, slid down a slope, and ran down a field edge. At the bottom of the field he came to a road. A car approached from the direction of the house and stopped with a screech of tyres. Decker squatted behind the hedge and drew the Heckler and Koch.

He heard voices giving orders, the crackle of a walkie-talkie, and footsteps running along the tarmac. He edged along the hedge-line until he reached the stile then checked along the road.

A security guard was standing at the crossroads with his back to him. Between him and the security guard was the gateway he needed to reach to get back into the village.

Decker climbed over the stile and walked along the road towards the gateway. He was metres away when the security guard turned round.

Pointing the Heckler and Koch at him, Decker put his finger to his lips. The security guard showed him his empty hands.

Decker climbed the gate and started running again.

Soon, he was walking through the village. A man was throwing a ball for his dog on the village green. Decker reached the Nissan, got in, and started the engine. Lowering the sun visor, he pulled out into the road.

Passing the church, a car came towards him. A couple sat up front, one of them speaking on a phone. Decker rested his elbow on the window ledge and held his head in his hand. The car drove past without paying him any attention.

Decker joined the A24 and headed north to London.

43

Taking a parking ticket, Decker drove to the top floor of a multi-storey near Hammersmith. He parked the car, left the building and boarded a bus. The bus headed west on the A4 where it started to rain. Windscreen wipers beat across the glass. The bus passed Hyde Park and turned up Park Lane. Wet leaves blew across pavements.

At the top of Tottenham Court Road, Decker stepped off the bus. He walked along the Euston Road. He was wearing a beanie with a hood pulled over it. He entered a hotel on the Marylebone Road and paid in cash at the front desk.

He undressed, took a shower, and put on clean clothes. He opened a can of coke, sat on the bed and looked at the photo album. He looked at pictures of Sachs and his father. In a couple of the pictures, it was just the two of them. In others, there were groups of people or just shots of buildings or scenery. He worked his way to the end of the album, to the picture of Sachs, his father and the third man. He took this picture out of its pocket and looked at it under the desk lamp. In the picture, his father was shaking hands with an Arab in front of a half-constructed tower block while in the background, standing in a group of Arabs, was Sachs and the third man.

Decker put the photo into his pocket and the photo album under the bed, then left the hotel and got in a taxi. At the bottom of Bloomsbury Street, he got out the taxi and entered an internet café and googled "Howell".

There were several new articles. Relatives were speaking out against the bondage and sex game allegations, claiming Howell to be a "loving son", a "loyal and caring brother", who had nothing to do with such allegations. A so-called "intelligence analyst" said his death had a "professional air" about it – clean, neat and tidy, going on to suggest that evidence was not being shared. There were reportedly missing SIM cards and memory sticks taken from his flat. In another article, with the headline "Who is Hatton Alharbi?", speculations ran deeper. Police were following up leads investigating links between Alharbi, Howell and the British secret service. Apparently, property tycoon Alharbi, had originally been given asylum in Britain and been paid a retainer by government intelligence agencies of £3000 per month in exchange for information about state-sponsored terrorism in the Middle East. The article seemed well-sourced and credible. Decker took out a pen and paper and made a note of the journalist's name, knowing there may come a time when he might need him.

Next, Decker checked the bulletin board he'd shared with Evie. There was a message saying she was staying with her friend in Oxford, that everything was fine. She was flying home tomorrow. He read the message several times. His lips moved as he read. Reeves had been true to his word then, he thought.

Then Decker opened the bulletin board he'd shared with Howell and found the following message from Reeves: "Evie is safe. She flies tomorrow. Now it's your turn, Martin."

Decker sat back in his chair and glanced round the café. Two Turkish men, sharing the same computer, were speaking in Turkish on Skype, and at different screens two white male youths and a grey-headed black man. Satisfied no one was watching him, Decker took out the hard drive and plugged it into the USB port and tried opening it in different applications but without success.

He put the hard drive away again and went back to the bulletin board, remembering the profiles Howell had sent him of Zishan and Bendjedid. Opening each of their profiles, he read through them again. Then he wrote the initials Z and B on the piece of paper and connected them up to Alharbi's initial. Then he wrote down an H for Howell and an A for Alharbi and connected them up with an S for Sachs. He studied the piece of paper: Z+B=A, A+H=S.

But there was something missing.

He remembered the photographs he'd taken of Howell and opened the folder and started flicking through them: Howell leaving his apartment; Howell running; Howell shaking hands with friends in restaurants; exiting the underground; climbing in and out of taxis; and walking along pavements …

Coming to the end of the folder, Decker sat back in the chair and rubbed his eyes.

He looked at his piece of paper again.

Z+B=A, A+H=S

He added another equation: S (Sachs) +F (his father) =?

The ? must be the person in charge of Sachs and his father, he thought – the man in the photo … the man at his grandmother's house all those years ago who had taken the photo album from him on the day of his parent's funeral.

Decker started looking back through the photos again. He reached the photograph of Howell standing beside the park bench just off the King's Road. Next to him, the grey-headed old man in the tweed coat, holding the wooden-handled umbrella and dry cleaning.

Thinking he had seen the old man before, Decker scanned back through the photos.

And there he was again: walking along a street several paces behind Howell, speaking on a mobile phone; then again, sitting in a taxi along a street; in a restaurant, tipping the waiter; and finally, back to the park bench off the King's Road.

The old man had thin grey hair, a distinctive hawk-shaped nose and taut, wrinkled mouth as well as a recent suntan.

Decker enlarged the image of the two of them on the King's Road to full screen and then took out the photograph from his father's album of his father, Sachs and the unidentified third man.

Decker put the photograph up beside the screen image. It was him – the man in the photographs with his father and Sachs. The same man, Decker bet, that had taken the photo album off him on the day of his parent's funeral.

Zooming in on his face, Decker looked into the old man's eyes so he wouldn't forget. This was the man Howell had trusted, he thought, bringing him information on what he thought was a leak between Sachs – his handler – and Alharbi. The man most probably who who'd had his parents killed. But where was he?

Decker zoomed out from the old man's face and panned round the photo, looking for something, a clue, a starting-point: a mother and a child; two teenagers holding hands; office workers; a street cleaner. Then back to the old man on the bench again; the item of clothing in a plastic cover folded over his arm. He zoomed in on the item of clothing, a woman's jacket, it looked like. He started to examine the writing on the cover. He zoomed in as much as he could. It was the name of a dry cleaning company. He couldn't make out the name but saw half a postcode. He entered the postcode into Google, adding the words "dry cleaner". He got a match. He wrote down an address near Regent's Park and left the internet café.

*

A coke can blew across the pavement outside Baker's Street station where a street vendor was handing out free newspapers. Decker stopped and lit a cigarette, checking the address on the slip of paper, and then crossed the road.

They were still open. Stamping out his cigarette outside, Decker pushed on the door and a bell rang. An Asian man came to the till and asked if he could help.

'Yes, my wife picked up some things yesterday. But one of the jackets was missing.'

'What was the name?'

'Howell. Mr Howell.'

The Asian turned the page of a large ledger and ran his finger down a column of numbers. Decker watched him checking them off with a column of names. It was a simple system, each person being given a number, then names and number being crossed out when items were picked up.

Decker looked round through the shop front. The street was quiet.

'I can't find your name here,' the man said. 'I'm sorry.'

Decker said, 'I know,' and grabbed the ledger.

The man saying, 'What are you doing? You can't have that,' as he tried to wrestle the book back off him.

Decker didn't have time to argue and pushed him out the way. The Asian man fell backwards into a rail of clothes.

Decker flicked through the pages of the ledger to the day of Howell's meeting. Then tore out the page and left the dry cleaners.

He dialled as he walked. He had a choice of three numbers. Decker reasoned the old man would have picked up the jacket on his way to see Howell. The first number Decker tried a woman answered and Decker asked her if her husband had picked up the dry cleaning. *No, she had, was something wrong? No, everything was fine, just routine, he was sorry to disturb her.* Decker went to the next number, a man this time. He tried the same spiel. *No, it had been his wife, is everything okay?* The third number rang twelve times before a woman answered by giving a company

212

name, then saying, 'Can I help?' Decker was writing down the name of the company as he hung up.

Leaves skated across the pavement. Decker turned twice, looking at the address he had written down. At a junction, he spotted the street sign. Google maps had given him an address for a firm of solicitors that matched the name the woman had given him.

He scanned his surroundings. There was a small park surrounded by black iron railings and a crescent of tall houses. On an adjacent road, pillared, white stucco-fronted buildings divided into flats and offices, one of them, the firm of solicitors.

Decker walked round the park, looking through the trees at the building. He stopped on the corner, lit a cigarette in cupped hands and remembered Evie.

He checked his watch. It was 17:37. Lights were on in the building. If it was an office people should be leaving soon, he thought.

Decker smoked and waited. The wind gusted through the tall plane trees.

At 18:06, Decker saw a young woman in three-quarter length grey overcoat and leather ankle boots leave the building. She looked late 20s, Decker thought. She was wrapping a red scarf round her neck and checking her phone for messages. She walked straight on towards the station.

Ten minutes later, Decker saw a middle-aged woman, short spiky blonde hair, blue raincoat, leave the building, followed by two men in suits.

Decker looked up at the windows of the building. The lights were still on.

He kept waiting.

An old woman walked her dog through the park. Decker took out his phone and pretended to be taking a phone call when she walked past.

He waited another hour, but no one else left the building. Maybe the old man had gone home earlier, Decker thought, or just wasn't at the office that day. There was a variety of possibility. He'd need to check again. It was getting dark when he returned to the hotel.

*

Lying on the bed, Decker looked at the photograph of Sachs, his father and the third man. He went through the photo album again. The TV was on in the corner. He'd bought a salami and mozzarella baguette on the way back. He'd opened a bottle of beer. A cigarette was behind his ear, although the hotel was no smoking.

Decker didn't remember much of his parents. Not really. He liked to think there were feelings, snapshots of memory, but they were mostly very distant, and many of them built around photos he'd seen. Decker turned the pages of the photo album, looking at each photo in turn. Most faces he didn't recognise. Some he felt he had seen before in other photos.

Then he looked at the photo of his mother and father on the ski slope. For years, he believed they had died in an accident. Accidents happened all the time, he had reasoned.

I think you've known all along. There are no accidents. No coincidences.

Decker wondered if this was what he had been taught to think or what he really thought. He wondered if he knew the difference anymore.

Whatever you're looking for, Martin, it isn't there. It's gone. Leave the past alone.

He looked at other pictures: Sachs' younger self; a view from a rooftop in Jerusalem; the foundations of a new building in Asia somewhere; pictures of people in offices, standing on bridges, in restaurants, on boats. Some subjects didn't look like they knew their photo was being taken. Others did. He wondered who was taking the pictures. They lacked the remove of surveillance photos yet were hardly tourist snaps – fell somewhere between. Someone on the inside, Decker thought; another work colleague, someone who'd become friends with his father. Then it dawned on him: the one person missing from the photographs – Mr Charles.

A long time ago I knew your father.

The long rectangular office; Mr Charles gazing out of The Compound windows.

We worked together on an engineering project in Abu Dhabi. He was a most likeable man. It was a terrible accident.

Perhaps Mr Charles was taking pictures for the company portfolio when his father had been killed. He must have known about Sachs and kept quiet. Twenty years on, Howell had found something out … the hard drive … contacted him. Set the ball in motion.

Lesson one. Remember: acknowledging something as a coincidence is a sure sign you don't know what's really going on.

Decker stood up, picturing Evie with her friend in a house in Oxford; one of Reeves' men parked up outside, drinking a Starbucks; Evie chatting with her friend, bottle of wine, cigarettes; but then, out of view, Schiller entering the house through the back, wearing gloves, treading softly.

Decker picked up the pay-as-you-go and rang Reeves; seven rings, then the hiss of white noise, the click, the voice.

'Hello Martin. I've been waiting for you to call. You got my message?'

'Where's Evie?'

'I told you. She's safe. She's flying tomorrow.'

'How safe?'

'Someone's with her now.'

'Let's hope so.' Decker checked the window; a helicopter passing overhead.

Reeves said, 'One of our men will take her to the airport tomorrow.'

Decker said, 'What about Sachs?'

'What about him?'

'He's involved.'

'Martin, I told you to leave this alone.'

Decker said nothing.

There was a pause.

Reeves said, 'I've done what you asked, Martin. It's your turn now.'

Decker said, 'He killed Howell.'

'It was unfortunate. Now where's the hard drive, Martin?'

'I'm sending you a photograph. Maybe it will jog your memory.'

'Leave it alone, Martin. Nothing good will come of it.'

Decker hung up.

44

The middle-aged woman with short spiky blonde hair and blue raincoat crossed the road and walked up the steps to the white stucco-fronted Regency building. She entered a code on a keypad, spoke into the intercom, and went into the building. She was the first to arrive.

Decker was sitting on a bench in the park, reading a free newspaper and drinking a black coffee. A groundsman had opened the gates at eight o'clock, emptied the bins, and driven off in a van. The sun was shining. A gap in laurel bushes gave Decker a view of the house.

He hadn't given up.

The young woman, in cropped leather jacket and heeled ankle boots, arrived next. She was wearing her hair up today, Decker noticed, maybe off somewhere after work. She walked straight up the steps, spoke into the intercom and went into the building. The suits arrived soon afterwards, one of them carrying a stack of files, his tie flapping round his neck as he hurried across the road, but still no old man.

It was 8:45.

Half a dozen pigeons landed on the grass, looking for food. Decker turned to the back of the newspaper and started on the crossword. A shadow line moved across the small square. The old woman walked her dog through the park. The pigeons flew up to the trees.

A little after ten o'clock, there was still no sign of the old man. Maybe he worked from home today, Decker thought, maybe he'd retired.

Decker folded up the newspaper and walked out of the park. Traffic crawled along the main road. He crossed at the lights and entered an internet café. Logging in, he scanned the photograph of Sachs, his father and the unidentified third man, and then uploaded it to the bulletin board for Reeves to see. Next, he typed in the address of the building he'd been watching – a firm of solicitors, Noble and Stiles. There was a legitimate-looking website, with a list of partners and support staff, although the old man's picture wasn't there. He then looked at the building on Google Maps. He wasn't sure what he was looking for. He wondered if he was wasting his time; wondered if he was at a dead end. He looked again at the surveillance photographs; look at the pictures of the old man sitting on the bench off the King's Road; zoomed in on his face, his wristwatch, his shoes, the writing on the dry cleaner's bag, compared it with the photograph of 20 years ago. There was no doubt it was the same man. Maybe then he'd got the wrong number from the dry cleaners, Decker thought. Or maybe the old man had given the number of his solicitors, not his place of work.

Next, Decker checked the bulletin boards and found a message from Evie saying she leaving for the airport today, and started to write back a reply, but didn't know what to say. He deleted his beginning several times then wrote that he would be in touch. But he deleted that as well. He ended up not sending a reply.

He left the internet café and entered a Starbucks across the street where he bought another coffee and pocketed two extra sachets of sugar on his way out. The sun shone through a gap in the buildings. A flattened cardboard box lay in the shade of a shop front. A street cleaner was sweeping the street.

Crossing the road, Decker weaved between the traffic and headed back along the main road, passing students stood outside an art college, smoking and speaking in Spanish, as the sound of the ambulance receded in the distance.

He checked his watch at 10:32. A few minutes later, he was approaching the solicitors' building when he saw a taxi pull in across the street and a man get out.

A tweed coat was folded over his arm. He used the wooden-handled umbrella like a walking stick. He was carrying an iPad in the other hand. You could tell the soles of his shoes were leather by the sound they made.

Decker swung left round the crescent. He saw two builders sat on a bench in the park eating sandwiches. Pigeons were gathered round them, picking up crumbs.

Decker stopped on the corner behind a van and peered round the side of it.

The old man walked up the steps of the house, buzzed and entered the building.

Bingo.

*

When the builders left the park, Decker sat down on the bench and continued with the crossword. Finishing that, he started on the Sudoku.

It was getting dark. The groundsman came round to lock the park and Decker left by the rear exit, walked to the end of the street, and waited round the corner.

The young woman left the building first, speaking on her mobile and running across the road in her heeled ankle boots. The old man was next to leave, buttoning up his tweed coat, umbrella under his arm, iPad in his pocket, and headed towards the main road.

Hood up, Decker was on him like a rash.

Reaching the main road, the old man stood at the kerb and flagged down a taxi. A hundred metres down the road Decker did the same.

The old man's cab stopped at a set of lights. Behind him, Decker could see him in the back speaking on his phone.

They continued along Victoria Embankment. Building lights reflected on the river.

They stopped and queued at traffic lights on Grosvenor Road, the old man's taxi weaving forward in the queue, then headed along Chelsea Embankment and turned right into Oakley Street.

Seeing the old man's taxi indicate to turn right again, Decker leant forward and said to the driver, 'What's down there?'

The driver said, 'Houses – expensive ones.'

Decker noted the road sign, Phene Street, and said, 'Keep going.'

As they passed the turning for Phene Street, Decker looked back over his shoulder to check the taxi wasn't just making a U-turn. It wasn't.

The driver said, 'What's going on, mate?'

Decker said, 'Pull up here.'

Decker paid the driver, crossed the road and jogged back down the pavement. Turning into Phene Street, he started walking. Ahead of him, he saw the old man's taxi stopped in the middle of the road and the old man walking up some steps to a house.

Decker hung back, making a mental note of the house number, and watched as the taxi went past.

*

Approximately 15 minutes later, Decker entered an internet café on the Fulham Road. There was no message from Reeves, which meant he hadn't seen the photo. Using street view, Decker checked the old man's house and surrounding area on Google Maps. He noted there was a small park at the end of the old man's street, a low stonewall, no railings, so accessible at all times of day. This presented opportunities. All he needed was for him to have a dog and he could catch up with him there.

He tracked along the streets, checking out each available exit route, and links to main roads and public transport. The area was quiet, the green space at the end of the road an added bonus – he could escape on foot to South Kensington in less than 20 minutes. From there, his options were various: Piccadilly Line to Heathrow, 50 minutes; Circle or District Line to Victoria, four minutes; Piccadilly Line to King's Cross St Pancras, 17 minutes.

Decker would do it in the morning, he thought, when the old man left the house. He reckoned he was an early riser. He could only hope he had a dog or liked a stroll. What if he ordered a taxi to his door or left with his wife? He didn't have time for a period of protracted counter surveillance. He would have to take his chances. Wait to hear from Reeves and then move.

Decker ate a steak and kidney pie in a pub. As he ate, he thought about tomorrow; thought about taking the Eurostar to Paris; thought about a room; about lying low for a while; then travelling south. He would book a ticket as soon as he heard from Reeves confirming the money was in place.

Leaving the pub, Decker stayed on foot. It was 22:19. Traffic streamed past in both directions, every other vehicle it seemed a bus or taxi at this hour. He stopped and lit a cigarette. Traffic lights changed in sequence along the road, the sound of police sirens in the distance. Across glass-fronted buildings, he observed acres of deserted office space, rows and rows of vacant computers and empty meeting rooms, and then along street level, shuttered shop fronts and sleeping bags in doorways.

The wind swirled, sheets of newspapers skidded along pavements, carrying the smell of petrol fumes and fast food. He headed north.

As he cut across the city, Decker's mind turned to Evie: thinking about how she would have she left the country by now; picturing a train ride from the airport; a car journey to the hospital. If her father was about to die, he thought, her mum would already be there, the brother too. All that was left was her; the father waiting for his daughter; waiting to die. He knew people were able to hold off death like this. Sometimes it worked the other way, of course. People died in hotel rooms, in bedsits, or slumped over steering wheels not having spoken to anyone for days.

Decker passed a pay phone and, checking round himself, stopped and went in. Reeves answered after just three rings.

'Good evening, Martin. How are you?'

'Who is he?'

'I take you are referring to the man in that picture you sent me.'

'Who is he?'

'His name was Giles Templar. Now let's talk about the hard drive.'

'What did he do?'

'You're back in London, aren't you?'

'What did he have to do with my father?'

'Martin, I've been very patient with you. But you need to get the hard drive to us.'

'You said "was".'

'That's right. Giles Templar is dead.'

Decker remembered the book in Sachs's study by Giles Templar; old buddies who had moved on to other things while his parents were in the ground.

'What was he to my father?' he said.

'He was head of your father's division.'

'He was giving the orders then.'

'Martin, it was 25 years ago. What do you hope to achieve with this?'

'He's still alive.'

Reeves said, 'What are you talking about?'

'He's still alive.'

'Martin, I have his file in front of me. Giles Templar died on—'

'The file is wrong. He was meeting Howell.'

'Martin, listen to me – Templar is dead.'

'No. Mr Charles and my father are dead. Sachs and Templar are still alive; still doing business. Otherwise people like Alharbi wouldn't be around. And people like Howell wouldn't be getting killed.'

'Martin, whatever you're thinking, leave it alone. The past is gone—'

'I will contact you tomorrow with the hard drive.'

'Martin!'

45

Decker checked out the hotel early the next morning. The receptionist stood beside him, saying, 'Is that all your luggage, sir?' Decker nodded, slipping his arms through the straps of the rucksack. The H&K was secured in a makeshift holster round his waist. He would get rid of it in a bin on the way to South Kensington after visiting Templar. He had already located the bin.

Decker crossed the Marylebone Road, thrusting his hands into his coat pockets.

Fog showed up in car headlights. The air was cold and damp and Decker hunched up his shoulders.

He entered Euston station, took the escalator down to the underground, and boarded a half-empty train. It was 7:00 by his watch.

Decker stood by the doors and looked at reflections in the carriage window, keeping his eyes to himself. Other passengers were reading newspapers or playing with their mobiles. When the train stopped and picked up other passengers, Decker looked up and made a note of who was getting on and getting off.

He changed lines at Victoria.

Boarded a District Line train and stood by the doors for one stop before getting off at Sloane Square.

Decker left the station, picking up a free newspaper on his way out, and headed down Lower Sloane Street. After about 200 metres, he turned right into Turks Row.

The fog was cold and damp on his face. He kept his hands in his pockets and looked straight ahead. A woman passed him walking a small dog on an extendable lead, then a man in a suit and bike helmet pushing a bike. Decker had the route memorised and didn't hesitate at any point.

Franklin's Row became St Leonard's Terrace.

He went into the small park at the end of Phene Street. He looked through the trees at the house. There were lights on in the top windows. He checked his watch: 7:45. It was getting to that time, he thought, imagining boiling kettles and popping toast.

He sat on a bench at the rear of the park. He took out the newspaper, folded it in half, and started on the crossword. A squirrel came down a tree and hopped across the grass, Decker raising his eyes. The squirrel climbed on top of the bin and began eating something in its claws. Decker watched it for a moment. Then, all of a sudden, the squirrel stopped eating, turned its head, and started flicking its tail over its head.

Decker looked towards the park entrance, hearing the sound of footsteps approaching along the road. The squirrel jumped onto the trunk of a tree and Decker put his hand under his jacket and grasped the handle of the Heckler and Koch.

A young man in suit and overcoat entered the park, walking briskly while looking at the screen of his mobile, headphones in, rucksack on his back.

Decker lowered his head and kept very still and watched him exit the park and continue along the main road, pretty sure the man hadn't even noticed him. Maybe only later tonight on his commute home, when checking news updates on his phone or looking at the *Evening Standard*, would the man realise what had happened and reality would strike as it dawned of him how someone had been shot on his route to work that morning; wondering if he'd seen anything or if he could have helped. Then maybe later, to a wife or girlfriend, he'd muse over a glass of wine about what may or maybe not have happened if he'd come along a moment later. Could it have been him? He would feel lucky somehow and would want to do something about it. At the very least, pay his respects to the dead. But the feeling would pass. And nothing would happen. Life would continue. He would remember it only occasionally.

The squirrel came down the trunk of the tree.

Decker released his grip on the H&K, took his hand out from under his jacket and looked at the house again. Several minutes passed before he saw any movement. A downstairs curtain opened slowly on a corded track. When it was fully open, Decker saw Templar pass in front of the window and leave the room.

Decker stood up and moved forward between the trees. He saw a door open at the back of the house and a woman appeared, calling a pet's name: 'Sukie... Sukie.'

A black cat climbed down through a wisteria growing up the side of the house and hopped down next to the woman.

'There you are,' the woman said.

Decker thought about ringing at the front. But he didn't want to involve the woman. Wait until Templar leaves the house, he thought, or for someone to arrive – a postm n or cleaner. Either way, he had Templar where he wanted him.

Decker took out his mobile and pressed the only saved number in the phone. Reeves answered after two rings; obviously waiting for him.

'The money?' Decker said.

'It's done. As you asked.'

'Good. The Thistle Hotel, Victoria Station.'

'Time?'

Decker saw the woman shut the French doors. 'I'll let you know.'

'You have the hard drive?'

'Yeah.'

There was a pause. Reeves said, 'Where are you, Martin?'

Decker shifted round the tree as a blind was lifted – the woman at the window this time. Decker said, 'Who ordered the killing?'

'What killing?'

'Stray dog.'

Reeves hesitated. 'They couldn't take risks,' he said. 'It needed shutting down.'

'Who carried it out?'

'There was a stray dog, Martin. It was never anything personal.'

'Sachs?' Decker said.

There was a pause. Reeves said, 'He was in your father's section. It had to be someone close ... on the inside ... who would keep it quiet.'

'And Templar gave the word and covered it up.'

'What choice did he have?'

Decker watched two wood pigeons fly into an ash tree in a neighbouring garden.

Reeves said, 'Where are you, Martin?'

Across the street, Decker saw Templar's front door open and then Templar emerge, pulling on his tweed coat. Decker flattened himself against a tree and peeked round the side. Templar was speaking on a mobile.

Templar turned to pull the door shut behind him.

'Talk to me, Martin,' Decker heard Reeves say down the phone.

Templar stood on the doorstep, turned round, and looked across the street. He held the phone to his ear but wasn't speaking now. Decker looked at him, then saw his lips move, saying his name 'Martin' into the phone.

At the same moment Decker saw him say his name he heard it over the phone.

'Martin…' The line crackled. 'Are you still there?'

The wind blew strands of hair off his head. So Reeves was Templar.

'Speak to me,' the man on the steps said.

Decker felt his jaw muscle flex. He said, 'What do you want to hear?'

'Tell me where you are?'

Decker removed the gun from his pocket. 'I'm with Templar.'

'You can see him?'

'Yeah. I can see him.'

The man on the doorstep looked left and then right. He started down the steps of his house.

'What does he look like?'

'Like a stray dog.'

'Stay there. We'll pick him up. Don't move, Martin—'

Decker stepped out from behind the tree, holding the Heckler and Koch at his side and dropping the phone on the grass.

The man on the pavement turned his head, saw him coming, and lowered the phone.

Decker levelled the gun at the man's chest.

'Giles Templar?' Decker said.

'Martin,' he said. 'You've got this wrong.'

Decker stepped forward, breathing steadily.

The old man said, 'Giles Templar died with your father. Twenty years ago. My name is Simon Reeves now. Leave the past alone, Martin.'

Decker raised the gun to the old man's chest. The old man didn't look away.

'You're making a mistake,' the old man said.

'I doubt it.'

Decker's finger closed around the trigger of the Heckler and Koch. Fog curled over rooftops. The two pigeons broke from the ash tree at the sound of the shot.

The old man held his chest. Blood spread across his coat.

Decker's eyes narrowed. He shot again. A second hole ruptured in his chest. The old man fell to his knees. He gulped for breath. Blood ran from the sleeve of his coat.

Decker shot him a third time, this time through the head. The old man collapsed on the pavement. Blood pooled.

Decker slipped the gun into his pocket and crossed the road.

46

A small delivery lorry stopped at the gates of Sachs's country estate. Through a window, the driver spoke into the intercom. He was wearing a baseball cap and orange fleece. His name was Martin Decker; he was here on a job. The gates opened and the lorry continued down the drive, accelerating through the gears. The sun was shining across the fields. It was mid-morning.

The lorry parked in front of the house. There were no other cars today. Birds were singing.

Decker walked round to the back of the lorry.

A young girl came through the door of the house. 'Hi, there,' she said.

Decker smiled and opened the double doors at the back of the van and looked at the order numbers on the crates. The real driver of the lorry was tied up in the back, his mouth taped. Decker found the right tray and followed the woman inside.

On his way out, Decker asked the girl if he could use the loo. She pointed him downstairs. 'Thanks,' he said.

Decker went up the stairs not down. He was drawing out the Heckler and Koch as he walked along the corridor. He could hear children's voices playing outside in the garden.

Sachs was asleep in his chair. An open newspaper lay on his lap. Decker saw the dog was running outside with the children. His wife was with them, talking to a gardener.

Decker stood in front of Sachs' chair and, removing his hat, pointed the gun at him.

Sachs woke up with a start, grabbing the armrests, the newspaper falling off his lap. 'What's this?' he said. 'What are you doing here?'

'It's over,' Decker said.

Sachs sat up. 'You little shit. Get out.'

'Templar is dead. Sit down.'

Sachs lowered himself back into the chair. Decker noticed he was wearing slippers. A recently drunk cup of coffee stood on the table beside him. Decker saw Sachs' eyes follow him round the room. Today, they weren't so cool.

'So you're the boy,' Sachs said.

'That's right.'

'And you've come back.'

'It seems so.'

Sachs pushed himself up in the chair. 'What do you want?' he said.

Decker's jaw tightened, his eyes narrowed. His finger rested on the trigger.

Sachs said, 'You want money, is that it?'

Decker said, 'You betrayed my father.'

'Oh, please, grow up. No one betrayed anyone. Just tell me what it is you want. And let's get this over with.'

Decker shot him three times in quick succession. Sachs slipped down in the wingback armchair, his arms hanging over the armrests and head lolling to one side. The back of the chair was covered in blood and there were holes in the upholstery where the bullets had passed straight through his skull.

The children were still running round outside. The dog was holding its head in the air, scenting the wind. Decker closed the door behind him, pocketing the gun.

He climbed back into the Sainsbury's van and started the engine. A loose bag blew across the driveway from under the van. Periodically checking his side mirror, Decker drove down the drive, keeping his speed steady, and re-joined the road.

After about half a mile, Decker pulled into a lay-by alongside a Renault Laguna, got out and opened the back of the lorry and ripped off the driver's gag. The driver sat there shaking and didn't move. Decker climbed into the Renault and drove off, dust clearing the hedgerows.

47

Later, the Renault passed through a small country village and turned up a dead-end track towards the downs. At the end of the track, where the tarmac ran out, the Renault stopped on the flint against the fence-line. With the engine turned off, Decker looked through the windscreen across the downland plateau. Beyond the grass headlands and undulations of plough, a glimmer of sea in the distance. He opened the car door. The hiss of downland wind whipped round him. He zipped up his coat and pulled up its collar.

He walked along the Ridgeway, a narrow chalk and flint track. The path rose to the horizon. Decker walked with his hands in his pockets. The wind ripped into the side of his face. Seagulls and crows lifted off a ploughed field. He came to an old barn. Corrugated iron sheets flapped in the downland wind. Cattle stood round a hayrack in the field, the ground muddy and well-trodden.

Decker sheltered in the barn and looked back the way he'd come. His could see the Renault in the distance, about half a mile away. He sat down on a bale of straw and looked at the view.

After a few minutes, a second car appeared up the slope and parked alongside the Renault. Decker moved his eyes but nothing else. The barbed wire juddered in the wind; chalk dust and hayseed blew off the track.

Decker's phone started to ring. He answered it on the seventh ring. A voice said, 'Hello, Martin. I got your message.'

'The car's open,' Decker said. 'You'll find it inside.'

Decker stepped out of the barn and looked towards the two cars. He saw a man get out, holding a phone to his ear, his jacket flapping in the wind. Decker watched him walk over to the Renault, open the door and reach inside. He retrieved the hard drive. The man shut the car door and looked round himself, still holding the phone to his ear.

'You sure you want to do this?' the man said over the phone.

'Yeah,' Decker said. 'I'm sure.'

The wind made a hissing sound, the line crackled.

The voice on the other end said, 'They cleaned up Templar. There's no word of it in the press.'

'And Sachs?'

'They found him yesterday.'

Remembering the boy, Decker said. 'Who found him?'

'His wife apparently.'

'Alharbi?'

'No one knows.'

There was a pause. The man said, 'What are you going to do?'

Decker looked across the rolling chalk downland to the banded grey horizon where you could see a shimmer of sea. 'Travel,' he said.

'I guessed you would.'

They both didn't speak for a moment. The wind hissed at either end of the line.

The man said, 'Well, if you need anything…'

'Yeah… I know.'

'I shall have someone pick up the car. Goodbye, then.'

'Yeah, goodbye.'

Decker watched as the car turned on the patch of flint and headed down the slope. When it was out of sight, Decker put a cigarette in his mouth and dug in his pockets for a lighter.

Lighting the cigarette, Decker narrowed his eyes in the wind. He saw a crow land on a fence post and caw against the leaden skyline. The moment reminded him of something a long time ago but he couldn't think what. Setting off in the opposite direction, Decker had something he had to do.

The downland track sloped away, a meandering, tapering white path, down to a water trough and muddy patch of ground where it rose again up the other side. With his hands in his pockets, Decker followed the track through the dip and up the other side, his figure growing smaller and smaller until he disappeared over the horizon.

*

Later that afternoon, Decker climbed a stile next to a metal gate and followed the footpath at a right angle. He walked along the edge of a field of kale; houses, a church in the distance. There were white chalk marks on his boots and the insides of his trousers. It had started to spot with rain.

Decker walked round the church. The loose gravel stuck to the mud on his shoes. The square tower, the flint walls, was as he remembered. A large beech tree stood at the rear of the churchyard, the wind tossing its upper branches.

Decker stood in front of a headstone, then, squatting down, read the inscription: "James and Annabel Decker". The rain pattered the ground. The wind whistled. He took his hand out of his pocket and wiped the rain off his nose. He stayed there for some time, the light fading.

When he looked up, an elderly man and a woman were walking towards the church. An outside light clicked on as they unlocked the door. The woman turned and noticed Decker standing in the churchyard. She had a wrinkled, weather-tanned face, and clear blue eyes. Decker felt a moment of connection with her like sometimes happens with complete strangers. They looked at each other for a second and the woman smiled before disappearing into the church.

Decker crossed the churchyard and left through the gate.

It was getting dark. A damp thin mist drifted in across the downs, the gloom closing in.

48

When he woke up, Decker stared at large advertising hoardings through the windows. He couldn't remember if the adverts had changed since he was last here but it seemed like they hadn't. A crane was lifting steel girders in the distance and the sun was shining. The train pulled into Gare du Nord.

Decker showed a recently made passport at customs. The woman in the booth looked at the photo in the passport and then at him and then passed the passport back. He took the escalator down to the Metro, where three buskers were playing guitars and an accordion in the underpass. Walking past, Decker felt like he had heard it all before, and it wasn't a good feeling.

He rode the train with his head turned to the window. He exited at Sèvres-Babylone near a park. He drank a coffee in a bar, consumed a sachet of sugar, tying the empty sachet neatly in a knot before leaving it on his saucer.

He waited on the opposite side of the street to a large, glass-fronted office block.

It grew dark. He followed a young woman from the glass office block. The woman's name was Annie, his old girlfriend. After ten minutes, he saw Annie enter a bar where she met with three friends – a girl and two men. Decker didn't recognise any of them. They drank and ordered food. Decker sat in a corner with a newspaper and completed the Sudoku. He observed them laughing and chatting over their food. After an hour, they moved outside and took coffee under the awning and smoked. They appeared to be enjoying life. Settling the bill, the four of them walked down the road together. At a junction, they said goodbye. Two of the friends walked one way while Annie and one of the men crossed the road.

They were holding hands and laughing.

They waited at a bus stop together and Annie put one of her hands in the man's coat pocket and kissed him. Decker stood on the opposite side of the street and watched. Then he watched them get on a bus and drive away. He didn't follow them, knowing enough not to. He said goodbye to that part of his life.

*

An hour later, he checked into an internet café and searched for information about Sachs. The first article he turned up referred to local landowner and property tycoon Jonathan Sachs being found dead at his home in Surrey. Cause of death: suicide. His death was not being treated as suspicious in any way. Then Decker changed his search to Howell and turned up an article with the headline: "An Inside Job – what happened to Daniel Howell?", published that morning, and read about the events leading up to Howell's disappearance from his contact with Bandar in Paris to his recent secondment to London. It talked about his maths and language abilities and his fast-track career. It looked again at previous reports of his body lying undiscovered for a week, the sex-games and bondage allegations. There were quotes from Howell's sister, claiming how you couldn't have wished for a more "loving brother", while an old neighbour insisted "he wouldn't have hurt a fly". Howell was a "private man", they all agreed, who "loved his work". There was another picture of Howell in running strip. They were still calling him "the marathon man". Family and close friends attended a private service.

Opening a new window on the browser, Decker background checked the sister, turning up a picture of her at a charity event at her children's primary school. There was a sibling likeness, nothing more.

Returning to the main article, Decker read about Howell's involvement with Hatton Alharbi. Several years ago, MI6 had indeed put Alharbi on a retainer contract for information about state-sponsored terrorism in the Middle East, only it had more to do with energy prices and real estate than terrorism. Concerned that something wasn't right, Howell had raised the alarm to his section chief, Jonathan Sachs. As Decker read this, he dragged the cursor over Sachs' name and highlighted it. The writer of the article was joining up the jots, as Decker knew he would when he'd decided to give him the hard drive containing all the names of those involved in the elite cartel that had

232

led to his father's death. This wasn't so much about terrorism as it was about money and greed; a group of individuals who helped each other become rich and stay that way; trading in passports, property, energy, intelligence – whatever it took. You scratch my back and I'll scratch yours. So long as no one finds out. But Howell had. Just as Mr Charles had and his father had before him. Then, in the next paragraph, there it was, the first mention of "Stray dog", an inside job that began over 20 years ago.

Decker booked a flight for the next morning, leaving out of Charles de Gaulle at just after ten o'clock.

Leaving the internet café, he crossed the river. Lights on the water, cruise boats –"the city of light", they called Paris.

On a side street, Decker went into a small restaurant. There was a television on in the corner; an older clientele, couples and solitary men. Decker ate a bowl of chicken stew and drunk a carafe of wine. Then he ordered a second carafe and sat outside on a plastic chair and smoked two cigarettes and finished the wine with some olives. Then he headed north.

He told himself stories about his parents. He thought about Annie, glad she had found someone else, knowing it was better like this. He'd come back because he'd said he would. Now he could leave.

He crossed the road ahead of some lights, losing his footing on the kerb and stumbling. He picked himself up.

The road was nearly empty. His breath smoked in the cold air.

He heard the car first, then footsteps tracking behind him. Without looking round, he turned off the road he was on, thinking he would lose the car, split his tail. But someone must have anticipated this and been waiting. A blow hit him across the back and he folded up like a bag of corn dropped from the back of a truck.

*

'Out celebrating,' a voice said.

The interior of the vehicle stank of stale cigarettes. There was a throbbing across Decker's neck as he sat up. He felt his hands tied behind his back.

'Or was it to help you sleep?' The voice came from the front of the car.

Decker saw there was also a man sitting next to him, and he was pointing a gun at him. That made three of them – two up front and the guy next to him. And he didn't recognise any of them. He glanced out the window and saw they were on the ring road heading out of Paris. It was still dark.

The voice from the front said, 'Someone wants to speak to you. Just sit back and relax.'

The man next to him motioned with his gun and Decker sat back in his seat. The driver accelerated across lanes, checking his mirrors.

In less than an hour, they were in the countryside, full beam on an empty road, the sat-nav giving commands in French. No one was speaking. The guy in the passenger seat was smoking a cigarette.

They drove on like this for about 20 minutes, then pulled off the road and followed a farm track. They drove to the end of the track where there was a line of poplar trees and an open-ended barn and stopped. The driver cut the engine and turned off the lights. No one spoke. The man in the passenger seat lit another cigarette. He lowered the window and checked his watch.

Within a few minutes, another car turned off the road and approached them along the track, headlights juddering up the slope. When the car was about 100 metres away, the man in the passenger seat flicked his cigarette out the window, turned round and said, 'Get out.'

Decker looked round. The guy next to him cut the tie round his wrist and gestured with the gun. Decker edged along the seat, opened the door and stepped out onto a stone track.

The wind blew in the tops of the poplars. The door shut behind him and the car started up and drove away, flicking up loose stones under its tyres.

Decker turned and faced the approaching car, squinting in the full beam. The car stopped in front of him, the engine left running, and two men got out. One of them was wearing a leather bomber-style jacket, the other a long navy overcoat. They walked towards him. The man in front had his hands in his trousers pockets. The man behind him was holding a gun and walked with a limp. Decker recognised the men to be Alharbi and Schiller.

'Hello again,' Alharbi said. 'You've been busy, haven't you?'

Decker didn't respond.

'I need a name,' Alharbi said, walking right up to him and looking him in the eye.

Decker just stood there and stared straight back at him.

Alharbi said, 'They're going to kill me, do you understand?'

Decker said nothing.

'This is not a game, you piece of shit! Speak to them.'

'That's not how it works,' Decker said.

Alharbi took out a Berretta 92 Inox with stainless barrel and slide and pushed the muzzle into Decker's cheek.

'No, this is how it works,' he said. 'You tell me what I want to know and I won't blow your fucking head off! You understand that?'

Decker looked into Alharbi's eyes, the whites flashing in the dark. Decker could feel Alharbi's chest beating, the adrenaline coursing through him, and could feel he was no longer in control and was afraid, but Decker wasn't surprised and remained calm. He said, 'Yeah, I understand.'

Alharbi swung his arm into the air and fired. *Boom!* The wind carried the sound off in the darkness. 'Tell me, you fucker. Who are they?'

Decker looked into his eyes, and said, 'I can't help you.'

The next shot came from behind them.

Schiller.

Alharbi dropped to his knees with a hole in his chest. Decker stepped backwards. Alharbi's blood splashed across the car's headlights.

Schiller walked towards Decker. Passing Alharbi, he fired another shot at him. It went through his ear. Alharbi slopped to the ground with a portion of his head missing.

Decker looked at Schiller. And Schiller looked back at him, pointing his gun at him, then got out a packet of cigarettes and pulled one out with his teeth and lit it.

Decker looked at Schiller in the flame of the lighter: the dark rings under the eyes; the ash coloured skin. A life of violence imprinted on his face and sucked from his soul.

Something like a smile came to Schiller's lips. Exhaling smoke, he said, 'Aren't you going to ask why?'

Decker shrugged. 'Does it matter?'

'I guess not.'

Schiller sucked on the cigarette. 'I bet you're glad you didn't shoot me now,' he said, 'when you had the chance.'

'I knew there had to be a reason,' Decker replied.

Schiller tapped ash from the cigarette and it fell down his overcoat. 'None of this is personal, you know,' he said.

'I know.'

'In the end, people are just people. You take a job. You get paid.'

'Yeah.' Decker looked up at the trees as the wind gusted. He wasn't so sure.

Schiller said, 'Think of it this way. In 100 years, no one is going to remember any of this.' He sucked hard on the cigarette again and then, tilting his head up to the sky, exhaled. The moon shone free of cloud. Putting the cigarette back between his lips and leaving it there, Schiller then said, 'Do you want a lift?' still pointing the gun at him, 'You can drive,' and shrugging.

*

On the outskirts of Paris, Schiller told him to pull up the car and Decker stopped alongside the kerb and turned off the engine. Schiller had his gun rested on his lap and kept looking straight ahead. 'You know how this will work, don't you?' he said.

'Remind me,' Decker said, knowing there had to be a reason why he was still alive.

'They'll wait to see who you contact, who you'll bring out into the open. And what you know. Then when you've served your purpose and they've taken all they can from you, they'll let you go.'

Decker nodded. 'It's like that, is it?'

Schiller smiled, turning to him, 'Just like that.'

'I see.'

'That way you'll know, you see,' Schiller said.

'Know what?'

'If you see me again, you'll know they're letting you go. And that it's nothing personal.'

Decker smiled. 'I'll remember that.'

Decker got out and watched Schiller walk round the side of the car, with his hand in his overcoat pocket holding the gun, and then get into the driver's seat and drive away, stopping for a moment at traffic lights before disappearing in the distance.

49

The plane touched down at Prague airport. Ledges of snow lay round the perimeter of the runway. Decker put on a pair of tinted glasses and a woollen hat. Walking through the airport concourse, he scanned from side to side. He approached a car hire desk. He left his glasses on as he spoke to a woman about hiring a car. The woman pushed a form across the counter. Decker filled out his details. The woman asked for his passport and driver's licence. Decker, not for the first time, took out documents with an identity different to the one he had used the day before, which was different again to the one on his birth certificate.

The woman returned his documents. Decker slipped them in his pocket. Announcements were playing over the tannoy. The woman started explaining terms and conditions. Decker stood there listening, with people passing through the airport behind him. Finally, the woman leant over the counter and pointed to an exit.

Decker was lighting a cigarette as he left the building. It had started to snow. A guy pulled up in a VW Golf, left the engine running, and got out. He walked across to Decker, scribbling notes on a form then gave Decker the form to sign. Signing the form, Decker left the cigarette smoking between his lips. The man gave him a copy and Decker got in the car, buckled the seatbelt, and pulled away.

Heading north towards Krkonoše, the roads were clear; steep conifer-clad slopes; shiny new crash barriers on sweeping turns; a panorama of mountains. Decker gripped the steering wheel in both hands, periodically looking across at a road map lying open on the passenger seat. A truck, stacked with lengths of timber, passed on the other side of the road, the sound of gritted snow under tyres.

After several hours of driving, Decker pulled into a service station and filled up with petrol. Holding the pump handle, he looked over the roof of the car at the mountains. Then he went into the shop bought a packet of cigarettes and a pint of milk and some chocolate. He drank some of the milk while sitting in the car and then drove off again.

*

The sky was still overcast but streaked with sunset when Decker turned off the main road and pulled into a hotel car park.

The woman at the reception was expecting him. Smiling, she handed him a set of keys, explaining how one key was for his room and the other was for the front door. Decker thanked her and climbed the stairs to his room, feeling tired from all the travelling.

In his room, he took off his jacket and put his bag on the bed and ran a bath. While the bath was running, he stood at the window and looked at the snow-covered landscape: clusters of houses amongst trees; smoke rising from chimneys; mountains severed by cloud; lengthening shadows and afterglow of sunset.

Then he took out a phone from his bag and dialled a number and let it ring.

Evie answered in Czech then added, 'Hello,' when she didn't get an answer. 'Who's this?'

Looking from the window at the darkening slopes, Decker gave no answer.

Evie said, 'Hello. Is anyone there?'

Decker watched thin flakes of snow falling from low-lying clouds.

Evie said, 'H-e-l-l-o?' and paused.

Then the line went dead.

Opening the window, Decker lit a cigarette. A buzzard was circling above a peak of conifers. Decker heard the sound of a lorry dropping gears as it strained up a hill. Snowflakes floated in the air. A crow cawed. Decker pictured Evie in her parent's house. About now, he thought, beginning to realise who it was. She was looking at the number on her phone, thinking whether to ring it back. She was walking out on to a veranda, phone in hand, looking down to a road.

Decker had to be sure.

*

It was only a short drive. Decker ate breakfast at the hotel first, checking the road map in the car, and lighting a cigarette before setting off.

Through trees, he watched a house the other side of the road. There

238

was a climbing frame in the garden, an abandoned bicycle, a football. He smoked a cigarette. Soon, Evie walked from the house and climbed into a car. Putting on a pair of sunglasses, she pulled onto the road and headed in the opposite direction. Decker waited a few moments before following her.

After a mile, they came to the outskirts of a small town where Evie pulled into a shopping centre. Leaving her sunglasses on, she crossed the car park and went into the building. Parked on the other side of the street, Decker jogged across the road and followed her inside.

Evie stopped and looked through several shop windows. She didn't look to be in any hurry, Decker thought. She went into a chemist and bought a basket full of items. She continued through the shopping centre, gazing through windows. At one point, she took out her phone and checked her messages. Then she went into a woman's boutique clothing shop.

Scanning the escalators and the balcony above him, Decker watched her look through rails of clothing. At one point, the shop assistant came over and asked if she needed help. She didn't. She walked round the shop and offered up clothes in front of mirrors. She didn't buy anything. As she was leaving, Decker was in position.

Brushing passed her, he whispered, 'There's a sightseeing spot north of the town ... near the cable car. I will meet you there in an hour.' Evie opened her mouth as she recognised who it was but before she could say anything, Decker was gone.

*

Decker arrived 30 minutes early. From the car, he looked at the cable car through binoculars. He scanned the woodland, the clearings between trees, looking for vantage points. A man in an army uniform was smoking a cigarette outside the cable car building. Decker looked at the other cars in the car park: skis, snowboards on roof racks; tourists mostly.

Evie arrived in time and parked on the other side of the car park. He watched her climb out of the car, glance over the roof, curl some hair back behind her ear and then walk across the car park. She was carrying a bag over her shoulder and wearing a suede coat with thick fur collar and suede gloves.

Decker got out his hire car, hands in pockets, and walked to the wall overlooking the steep-sided valley. He put a cigarette in his mouth and lit it. When he turned to his side, Evie was standing beside him.

'How's your father?' Decker said.

'Stable. He was operated on last night. It was you, wasn't it, on the phone?'

'Yeah.' Decker looked at the view. 'Are you okay?'

'How long have you been following me?'

'Two days.' Decker offered her a cigarette.

'No, thanks,' she said. 'I've given up.'

He caught her eye. Evie smiled. 'What about you, did it work out?'

Decker took some time to say, 'Yeah, I suppose.'

'That's good. It's over then.'

'Yeah, it's over.'

Evie looked round. 'I don't want the money.'

Decker hesitated.

Evie said, 'That's why you came, isn't it?'

Decker said, 'You earned it.'

'Did I?'

'Yeah. The money's yours.'

A cable car passed into view, mist swirling above the cables.

Evie said, 'You know I have dreams – about us.' There were tears in her eyes as she spoke. 'We're running. They're chasing us. Then I don't want to run anymore. I want it to stop. But you say we have to keep going. Keep moving. Then there's the blood ... blood everywhere.'

Decker kept looking across the valley. 'I'm sorry.'

Evie wiped an eye with a gloved hand. It left a damp mark on the suede.

Then she said, 'What are you going to do?'

Decker's eyes focused in the distance. 'Travel,' he said.

'And then what?'

Decker didn't reply.

Evie looked at him, her eyes glistened. 'You know, you could stay for a bit... if you wanted.'

Decker said, 'I'm flying tonight.' Looking round, he noticed the security guard was walking across the car park towards them.

Evie said, 'This is it, then.'

Decker put out the cigarette on the wall and, looking across the valley again, said, 'In a minute, I want you to turn round and start pointing me in the direction of the town. If someone asks, tell them I was asking for directions ... I was lost ... that you've never seen me before. Do you understand?'

'And you're just going to disappear…?'

Turning, Decker caught Evie's eye and, for a moment, felt all that life could be but wasn't.

Pointing now over his shoulder, Decker said, 'Is the nearest town in that direction?'

Evie hesitated before saying, 'That's right. Follow the road…'

As Evie was pointing and explaining the way, Decker slipped the envelope of cash into her bag. There was enough money in it to fly her round the world several times over. Then he walked back to his car, reversed up and pulled out onto the road.

*

The road stretched out in front of him, steep coniferous slopes one side and snow-ledged crash barriers the other. Putting a cigarette in his mouth and lighting it, Decker imagined Evie at that moment finding the envelope in her bag as she retrieved her car keys, stopping for a moment before realising what it was. She would look over her shoulder, see the security guard and get into her car. Her heart would be beating quickly. She would peek into the envelope and see the cash. She would hold the steering wheel for a moment and then remember what he had told her. She would drive away. She would say she had never seen him before.

Decker turned on the windscreen wipers as fresh snow began to fall.

50

The sound of chickens filled the yard; the sun rising through poplar trees. The temperature was already 20 degrees. A door opened in a stone shed and a dog ran out into the yard. Next, a man stepped out, rubbing his face and the back of his neck. He was about 6ft, slim, and had short fair hair and a deep suntan. He picked up a pair of boots and clapped them together. Dried mud fell off the bottom of the soles. The man sat on the doorstep and pulled on the boots, then walked out into the yard, carrying a fishing rod, a folding landing net and canvas shoulder bag. He stroked the dog's head as he walked across to a red Peugeot 206. There was mud down the side of the car and a dent in the door panel. The man opened the boot, put in his fishing equipment, and held the door open for the dog. The dog jumped in and lay down on the back seat. The man started the engine and drove down the road. After a mile or so, he could see a river through the trees and the sun glinting on the water through the trees. The man parked in a small clearing off the road where there was a sign in French warning people the land was private. There was no one about. The man took his rod, net and bag from the boot of the car, and walked through the trees down to the river. The dog followed him, sniffing the undergrowth and urinating along the way.

The man's name was Thomas Fielder. He worked on a game farm in France, rearing pheasants and partridges. He'd been there for nearly four months, living alone with his dog, Arun. All anyone really knew about him was that he was in the army once and that he was a good worker. Some people thought that maybe he suffered from post-traumatic stress after serving in Afghanistan. Certainly, no one knew his name was once Martin Decker and that he'd killed people for a living. 'He kept himself to himself,' the locals said, when his name came up. And they were right. He wasn't there to harm anyone. Today was his day off, and on his day off, he went fishing.

It was early summer.

Decker could hear the sound of the weir pool as he approached the river through the trees. He saw the water lipping the edge of the weir as smooth as a sheet of glass before tumbling into the frothing pool. Sticks and loose debris collected at the side of the pool in the foam. It was dank and cool at this time of day before the sun had cleared the small copse.

Decker sat on the trunk of a fallen tree, got out his penknife and stuck it into the wood beside him and looked at the water for a moment. His dog, Arun, lay on the grass at his feet. Then Decker assembled his rod, lining up the eyes, and threaded the line through the eyes. Then, opening his bag, he took out a metal fly box and inspected the selection of flies. He chose a nymph he'd tied himself with wool and copper wire for weight, and tying it to the end of the leader, he spat on the knot before drawing it tight.

Then, crouching, he walked towards the weir pool, drawing out line and casting overhead. When he reached the water's edge, he released the line out across the pool and watched the weighted nymph sink the leader and the current start to bow the main line before he retrieved the line in through his fingers and repeated the process. On his third cast, he saw a trout trailing his nymph through the water, but then turn away again at the last moment and dive deep into the pool.

He lifted the line from the water and cast again. He knew there would be others. Once more, he watched the leader sink and the mainline start to bow before retrieving the nymph. This time, though, he felt a hit on the line almost instantly. He struck hard, lifting the rod above his head, and felt the line judder. He kept the rod tip up and the fish came splashing to the surface.

The fish was only a small one and tired quickly in the strong current. He reached for the landing net hooked to his belt and snapped it open. The fish splashed at the surface. He kept the line taught and brought the fish over the head of the sunken net and lifted the net under the fish, out the water and onto the bank.

He knelt down and took out the hook from the fish's mouth. The fish weighed about 12oz – a clean, smooth wild trout. A little bigger and he would have kept it. He carried the fish to the river, put his hand in the water with it, and let it go. The fish swam off. He rinsed his hands in the water and wiped them on his trousers and then picked up his rod and began casting again.

Gradually, the sun came into the copse and burnt the dew off the grass. He walked downstream, casting and retrieving the line through the water. He felt the sun on his neck now. Near an overhanging tree, he saw a larger fish taking gnats on the surface. He stopped casting for a moment, lay down the rod and opened his fly box and selected a small dry fly. He tied on the fly, wetting the knot with saliva again and began casting. He landed the fly several metres in front of the circle of ripples.

The leader line quickly straightened up in the current, bringing the fly on course to pass over the ripples and the fish underneath. As it did, Decker saw the flash of silver rise up under his fly. He gripped the line between his fingers as the water bubbled up under his fly. Then there was a tug on the line and he lifted the rod, pulling the line tight, and was in. The fish dived, moving into open water, taking out line, then ploughed towards a bed of rushes, the rod tip pounding. He applied pressure and turned the fish away from the rushes and then the fish darted across the river at a right angle, leaping clear of the water and shaking its head. For a second the line went slack and he thought he might lose it, but he quickly angled the rod tip in the opposite direction, the line tightening, and regained contact with the fish again.

Decker never pictured the car pulling into the lay-by; just as he hadn't been aware of the same car parked down the road from his house these last few days. The same man who had been staying in the local hotel, asking questions in town.

This man now brushed through the undergrowth along the riverbank. He was holding a SIG Sauer fitted with a sound moderator in his right hand. His name was Peter Schiller. He killed people for a living.

Decker was lifting the fish out the water in the net. Laying it on the bank here moved the fly and then hit the fish over the head with a wooden priest. The fish was about a pound and a quarter and enough of a meal for one. He then unwrapped a canvas sack and wet the sack in the river and laid the fish inside. He secured the sack with a stick to the bank. He then washed his hands in the river and wiped them dry on his trousers again. Bending down to pick up his rod, he was about to call his dog, Arun, when he saw Schiller standing on the path in front of him.

The two men looked at each other. Schiller offered half a smile. Decker saw the patch of flattened grass where Arun had been lying.

The sun glinted on the river. The breeze was enough to move the rushes.

Schiller glanced across at the river and then back at Decker again. 'It's a nice spot,' he said. 'You know, this is nothing personal, don't you – whatever happens?'

Decker heard the breeze in the rushes again as the sun flickered through the upper branches of a tree. He narrowed his eyes and kept his hands where they were, hanging by his sides, and said, 'And what's going to happen?'

Schiller took a step towards him. '"Find him," they said, "and see what he says…"'

Decker glanced at Schiller's gun, a SIG 9mm, some of the blacking chipped on the sound moderator, and then looked at Schiller, pale and unshaven as always.

'"And if he doesn't agree, well…"' said Schiller smiling. 'You know the rest.'

Decker nodded. 'I can guess.'

'They have a job for you,' Schiller said. 'It seems there's a shortage of people like us in the world today.'

'Like us?'

Schiller smiled again. 'You see, I told them you would be like this. But they insisted. "Be nice, talk to him."'

'Who is it this time?' Decker said.

Schiller tipped his head to one side and frowned. 'Since when did that become an issue?'

Decker said nothing.

Schiller glanced across at the river and back again. 'Anyway I find people are all the same after a while. Don't you?'

'Not really,' Decker said.

Schiller shrugged. 'You made it personal, Martin. That was your mistake.'

'Is that right?'

Schiller's expression went blank all of a sudden, cheeks drawn, eyes grey and lifeless. 'You know, I would love to chat, Martin.' He raised the gun.

Decker knew Schiller wouldn't hesitate, most likely a chest shot first, then head, with the sound of the river, the breeze, swallowing up the shots. He knew he wouldn't get to see Schiller unscrewing the sound moderator, pocketing the gun and checking about himself, as he had done countless times before.

Schiller smiled briefly, and said, 'I was like you once. Sure there was a right and a wrong – a good and a bad.'

Decker took his turn to smile now. 'And then you grew old and wise.'

'Don't kid yourself, Martin. Right and wrong – good and bad – have got nothing to do with it. If anything, we're the ones ...' Schiller gestured with a tilt of the gun to indicate people in their profession, '... who bring a little clarity to the picture, a little good ... Now, what's it going to be, Martin?'

Decker shrugged. 'You tell me,' and he turned his back on him and started walking.

51

Walking back down the track alongside the river that day, having turned his back on Schiller, Decker had often wondered since why Schiller hadn't pulled the trigger on him. Because Schiller had thought he was once like him? Was it because there was still something to be gained by keeping him alive –or nothing by having him dead? Decker couldn't explain it.

Sometimes, sitting drinking a beer by the fire – it was winter now on the game farm – Decker would remember that day by the river. It came back to him in a series of freeze frames: the weir pool; the sun glinting through the trees; playing the trout; unhooking it on the grass; Schiller standing there, gun pointed; the chipped blacking on the silencer. He'd think that maybe some things were not meant to be explained – that coincidence did after all exist. And leaning forward, he'd chuck another log on the fire, and embers would fall through the grate, and Arun, his dog, would lift his head to see what was going on, and Decker would stroke his head and he would return to how he was.

Then Decker would find his mind wandering and thinking about Evie and this would make him get up and fetch another beer. The TV would be on, his body would be tired after work, his thick socks flapping half off his feet, as he squatted down by the fridge.

Once or twice, Decker said her name out aloud, just to hear it.

'Evie... Evie...'

And sometimes, like tonight, after locking the rearing sheds, on his walk back to his house, Decker stopped and looked up at the moon and thought how it looked like the same moon as when they'd spent the night together in the car. And standing there for a moment, as Arun walked ahead of him, Decker found himself out of nowhere feeling he wanted a cigarette until he remembered he'd given up and hadn't smoked in months. And this made him smile. Sometimes, kind of stupidly, like now, he allowed himself to imagine that maybe somewhere Evie was doing the same thing and thinking of him.

A breeze blew through the pine trees behind the rearing sheds. In two weeks it was Christmas and Decker was taking some time off. It would be his first holiday since starting work at the game farm. He'd heard the skiing was good in the Czech Republic, especially around Krkonoše. He wondered if Evie skied. He would be surprised if she didn't. Now there was a thought.

Arun was waiting for him along the track. Decker had an early start at work in the morning. He looked round. The sky was cold and bright with stars and you could smell the pine needles and the damp under the trees.

Printed in Great Britain
by Amazon